"LET ME OUT OF THE CAR!" SHE CRIED, HER VOICE TREMBLING IN TERROR.

"Shut up!" he snapped. "Nobody's hurting you!"

The darkness on either side of the headlight beams was impenetrable. The car careened and fishtailed around the tight corners of Central Park, and the girl was grabbing at the locked door handles, sobbing audibly now. Too fast, was her only thought. He's going too fast.

Trees blocked out any light from above, and she watched desperately as the man beside her leaned forward over the wheel, swerving toward the distant lights along the Hudson River.

Then they were turning under the West Side Highway and over onto the grass. He stopped.

"Let me out, for God's sake!"

He put a hand over her mouth. "You just got a free ride," he said softly. "That's worth something."

Blood Red Rose

Arthur Wise

PLAYBOY PAPERBACKS

For Jim and Liz Trupin,
without whom
Manhattan would have been a jungle

This book was conceived and largely written in suite 608 of the Hotel Olcott on West Seventy-second Street, Manhattan, N.Y. I want to record the gratitude I feel toward that magnificent establishment, its staff, and, above all, its manager, Joseph Pollack.

ARTHUR WISE
New York, 1980

▼▼▼▼▼▼▼▼▼▼▼▼▼▼▼▼

CHAPTER 1

▲▲▲▲▲▲▲▲▲▲▲▲▲▲▲▲

It was one hell of a party.

Someone had put the lights out in the bedroom and the place was full of sweet moans. Janey stood in the doorway wondering where Derek had gone. The flashing neon sign from the deli across University Place threw periodic shadows on the walls. A locked couple leaned against the wall. The floor rippled with human shapes. Somewhere under the heaving mass on the bed was the hostess. She'd had her pants ripped off, and her glasses lay twisted underneath her. She didn't give a damn. Someone was into her and there were lips covering her breasts, and she had her fingers buried in the thick mat of hair on some male chest.

A voice cried, "Ride me, cowboy!"

Janey said, "Derek?" She said it tentatively. She didn't really believe he could be in there. She didn't know him well, but she'd formed certain opinions about him.

A figure got up from the floor. It was a male—tall, broad. Although she couldn't see more than his silhouette against the red flash of the neon, she could tell that he was naked. He came toward her, feeling his way with his feet through the writhing bodies on the carpet.

"Derek?" she asked.

"Right here, honey." The man put out a hand toward her.

But it wasn't Derek. She knew Derek's voice. Before the man could touch her, she had backed into the living room and closed the door.

The sound of the stereo pulsed in her ears. She didn't know how much she had drunk. Everyone had pushed glasses at her. The vodka had lost all taste, so that she didn't know whether she'd been on straight tomato juice, as they'd promised, or loaded Bloody Marys. The man who had introduced himself four hours earlier as an assistant professor of English at NYU was sitting on the floor by the window with a plastic bag of melting ice and a gallon jar of white wine between his knees. He didn't notice her. He was past noticing anything.

Though the windows were wide open, there wasn't a breath of air in the room. She felt stifled. With a wad of Kleenex she kept dabbing her forehead, but it made no difference. The minute one bead of sweat had been mopped up, another oozed to take its place.

She looked for Derek among the dancers, leaning into one another with glazed eyes. He wasn't among them. In the corner, where two bookcases were joined at right angles, the white-haired man who had been introduced as a publisher had his arm around the neck of a young blond man. He was saying, "What's wrong with it if it's honest? I mean, if it's a genuine human feeling . . ."

She moved away.

The air was blue with smoke. The sweet smell of grass made her feel sick. She began to lose her sense of balance under the vibrant boom of the music. Unsteadily she made her way to the kitchen, where she had to blink against the glaring fluorescent light reflected off the gloss-white walls and the tiles and the glass-fronted cupboards. Someone had been sick in the sink. At the sight of it, she felt a great flush of heat rise up into her face and head. She put her hand on the cold enamel of the refrigerator and felt herself begin to slip.

A man's voice said, "Let me take you home. You look terrible."

She couldn't remember having seen him before. He was smiling. It was a friendly, open face with a close-knit pepper-and-salt beard.

She said, "I was looking for Derek."

"He left."

"Left?"

"Passed out. They put him in a taxi." He had a hand out toward her. "I've got a car outside. Do you live in the Village?"

She shook her head. "No," she said. "West Seventy-sixth, between Broadway and West End Avenue."

"Come on," he said. He was still smiling, and in the end she let him take her arm and lead her outside.

The air in the street was suffocating. There wasn't a breath of movement. There was going to be one hell of a storm. Nothing else would break the tension. The red light from the deli flashed on and off. From Washington Square to her left, the sound of jazz vibrated through the night. A swarm of laughing people carrying balloons and bottles came down the street toward them, a wave of movement and color and sweat that was going to break over them and, if she didn't look out, drown her. It wasn't air she was breathing but oil and carbon monoxide. She climbed into the car, thinking that if she didn't get into the fresh air soon she was going to die. The whole of New York City was drowning in human sweat.

The man was looking at her, leaning back into his seat, elbow through the open window, one hand on the steering wheel. He had her in profile—upturned nose, long, narrow throat, little mounds of breasts not much more than a boy's—and beyond her the lighted shopwindows of Madison, a flashing, shimmering, psychedelic backdrop. He had had his eyes on her ever since she'd walked into the room.

"Do you live alone?" he asked.

"Mmm."

"Don't you ever get scared?"

"I don't think about it," she said. "I can take care of myself."

"What about the killings?"

"I take care. They'll catch him in the end. He'll make some mistake."

"Let's hope so."

He drove as far as Seventy-ninth Street, then turned west and into the park. The walls of the underpass rose up black on either side of the headlight beams. A cyclist came into view—a man crouched over the handlebars, riding in the middle of the road. There wasn't enough room for the car to get past without crossing the double yellow line.

The driver honked, the sound reverberating from the stone walls of the underpass. The cyclist put a single stiff finger up in the air, but he didn't change his position in the road.

The driver hesitated. "Jesus Christ," he muttered. There was no car ahead and none showed in his rearview mirror. As he slowed, the scorching air trapped in the underpass came in through the open windows. Sweat trickled down his face. He could smell the perfume of the girl next to him, and began to feel that his opportunity was slipping away from him. He snatched at the wheel, a gesture of sudden irritation, and pushed down on the accelerator. The car crossed the double yellow line and came even with the cyclist. Abruptly the driver made a sharp right, cutting across the cyclist's path, and a second later there was a yell from behind and the sound of metal on metal.

"My God!" gasped Janey. She couldn't believe what had happened. "You hit him! Aren't you going to stop?"

The man beside her took a glance in the rearview mirror. The cyclist had disappeared into the darkness. "He's okay," he said, taking a handkerchief out of his pants pocket and mopping his face. "They're crazy, the lot of them! You'd think they owned the place. Jesus, what's a guy doing cycling through Central Park this time in the morning, anyway?"

The nausea that Janey had been feeling at the party had gone. Uppermost in her mind now was a sense of growing apprehension. What was she doing? She must be crazy, letting a perfect stranger drive her home alone through the park at this hour! Suppose this was the guy the whole town was talking about, the guy the *Daily News* had christened "Bald Eagle"? Panic began to build in her gut. "You can make a left down Central Park West," she said, keeping her voice as even as she could manage.

"Let's see if the lights are with us," he said. "It might be quicker to go straight, then cut down West End Avenue." He was wondering where to take her. He figured she'd never let him go home with her.

She was on the point of asking him to stop and let her out right where they were, when she realized that that would be playing into his hands. The darkness on either side of the headlight beams was impenetrable. The trees leaning over the underpass blocked out any light from above. She'd have to control herself. Once they reached the lights of the West Side, she'd be safe. Yet, even as she kept telling herself that, simple fear gave way to terror, and she had to summon all her willpower to control it. She could sense the tension in the man beside her. He had lost that easy, casual air he'd affected at first and was now leaning forward over the wheel, his eyes riveted on the row of stop lights along Central Park West. The only thing she knew about him was that they'd been guests at the same party!

The lights were green when he reached them and

he drove right across Central Park West, the car pitching and rolling on the broken road surface.

The lit streets were an enormous comfort to her. Ahead, she could see the lights of Jersey across the river. The raw edge of panic subsided. She began to think that maybe in the darkness of the park she'd got things a little out of proportion. She knew what this man was after—the same thing they were all after, nothing more. Statistically, what were the chances that this was Bald Eagle sitting next to her? The thought almost brought a smile to her lips. Almost, but not quite.

He made a left down Columbus, then a right at Seventy-ninth Street. As they crossed Amsterdam, she could see that the lights at Broadway were red. He was going in the right direction. It was okay. Even so, when he came to a stop at the Broadway intersection, she figured she'd stick with her intuition. "This'll be fine, thanks," she said. "I can walk from here."

He had a place in mind now. All he had to do was soothe her worries for a couple more minutes. After that, it would be too late. "Sure," he said, his voice soft and reassuring. "But I don't think it's too good an idea." He nodded to a black man sitting on the bench halfway across the intersection. He had a brown bag of liquor in his hand and he was watching them. Beyond him, two figures lay asleep, features distorted by the light from the sodium lamps. The stink of dog shit came in through the open windows.

"Okay," she said at last, leaning back against the seat. "You can make a left at West End Avenue."

The lights flashed to green and they crossed Broadway. But he didn't make a left at West End Avenue. He drove through the lights there and across Riverside Drive and down to the river. They were under the West Side Highway before she realized what had happened. Panic suddenly overwhelmed her and she screamed in terror, "Let me out! For God's sake, let me out!"

They were along the riverside walk and onto the grass before he stopped. Lights bobbed on the water from the boat basin. Someone had a radio on in the distance, crooning softly into the night.

"Aw, come on," he said, his right hand on her knee. "Be friendly. You just got a free ride. That's worth a little——"

"Let me out!" she howled, tears streaming down her cheeks, fingers struggling to unbuckle the safety belt.

He snapped, "For Christ's sake, shut up! Nobody's hurting you!"

He put a hand over her mouth. She bit it. At the same time, she got clear of the safety belt and opened the door.

"You goddamn bitch!" he yelled. "You get me going and now . . ."

He leaned over and grabbed her by the skirt. She hit him with her purse, but it wasn't heavy enough to do any damage, so she untied the knot on her wraparound skirt and pulled herself clear. Once out of the car, she turned and started to run back toward the lights of the boat basin.

By the time he got out of the car, she had disappeared, but he could still hear her footsteps. He knew she would want to get out of the dimly lit park as soon as she could. He broke into a cautious jog, the river on his left, the dark stretch of park on his right. He couldn't leave it like this. He had to get to her, now that she knew who he was. He'd never messed anything up like this before. What a lousy piece of luck picking a bitch like this!

"Aw, c'mon!" he called. "I was only fooling! Hey, lemme give you a lift home. You're not safe in here alone!"

There was no answer. Where the Christ had she

gone? He came to a stop and listened. He couldn't hear her footsteps anymore. Had she got out and onto Riverside Drive already? He didn't know the park well. The East Side was really his scene.

He turned toward the drive and climbed a ramp and found himself in a great concrete amphitheater. There were no lights, and he could barely make out the stone columns supporting the traffic circle above, and the circular shape of the central fountain. It was another faded dream—magnificent until the money had run out. In the heat of the night it stank of urine.

His footsteps echoed from the enclosing walls. What was he doing? He was alone in Riverside Park, chasing some cockteaser. Was he crazy? He turned to go. As he did so, he heard her. He froze and listened, then began moving his head this way and that to bring the faint sounds more clearly into focus. He could hear her feet now, making little scratching noises on the concrete floor as she groped her way toward the exit.

Then he saw her, a black shape in the darkness, crouching by the wall. He moved toward her infinitely slowly, controlling his eagerness, lifting one tiptoed foot after the other. Everything was at stake now. He had to reach her before she realized he was there. At all costs, she mustn't cry out. He had to put his hand over her mouth and hold it there until he'd explained that all he was after was a little harmless fun. He hadn't wanted to upset her and he was sorry he had. Above all, he didn't want her going to the cops and complaining about him. The idea of opening the *Daily News* and seeing his picture there in connection with some sex rap was more than he could bear.

He was within a yard of her, poised above her. She was absolutely unaware of his presence. He lunged finally, pinning her shoulders with his hands, groping for her head, trying to get a hand over her mouth. She slipped and he fell with her, struggling to keep his grip on her, squeezing her into silence. She made no sound at all, nor did she offer any resistance.

A trash-can lid clattered nearby, and suddenly panic seized him. He was on his knees on the concrete. What was going on? Where was he? Strange sounds were all around him. The place was crawling with dark shapes. He could feel hands groping for his wallet, tearing at his pockets, ripping the gold ring off his finger. They were coming at him with knives and lengths of iron piping. He'd expected to be into soft thighs and sweet female flesh. Instead, he was being mugged!

He managed to tear himself free and ran—back past the children's playground and the stone rest rooms and the bobbing boats in the boat basin, sweat pouring off his forehead and down his face and soaking into his striped cotton shirt. He finally reached the car, locked himself in, and got it started. The headlights blazed and blew the night apart. The path ahead was empty. Black shapes loomed to his right. He made for the exit, tires screaming on the asphalt surface.

When he reached the highway, he turned left along Riverside Drive, then made a right on Seventy-ninth Street. A guy was jogging ahead of him. Behind, a cyclist came into his rearview mirror and began racing after him. A dog flashed through his headlights, heightening the tension inside him. New York was out of its mind! It didn't have any rules, any form, any order.

The minute he got into the underpass and headed east through Central Park, the panic in his gut began to ease. Beyond the park lay civilization, and he wanted to get back into it. Then, as the lights of Fifth Avenue came into view ahead of him, he took to wondering whether anyone had seen him. Would they recognize him if they saw him again? Would he have to offer some explanation? Time would tell whether the affair remained a secret or whether it got dragged out into the open. The only one who really knew anything was the girl, and she wasn't likely to talk. One thing he swore to himself as he crossed Fifth Avenue and headed for Yorkville: Whatever temptation came up in the future, he'd never again get into that kind of hassle.

Nothing stays secret in New York City. Sooner or later, every corner gets probed by a sodium lamp or some derelict's fingers poking among the garbage for breakfast. And in the summer stew there are the flies —the best detectives of them all.

Anton Stern kept a liquor store on the west side of Columbus at Eighty-second Street. It was a good location. It faced east, and facing east, Stern wasn't troubled by the sun. Anyone facing west daren't put decent German wines in the window in case the heat ruined them. They had to fill their windows with spirits and California wines and that kosher pap coming in from Israel. And anyone facing south on one of the cross streets might as well close up for the summer, or maybe brick up the window and put in deep refrigeration and open a funeral parlor. Except where would anyone park?

Stern was in his fifties—medium height, blond hair, military bearing. He had served under Rommel and been taken prisoner by the British and spent four years in a camp in Egypt. After that, he had come to the States. He was a naturalized citizen now, married, with a daughter and two sons, but he had never got over the feeling that it was all temporary and that if he didn't stay alert every waking moment, they would find something wrong in Washington and deport him to Germany.

At seven that morning, he got up and put on a white T-shirt and jeans and went down into the cellar to bring up the new stock for the day. His wife, Maria, got up with him and made a solid German breakfast, and at eight the boys came down. They were the problem at vacation times. The girl was no problem. She was thirteen. She was up in her room until midday and then she went out with her friends. But the boys had too much energy and no idea how to direct it. Thank God for the bicycles, he thought. Maria could send them off around eight-thirty with a couple of sandwiches, knowing they were getting healthy exercise and wouldn't come back till lunchtime.

"Remember who you are," she called as they rode off. What she meant was, Don't do anything that will bring shame on your father and me. She had tiny hands and feet, a tiny, unwrinkled face, and a body as tight and round as a pool ball. However many documents Washington gave her to prove she was an American, she would never be anything but a German hausfrau from Baden-Württemberg.

The boys rode up Columbus, against the traffic, Thomas in the lead. Nobody honked at them to tell them they were going the wrong way; to tell them that even in New York City, there are certain rules you've got to obey to prevent the whole kettle of fish from getting fouled up. Somebody waved to them and called, "You take care of yourselves, now!" It was Officer Callaghan, riding past in his police car.

Thomas was ten. He called to his brother without turning his head, "Where you wanna go?"

"I don't care," called Rudi. He was eight, and he had his father's blond hair and square-jawed face. When he grew up, he was going to be a stunt man like Duke McGlade. In the meantime, he had his eyes fixed on the ass of his brother's blue jeans ahead of him. One day he'd be up there in front of his brother, with nothing ahead of him but the open road. Let Thomas stare up *his* ass for a change.

They rode as far as Ward Burton's bicycle shop on Eighty-eighth Street. Thomas was going to collect some literature on the new Fuji so he could start putting pressure on his father in plenty of time for Christmas. But he rode past the store when he saw that the grills were still over the window and the double doors were chained and padlocked.

They turned for the river, jinking around the cars parked amid the dog shit in the gutters. It was hot already, and air-conditioners were trickling water onto the sidewalks. A group of Hispanics sat on the stoop of a crumbling brownstone drinking from beer cans. Duke McGlade said they stayed there all night. They wanted to be first off the base if there was another blackout like last summer's—another chance to kick in a few windows along Amsterdam and furnish a one-room without having to dip into welfare money.

"What do you wanna do?" called Thomas.

"What do *you* wanna do?" asked Rudi.

The river was heavy with mist. A long string of barges, deep in the water, was being pulled upstream by a tug. Overhead, the police helicopter watching the traffic coming in down the West Side Highway clattered like a kid running a stick down a row of garbage cans. A middle-aged man jogged past in white shorts and T-shirt, pain all over his face. Two cyclists and a dog shot up the track from the boat basin.

"You hungry?" asked Thomas, leaning on the rail at the edge of the pathway and looking down at the houseboats bobbing on the water.

"Yeah," said Rudi.

They chained their bikes to the fence and went with the lunch box into the children's playground. The place was empty except for a blue jay chattering somewhere above and a squirrel that had dropped out of a tree and come up behind them, waiting for handouts.

"You got a ham roll?" asked Rudi, looking at the lunch box.

Thomas opened the lid and looked inside. There was the usual stuff. "It's kinda early," he said. "Let's go up to the circle, watch the traffic coming in." He knew that once they started eating, they were going to go through it all, and lunchtime was still a long way off.

Rudi said, "We can break one in two, half each."

"Let's wait," said Thomas, closing the lid.

They walked up the ramp. Three men were hitting a softball in the diamond below.

Inside the rotunda, they went over to the fountain and sat on the edge of the basin.

"Why do they have to paint the inside of this thing blue?" said Thomas. "Why don't they just fill it with water?"

"What's in the thermos?" asked Rudi.

"Lemonade," said Thomas, unscrewing the top. It was always lemonade.

They took a couple of mouthfuls. The traffic passing overhead set up a strange humming sound among the stone columns.

Rudi handed the thermos back to Thomas and said, "I don't like it here; it's creepy. Let's go up into the park." He got up and walked toward the steps and disappeared around the corner.

Thomas screwed the top back on the thermos and followed his brother. They could sit for a while on the grass along Riverside Drive. "Hey, wait, Rudi," he called, making for the steps.

Rudi hadn't climbed the steps. He was standing just around the corner, looking at something in his hand.

"What you got there?" asked Thomas.

"I dunno," said Rudi. "Some kind of picture."

"Here, lemme take a look," said Thomas, putting out his hand.

It was a card, the size of an ordinary business card. There was a bird on it, and below the bird some printed words. It was a nice picture. The bird had its head lifted and its beak open. Before he got to reading the words, he became aware of his brother saying his name over and over again—"Thomas . . . Thomas"— very flat and quiet.

"Yeah?" he said, without lifting his head. Then, when he looked, he saw that Rudi was staring at a pile of garbage that had been dumped in the shadows behind the steps.

"It's a woman," said Rudi, his voice as quiet as if he was speaking in church.

Thomas looked. The pile of garbage came together. The shadows and highlights took on a significance. He could make out an arm, a hand, a bare leg. Finally the face. It pointed upward, and the flies swarmed black all over it.

They stood there side by side, looking down at the body. Finally Thomas said, also quietly, "Come on."

They walked back down the ramp, Thomas in front, Rudi right behind. Thomas unlocked the bikes, put the chains, the lunch box, and the thermos in his saddlebag, and pushed the card into the pocket of his jeans.

They were crossing West End Avenue, driving down on the pedals, shoulders rocking from side to side, when Rudi suddenly screamed, "Did you see the flies? All over her face!"

▼▼▼▼▼▼▼▼▼▼▼▼▼▼▼

CHAPTER 2

▲▲▲▲▲▲▲▲▲▲▲▲▲▲▲

As far as Ward Burton was concerned, the bicycle figured large in the Declaration of Independence. It was one of the truths that was self-evident: the right of every man to ride his bike in Central Park without let or hindrance from any other vehicle, from pedestrians or from God himself. Jefferson's very words, and if they weren't the words they taught you at P.S. 77, that was because the teachers didn't want the truth to get to you.

Burton lived on Eighty-second Street, just around the corner from Stern's liquor store. Every morning, he made for Central Park on his steel-blue *Le Champion* Motobecane with ten-speed Campagnolo derailleur, two electric horns, and AM/FM radio. It was a beautiful, beautiful machine, and if he'd ever found a woman as steely blue and strong and tubular—a woman with tape-wrapped drop handlebars and AM/FM radio between her breasts—he might have married her. Except she'd still have been a woman, wanting to know where he went when he wasn't home, wanting to curb his freedom and cramp his style. No—even a Motobecane woman wouldn't have suited him. He was a man on a bicycle.

Burton was finishing his lap of the park and making for the Seventy-second Street exit. There was a taxi on his right, coming up fast. He had a sharpened file in his hand that he always had ready in traffic. They thought they could do anything to a man on a bicycle —crowd him off the road, push him straight up onto the sidewalk. Well, they couldn't. They kept their distance or they were in for a repaint job.

The taxi slid past. Burton eased to the right, his big yellow direction indicators going *bleak! bleak! bleak!* Ahead of him lay the spires of Central Park South and the whole run of the Avenue of the Americas. New York, New York—the greatest act of human worship on the face of the earth!

He made a right down Seventy-second Street, cutting straight through the red light, jinking this way and that as the traffic braked and honked at him. He grinned and waved his file. He was self-sufficient. He could look after himself. He didn't need traffic lights to tell him what to do.

As he rode past the Hotel Olcott, he could hear a singer practicing in one of the upper rooms—a soprano voice so pure and free it seemed to come not from her throat at all but straight from her soul. That was freedom! When you didn't have to climb any obstacles. When just wanting something was enough to make it happen.

It was at Columbus and Seventy-ninth Street that he heard someone calling, "Mr. Burton! *Hey,* Mr. Burton!"

He thought it was a girl's voice until he screwed his head around and saw that it was the Stern boys from the liquor store. "Yeah?" he called, but he didn't slacken pace.

Thomas knew they'd never catch up; he couldn't get his legs to work like Burton's. He shouted, his voice high-pitched and panicky, "Mr. Burton! Can you hold it, Mr. Burton? We've found something!"

Burton stopped pedaling and slipped down through the gears. He was over in the right lane, with the traffic coming straight at him on its way downtown. He was keeping his balance between the line of parked cars and the moving traffic, waiting for the boys to catch up with him. When they were within earshot, he called, "Yeah? So what've you found?"

Even before Thomas drew alongside Burton, he could smell the sweat on him. The man was steaming. Breathless, he gasped, "We found a . . . a woman."

"So?" said Burton.

Thomas said, "Dead."

"Where?"

"By the river. In the Rotunda."

"Anyone you know?"

"No."

"Who did you tell?"

"Nobody."

"So?"

Thomas admired Burton. Watching him flashing down Columbus on his Motobecane, jinking through the traffic, ignoring the signals, was like watching St. George on his way to slaughter the dragon. He had looked to Burton for help. Now that Burton had thrown him back on himself, he didn't know what to say.

"Show him the card, Thomas," said Rudi.

"What card?" Burton asked.

"Rudi found a card," Thomas said, putting his finger and thumb behind him and into the top of his back pocket.

"Let me see." Burton put out a hand to Thomas.

Thomas, straddling the crossbar of his bike, looked up at Burton. He was a tall man, dark and good-looking. Thomas watched his face, wondering what he was going to say.

Burton handed the card back. "You better tell your pa," was all he said.

"What are you going to do, Mr. Burton?" asked Thomas.

"Gonna take a shower and open up the shop," said

Burton. He had already remounted and begun to move away.

"You gonna tell the police?" called Thomas, trying to catch up with him again.

"What for?" called Burton, now facing forward and drawing away fast. "I got a business to run."

The boys left their bikes in the yard and went into the liquor store through the side entrance.

Duke McGlade was having breakfast in the Sterns' back room, the way he'd been having it every morning since the blackout had made a folk hero of him. That terrible night when the lights went out, the Sterns had been in Queens visiting with Maria Stern's sister. McGlade was the reason the liquor store wasn't looted. He'd taken a baseball bat and stationed himself in the doorway and stayed there till it was daylight. They'd even put his picture on the cover of *Westside TV Shopper*.

He said to the boys, "I thought you guys had gone to the Cloisters."

Maria Stern closed her eyes when she saw the boys standing together in the middle of the back room. She said, "What now? Didn't I say lunchtime? Not before twelve-thirty—didn't I say that?" Everything about America was a strain to her these days.

"Where's Pa?" Thomas asked.

"Anything wrong?" asked McGlade, wincing as he shifted in the chair. He wasn't at his best. His back was paining him. He worked as a stunt man, and in the spring he'd injured himself doing a twenty-foot fall into wet concrete for a cement commercial. He was drawing workmen's compensation and he hated it. It smacked of some kind of handout, which put him in the same category as all the derelicts sitting on all the brownstone stoops swilling Budweiser. It took away his dignity. Dignity was something that went very deep with him. He never forgave anyone who took it away from him.

When neither of the boys said anything, McGlade turned to Rudi and asked, "Anything you want to tell me?"

Rudi wasn't sure where to begin. All he could see in his mind was the upturned face of the woman and the flies covering it. He said, "We were . . . we were along the river, and Thomas had the lunch box, and we went up to the rotunda——"

Thomas cut in: "We'd better tell Pa."

McGlade shrugged. His heavy, drooping mustache added to the general sadness of his expression.

Stern was through the connecting hallway in the store. There was still a while to go before he opened and he was arranging stock on the shelves. He caught sight of the boys through one of the circular surveillance mirrors and, without glancing up, said, "Thomas, we had an agreement, huh? I buy you bikes for the vacation and you don't come in here. I got a business to run, you know that."

It was what Burton had said.

"We . . . found a body, Pa," said Thomas.

Rudi was standing immediately behind his brother, almost touching him. Thomas had said the important thing. That was what *he* should have said when Duke McGlade asked him, instead of talking about the river and the lunch box. It was finding the body that was important.

Stern said, "You——" He put down the bottles and came to stand in front of the boys. His freshly shaved face looked polished under the fluorescent lights. Very serious, he looked straight at Thomas. Thomas looked straight back into those very blue eyes. "You found . . . a body?" Stern said.

Thomas nodded.

"What kind of a body?"

"A woman's, Pa. In the rotunda under the traffic circle, bottom of Seventy-ninth Street."

Stern didn't doubt the boy. He admired the way he stood there and spoke out. That was the way he'd tried to bring the two of them up, to be forthright, courageous, honorable—all the best qualities of the old country—because however much America offered a man in the way of freedom and opportunity, Stern believed there were still deep human values that the fatherland could contribute.

"Did you tell the police?" he asked.

"No," said Thomas.

"Did you tell anybody?"

"Mr. Burton."

"Mr. *Burton?*" said Stern. "You mean from the bike shop?"

Thomas nodded.

Burton was a bum! He never made any contribution to the neighborhood. He wouldn't join the block association, and in the blackout he'd protected his own property without doing a thing to help the other shopkeepers. He was the only one in the neighborhood who could generate his own electricity. He hadn't any social conscience. He was an anarchist. Why would the boys go to him before coming to their own father?

"Why Mr. Burton?" asked Stern. He tried to speak softly. He could sense the tension in the boys and he knew it wouldn't take much to have them both in tears.

"We met him on the street," said Thomas.

"He was going home to shower," added Rudi.

"What did he say?"

"He said to come and tell you," said Thomas.

"Quite right," said Stern. It was more than he'd expected.

"We showed him the card," said Rudi.

"Card?"

Thomas gave the card to his father. When Stern looked at it, his heart sank. Ever since coming to

America he'd tried to stay invisible, doing whatever was required of him by his adopted country, staying strictly inside the law. How many people lived on the West Side? A quarter million? Half a million? Why, out of all those hundreds of thousands, had this happened to him?

"Did Mr. Burton call the police?" he asked.

"No," said Thomas.

"Did he say he was going to call the police?"

"No, Pa."

"Well, what *did* he say?" Stern knew his anger was showing now. He couldn't prevent it.

"He said he had a business to run," said Thomas.

Stern looked at the card in his hand. "I see," he said. "A business to run."

He called through the connecting hallway, "Maria!" When his wife appeared, he asked, "Where's Elsa?"

"Upstairs," said Mrs. Stern.

"You sure?"

"She's in her room. Why you looking so worried?"

"Don't let her out," said Stern. "Take the boys upstairs. Keep them there till I tell you."

She didn't question him. There were generations of female obedience behind her; no Equal Rights Amendment was going to change that. She took the boys upstairs to the living room and waited for her husband to tell her what to do next.

From the back room, McGlade called, "What's happened, Tony?" He was always careful to use Stern's Americanized first name. He knew Stern preferred it.

Stern came through the hallway from the shop. "There's been another killing," he said.

"Jesus!" said McGlade, straightening his back carefully and turning from the waist to look at him.

Stern picked up the phone in the hallway and dialed the emergency number. Over his shoulder, he said to McGlade, "The boys found her."

"Christ Almighty!" said McGlade.

Stern had got through to the police. He was saying, "They told that Burton guy. You know—the bike shop on Columbus, around Eighty-ninth. What? Well, they met him on the street, I guess that's why. . . . No. I asked them did he call you. They told me no." Stern put the phone down and stood looking at McGlade.

McGlade said, "They told Burton and he didn't call the police?"

"What do you make of that?" cried Stern. "You'd think we live in some cow town out of the movies instead of New York City!"

"Maybe it wasn't the same killer," said McGlade. "Maybe this dead woman they found met with some accident."

Stern handed him the card. McGlade held it at arm's length, but even before it came into focus he knew what it was. Similar cards had been shown on TV and plastered all over the papers. It bore the outline of a bald eagle, the kind of thing you saw on conservation posters. It was beautifully done—very neat, in india ink. At first glance, it looked as if it might have been printed. Someone had taken a lot of trouble over it. The words underneath read: "New York is a pile of dog shit."

In the evening, McGlade picked up the first edition of the *Daily News*. It carried the headline TEN THOUSAND DOLLARS FOR BALD EAGLE, and under it, a seven-column piece beginning: "For the third time since April 25, a young woman was strangled on the West Side. The all-too-familiar card depicting a bald eagle was discovered at the scene. The *Daily News* offers $10,000 for information leading to the capture of the killer. . . ."

"Ten thousand bucks!" McGlade muttered when he read the story.

To a guy drawing workmen's compensation, $10,000 was an awful lot of money.

CHAPTER 3

The police came twice to talk with the Stern boys.
McGlade didn't see them. Since his accident in the
spring he spent a lot of time in his room, though he
still did what he could to keep fit. As a stunt man, his
capital equipment was fitness. He kept telling himself
that his present disability was only temporary. It had
happened to him before and it would happen to him
again. It was one of the risks of the business.

Every day, he examined his naked body in front of
the full-length mirror in the bathroom, looking for the
first signs of age. But his pectorals still looked good,
and his abdominal wall could take any punch that was
thrown at it. This morning was no exception.

He went to the window. It was wide open, but it
made no difference to the air in the room. Inside or out,
you might as well have been breathing liquid carbon
monoxide. The enclosed backyards below held the heat
and the fumes like an oven. Down there were some of
the stinks that made up New York City in the summer:
the drift of stale cooking oil, the smoke from the
hibachis, the fumes of burnt gasoline.

At least he was above the worst of it. From his
window, he could see the deck where Burton sometimes sat in the evenings with his dog. It was the flat
roof of a two-story addition to the brownstone that had
been built out into the yard behind. He had never

spoken to Burton, just looked down at him from the superior height of his own fourth-floor room. Twice when he'd had direct eye contact with the guy he'd nodded. Burton had nodded back, but it wasn't a gesture that encouraged human contact. If it said anything, it said the same thing as the wicker fence Burton had put up to define his aerial territory: Keep your distance.

McGlade put on a black sweat suit and sneakers and went downstairs and knocked on the Sterns' living-room door. Mrs. Stern opened it. There was an air-conditioner working in one of the windows and the air was clammy.

McGlade said, "I was going into the park. I thought maybe the boys would like to get out. I'll keep an eye on them."

"I don't know," said Mrs. Stern.

McGlade was looking past her to where the boys were playing checkers on the floor. They looked tense. Behind them, seated on the sofa, Elsa was turning the pages of *Photoplay*. She lifted her head and gave him a long, cold stare.

McGlade said to the boys, "I'm going into the park. Giving the back a workout. You wanna come?"

Rudi looked up and hesitated, then glanced at his mother. He couldn't bear sitting cooped up in the room.

"Is that okay, Mom?" asked Thomas.

"Your father said to stay here," said Mrs. Stern.

"C'mon," said McGlade. "I'll go and see Tony."

The boys followed him downstairs and into the store. Stern was at the cash register serving a customer.

Thomas said, "Can we go to the park with Mr. Mc-Glade, Pa?"

"I'll look after them, Tony," McGlade said.

"Please, Pa," Rudi pleaded.

The customer left and Stern turned and looked at his sons. He was conscious of what they'd been through already. He didn't want to make any more of it than was absolutely necessary, but the fact remained that they were both involved in a murder. In the end he said, "Okay. But you stay with Mr. McGlade, now, you hear me?"

On the face of it, the new murder hadn't changed anything in the outside scene. The haze that had hung over the city for a week was still there, like a lid on a casserole. In the school yard opposite, a group of blacks flicked a ball through a basketball hoop. But McGlade could feel the tension under the surface, strung like piano wires. People still lounged on the brownstone stoops, but no one was speaking anymore. Bald Eagle had really got to the West Side. The place must be crawling with undercover cops.

In the park, he broke into a jog. It was a stiff, staccato action, and he didn't move forward at more than a walking pace. Now and again he clenched his jaw and tried flexing his spine as his knee came up and down. Maybe it was getting a little easier; maybe not.

He said, "What did the cops say?"

"Nothing," said Thomas. He was keeping up with McGlade just by walking.

"Did you tell them about Mr. Burton?"

"Yeah."

"What did they say?"

"Nothing," said Thomas.

"Nothing? Nothing at all?" McGlade asked.

"They were going to go around to see him, Duke," said Rudi. He was in a slow jog on McGlade's left.

"They said that?" McGlade asked.

"Yup," said Rudi.

"What do *you* make of it?" asked McGlade. "If someone came to you and told you about a murder, what would *you* do?"

"Tell the cops," said Rudi.

"You'd tell Pa," said Thomas.

"I'd tell the cops," said Rudi.

"Sure you would," said McGlade. "So why didn't Mr. Burton?"

"He told us to tell Pa," said Thomas. "He knew Pa would call the cops."

McGlade put his arms across his chest and pressed back against his shoulder blades. He was stiff as a poker down his spine and it depressed him. He was going to have to go the full period on workmen's compensation. He was sweating more than he should, too. He'd put on weight. He'd have to drop ten or fifteen pounds before he started work again. "Let's take a breather," he said.

They sat on a bench overlooking the Great Lawn. A group of kids were playing softball at the nearest of the diamonds.

McGlade said, "Now, look at that. You don't get anywhere in a ball game unless everybody does what's expected of him."

He addressed himself more to Rudi, sitting on his left—he hadn't had the same pull with Thomas since Burton had opened up the shop on Columbus and come to live around the corner the year before. But it was Thomas he was aiming his sermon at.

"No," said Rudi. He'd no idea what McGlade was talking about.

McGlade nodded stiffly toward the kids beyond the protective wire fence that stood between the bench and the ball game. He said, "Just watch."

The pitcher threw. The batter hit. The center fielder came in and took the ball on the second bounce and flung it low to first base. It beat the batter by a yard. It was a little cameo of perfect human cooperation— neat, ordered, successful.

"You see that?" said McGlade, as if he'd set the whole thing up to illustrate some Sunday School parable.

"Great," said Rudi. He still didn't understand.

But Thomas understood. He said, "It didn't have

anything to do with Mr. Burton. We were the ones who
... you know. *We* should have told the cops."

"No," said McGlade, getting up. "You're kids. Nobody expects that of kids. But a grown man—a guy
like Mr. Burton—that's different. You expect a grown
man to ... like, do his duty."

They jogged slowly round the Great Lawn and
back toward the Delacorte Theater. In the spring, Mc-
Glade had been hired to arrange the wrestling match
in *As You Like It* there, but the accident had put an
end to that. He said, "Why don't we all go over to
Gracie Mansion on Saturday and watch the carnival
of sailing ships on the East River? Maybe afterward
we'll go up to the Cloisters and have a picnic. If it
wasn't for this back of mine ... Hey, why don't I go
see Mr. Burton, get him to rent me a bicycle?"

It was Friday when McGlade called at Burton's shop.
Outside, a rack of rental bikes stood chained together.
The window was so plastered with ads for Schwinn
and Fuji, the shop, visible through the wide-open double
doors, seemed dim despite the stripes of fluorescent
lighting.

The second McGlade walked through the doors, a
warning buzzer bleeped. He'd broken some electronic
circuit. There was no one around. Two fans hummed
in the ceiling, driving the hot air around the shop without cooling it. On either side, there were cycles suspended from wall racks six feet from the ground, and
below them, glass-fronted cupboards full of spares.
A stripped-down machine lay on a bench halfway down
the shop.

McGlade called, "Mr. Burton?"

There was no reply.

McGlade couldn't believe it. Putting an average
figure of $200 on each bike in sight, he figured there
must be $10,000 on the walls alone. How could a guy
leave stuff like that unguarded, with the doors wide

open? He glanced at the ceiling for the TV cameras surveying the place. There were none.

Ahead of him and to his left was a counter and the cash register. He stepped forward and put out his hand. He wasn't going to touch the register—it was the last thing he'd ever have done—but he wanted to see how far a stranger walking into the place could go without being detected. There was a pile of literature beside the register. If he could pick up two or three sheets of that, then anyone else could as easily have opened the register.

But, as his hand touched the counter, there was a deep-throated growl from the shadows, and a moment later a German shepherd had flung itself forward, locked McGlade's bare right forearm in his teeth, and hurled him back against the wall just left of the doorway. If it hadn't been for the wall, the dog would have had him over on his back and been on top of him. He shook his arm and kicked at the animal, but he couldn't get it loose.

He shouted, "Burton!"

Burton came out of a door at the back of the shop, a towel in his hand. He didn't make any attempt to order the dog off. "What were you doing?" he asked.

"Nothing!"

"He doesn't go for people doing nothing."

"I wanted some literature!" yelled McGlade, still trying to shake the dog loose. "I went to get it and he came straight at me!"

"Why didn't you ring the bell?" asked Burton, nodding to a length of rope hanging from the ceiling.

"I didn't see the bell! The buzzer went off—isn't that enough? Get this fucker off me!"

"Stay where you are," said Burton, still drying his hands on the towel.

"Christ Almighty, don't you recognize me?" McGlade howled. "I live over the liquor store. You've seen me from your deck!"

"Sure I recognize you," said Burton. "I recognize a lot of people. What difference does that make?"

"Please!" McGlade begged. There was desperation in his cry. He was trying to reach a length of steel tubing propped against the wall to his left, but the dog was resisting. He didn't want to rip its teeth through his flesh by dragging his arm away.

At last Burton said, "Okay, Blue, let him go."

The dog hesitated.

"Let him go!" snapped Burton.

The dog released McGlade and went to Burton. Burton struck him twice sharply across the muzzle with his open hand. "I said, let him go!" The dog took it without a protest and turned away and dropped down again in the shadows.

McGlade bent his arm and looked at it. A full set of tooth prints was clear, and blood trickled down to his elbow. He screamed, "You oughta have the thing put away!" There was hysteria in his voice. His brushed-forward, thinning hair was dark with sweat, and his cheeks were puffed and red. "Christ!" he cried. "You never heard of people? *People!* That's what cities are built for, not these fucking wolves!"

Burton said, "Yeah, I've heard of people. I prefer wolves." He dropped the towel on the bench that supported the stripped-down bike, went to the counter and picked up a pile of literature, and walked over to where McGlade was nursing his arm. "Here," he said. "If you want some literature, here's some literature. Have a good day."

He would have turned and gone back to the bench, but McGlade said, "All right, I'm sorry! I should have looked for the bell. I should have called louder. I should have known you raised wolves."

The dog growled at the raised voice, a deep rumbling sound in the shadows.

Burton said "Shut up" without turning his head. The growling stopped at once.

"Can't you keep it on a chain?" McGlade asked.

"What use would he be on a chain?" Burton snapped. "You forgotten the blackout? Nobody put *those* animals on chains. Why should I put Blue on one?"

"Suppose it hadn't been me that came in? Suppose it had been some kid?"

"Kids are the worst," said Burton.

McGlade's heartbeat finally slowed. Some of the high color was leaving his face. He took a handkerchief out of his back pocket and mopped his forehead and neck. "You got anywhere I can wash my arm?"

"In back," said Burton. He turned and picked up the towel from the bench behind him and tossed it to McGlade. "Don't get any blood on it. And keep your hands off the soap."

The dog had been well trained. The bite hadn't done more than break the skin on McGlade's arm. But he was still shaking from the shock of the attack, and just below the surface was a barely controlled fury at the way Burton had behaved. What kind of a guy was this who set dogs on customers, and then didn't even offer a word of apology?

When he returned to the shop, he saw that Burton was reassembling the derailleur of the bike on the bench. He had put a small portable fan beside him, and it was blowing his dark hair across his forehead. He seemed totally unaware of McGlade, standing not three feet from him.

McGlade stared at him. The guy was tall and strong and well built. He looked somewhere in his late thirties. He'd kept himself very trim. There was no sign of his running to seed. Everything about him showed a control of his situation: the way he moved, the way his hands worked on the gear wheels, the way he ignored McGlade.

Fascination began to replace McGlade's earlier fury. It brought him back to the real reason for his presence in the shop—an uncontrollable curiosity. Why hadn't

Burton called the police when he heard about the killing from the Stern kids? A citizen had a *duty* to respond. Jesus, everybody else was responding: the press, the TV channels, the mayor. Burton must be the only guy in New York City who hadn't. Why?

McGlade tested various approaches in his head. He might come right out with it and say, "What the hell were you playing at, sending those two kids home? You should have got right on the phone to the cops." Or: "Look, Mr. Burton, let me ask you a question. You're riding through Central Park. There's a woman ahead. A guy comes out of the bushes and attacks her. What do you do?"

In the end, he asked, "How much do you charge for rental?"

Burton put down the derailleur, then turned and looked at McGlade. "Is *that* what you came in for?" he asked finally. "You wanna rent a bike?"

McGlade nodded.

"Why didn't you say so in the first place?" snapped Burton.

They stood facing each other for a moment. Then Burton went to a cupboard and took out a jar of antiseptic cream. "Here," he said, handing it to McGlade. "Put some of this on that arm. I don't wanna go losing a new customer."

▼▼▼▼▼▼▼▼▼▼▼▼▼▼▼▼▼

CHAPTER 4

▲▲▲▲▲▲▲▲▲▲▲▲▲▲▲▲▲

McGlade rented a battered Raleigh tourer. It looked about on its last wheels. Burton wanted $50 through August. McGlade got him down to $35, but agreed to pay in advance.

When McGlade got the bike back to the liquor store, Stern said, "Chain it up in the yard next to the boys' bikes."

"Suppose I give you a couple of bucks a week," said McGlade.

"I don't want anything." Stern was grateful to McGlade for the interest he took in the boys. If he took them off to Gracie Mansion to watch the sailboats in the morning, that was all the payment Stern wanted.

"Well, let me owe it to you, Tony. I don't like being obligated. I'll let you have it when I get started work again."

"You're not obligated. The boys like you. They stay out of trouble with you. If it wasn't for you, we might have had to send them upstate to one of the summer camps. You know who they send up there—kids from Harlem, kids from the South Bronx. I don't want my boys picking up bad ways. I'm grateful. Believe me."

It was a quarter to midnight when Maria Stern went to bed. She was dead with tiredness, the way she always was. If she'd lived in a shoe box, she'd still have found enough housework to keep her occupied every waking minute of her life.

Stern began to check the day's sales and get the empty crates ready to carry down through the trapdoor into the cellar. Most of the liquor stores were closed by eleven, but not his. He'd have stayed open beyond midnight if the law had allowed it. Life was work—that's what he'd been brought up to believe. Now it was part of his nature. It would have bothered him to think he'd missed a customer by closing a second before he had to.

It was two minutes to midnight when the warning bell pinged. When he looked up, there was a black guy coming into the store. He was tall—a couple of inches over six feet—and heavily built, maybe two hundred and fifty pounds. He wore a green sleeveless vest and cut-off jeans. His eyes were bloodshot, and he moved toward Stern a little off balance.

Stern was standing by the cash register on the counter. There was a sheet of bulletproof glass in front of him, and on either side of that, a wire grill. To get to him, the man would have to come around the counter, and long before he reached him, Stern would already have picked up the loaded automatic pistol from the shelf underneath.

But the man wasn't a threat to Stern. He came in late most nights and picked up a final pint of vodka. He lived with a beautiful young Hispanic woman in one of the brownstones that backed onto the rear yards. What the hell she saw in him, nobody knew. She could have had any man she wanted. Anyone watching her crossing Grand Army Plaza in her Calvin Klein creation would take her for a film star staying at the Pierre.

The man said, "Gimme a pint of Buckmaster." He fumbled with a roll of notes, then pushed a five-dollar bill toward the slit between glass and counter top.

It was his third visit that day. Stern wondered where he got the money from. Apart from his visits to the store, the only thing Stern had seen him doing was sitting on the stoop of his brownstone sucking beer from a can through a straw. Maybe he sent the girl out to work. How could you talk about integration with people like that? thought Stern. It wasn't the fact that they were black. God Almighty, they could be any color they liked, for all he cared. Color had nothing to do with it. What mattered was that they took a whole different view of life.

He reached behind him, picked up a bottle, and passed it through the bars, aware that the man was watching every move he made, keeping the tips of his fingers on the five-dollar bill as if he expected a rip-off. There'd never be any trust between them, however many times they did business. Guys like that never trusted anyone.

When the man had gone, Stern closed and bolted the grills on the store windows, then locked the door. He left the light on over the counter so that the night patrol would have a clear view of the place, and tripped the burglar alarm. Finally he picked up the automatic, pushed it into his belt, and went upstairs.

It took him an hour to make his daily entries in his books and balance his cash receipts. He worked in a room overlooking Columbus, immediately underneath the boys' bedroom. The window was wide open, and the beginnings of a little breeze touched his bare arms and face. It might be the start of a break in the weather. What they needed was a couple of days of rain to swill the garbage out of the streets and bring some breathable air down from upstate.

It was a little after one o'clock when he climbed the final flight of stairs to the bedrooms. He listened at the open doors of the children's rooms. There was no sound from Elsa's room, but when he stood outside the boys' room, he heard Thomas whisper, "Is that you, Pa?"

"Go to sleep," Stern whispered. "It's late."

"I can't sleep," Thomas whispered. "It's so hot."

"There's gonna be a storm. It'll be better after that."

He heard Thomas slip out of bed and tiptoe across the room. Stern was tired; he'd been on his feet for more than eighteen hours. He braced himself for a scene with the boy.

Thomas came out of the room and stood in the doorway, silhouetted against the lights from Columbus Avenue that shone through the window. Stern looked at him with some surprise. It seemed that he'd grown without Stern noticing. He was turning from a boy into a young man. Where had the years slipped away to?

Stern said, "Thomas, it's after one. I've gotta get to bed."

"I don't wanna go off with Mr. McGlade and Rudi, Pa. I wanna get a job."

"Listen," whispered Stern, "I've gotta be up early, you know that."

"I'm serious, Pa," said Thomas. "I wanna help."

"Go to bed, Thomas."

"I'm old enough."

"You're ten. Ten! You should be getting your sleep."

"I'll be eleven in a couple of months, Pa. You were working before you were eleven."

"Who told you that nonsense?" said Stern.

"You were working on the farm—helping with the harvest, driving the horses—back home in Germany. You told me so."

"I *left* Germany," said Stern. "I came to America so you could have a better life. Now, go to bed!"

"Pa, I'm on *vacation*."

The boy wasn't going to give an inch. He'd somehow got Stern into a position that he couldn't get out of. Stern could have ordered Thomas back to bed—used his authority as head of the family, the way his own father used to do—but it didn't seem right anymore. The boy was so obviously serious. He'd made a reasonable statement: He wanted a vacation job. In fact, it was more than reasonable; it was *creditable*. He'd said he wanted to help. How many other kids of his generation would be that thoughtful? He felt a sudden surge of pride in his son.

At last Stern said, "What kind of a job, Thomas?"

"With Mr. Burton."

"Mr. Burton?" Stern was trying to collect his tired thoughts. It was the last thing he'd imagined Thomas saying. Yet, if he'd spent more time with the boy, he'd have seen it coming.

"Everybody's renting bikes this time of year," said Thomas. "Particularly weekends. He's gotta need somebody to help with the cleaning. I can take care of a bike. I can adjust saddles and handlebars. I know about lubrication—that sort of thing."

"You're not working for Burton," said Stern. The time had gone for being reasonable. The boy didn't know what he was talking about.

"But, Pa——"

"I said no!"

"Can we talk about it?"

"No."

"I don't mean now, but tomorrow maybe?"

"No!"

"But, Pa, why not?"

Stern's patience snapped. He said, "Go to bed! I don't want to talk about it again. You hear me?"

Stern turned and went into his own bedroom and closed the door behind him. His wife had left the air-conditioner on again. He turned it off, clicking his tongue in disapproval, the way he did every time it happened. It cost more to cool a room in a New York summer than it did to heat in the winter; but no matter how often he explained it to Maria, she never seemed to understand. More often than not, when he came into the room at night, the machine would still be humming. Maybe she was too tired to notice. But he sometimes wondered if she was making some unconscious protest about the way they lived.

He slipped into bed, trying not to disturb her. He could feel the heat of her body beside him. Despite everything, he still felt protective. She was ten years younger than he, and he'd never been able to get in touch with her. There was always a part she kept hidden, and it left something in him unfulfilled. He loved her in the dutiful way he felt he ought to; but there'd never been any passion between them. He was resigned to that now. He kept his strongest feelings for his children.

He lay on his back and closed his eyes, but sleep wouldn't come. He couldn't relax. He was already beginning to regret the way he'd spoken to Thomas. He thought of what had happened to the boys during the past few days: stumbling on a murdered woman, facing the police and the press . . . He thought of his daughter, growing from a girl into a young woman in such an environment. How long would it be before something happened to *her?* But what could he do about it? He couldn't move. All his capital was tied up in the store.

Through the closed windows, he could hear the distant wail of an ambulance siren. Somebody was dying out there in the gutter, but who cared? He slipped his hand out and touched the gun, now lying on the shelf under the bedside table. Even after all these years, this culture went against his grain. He'd been brought up to believe that society protected its members. If you subscribed to society, it looked after you. And God knows, he'd subscribed to it. As a boy in Germany, he'd joined the Hitler Youth and given the right salutes. The war had changed his views, of course. Adolescent obedience had given way to mature skepticism. But the basic view he took of society was too deep to be eradicated.

New York *wasn't* a society—that was its problem. It was a collection of Indians all going their own ways. There wasn't a man or a woman in the place who'd give up an ounce of personal freedom for the common good. *Freedom!* He was sick to death of the word. Why didn't someone talk about responsibility?

A sudden flash of lightning lit up the room, followed by a crushing peal of thunder. The rest of the country was suffering a cold spell. In Vegas, the temperature had reached the lowest for any August on record. But New York . . . New York was different. New York wasn't America. New York was a jungle; every paper you picked up used the phrase.

No, he thought. Jungles had rules; otherwise nothing would survive. New York had no rules. You couldn't even predict from one second to the next what the guy coming toward you on the sidewalk was going to do. The law of the jungle was the survival of the fittest. Who were the "fittest" in New York? Who was New York selecting for survival? The gays with the biggest German shepherds, and the brown baggers, who weren't worth ripping off. New York was breeding a future of wolves and derelicts.

Stern took his hand off the gun and turned on his side. He slipped into sleep, reconciled to the fact that he was going to have a sleepless night.

When he woke, he thought for a moment that what he heard was simply a continuation of wakefulness. He got up, went to the window, and peered through the slats in the venetian blind. It was raining—a steady, solid downpour that dimmed the lights on Amsterdam Avenue and formed great pools in the yards below. But it wasn't the rain that had roused him; it was another sound—a human sound. He thought at once of his daughter.

He pulled on his pants and went onto the landing. The hot, damp air outside the bedroom pricked his eyeballs and brought the sweat to his face. He went straight to Elsa's room. Through the open doors, he could make out her bed against the right-hand wall. The sheet had been thrown off and the bed was empty. The rain hissed outside the open window, a continuous sheet of falling water. Thunder crashed again over the park, and lightning tore the sky apart.

He whispered, "Elsa? Are you there, honey?" He tried to keep his voice light. He didn't want to admit, even to himself, the panic he was feeling.

There was no reply.

"Elsa?" he said, going up to the bed and putting his hand on the rumpled sheet.

A voice said, "I'm here, Pa."

He turned. She was sitting in the corner by the window. "Are you all right?" he asked.

As he spoke, he could hear his voice tremble with relief. She was only thirteen, but youth hadn't protected the other three girls from Bald Eagle. What could Stern do as a father to make life safer for her? The other girls had had fathers. Two of them had made appeals to Bald Eagle on TV, asking him to please consider what he was doing. One of them had talked about "this terrible waste of beautiful young people," and Elsa was beautiful; everybody told him so. The other had said, "Let me appeal to you as a parent. If only you knew the terrible suffering you are causing, I believe you'd come forward and give yourself up." It hadn't made any difference. It hadn't saved that girl in the rotunda. All you could do was warn a daughter of the things that lay in wait for her in the streets, and hope to God she'd listen.

"What's the noise, Pa?" the girl asked. She was huddled in the chair with her arms around her knees.

"It's raining," said Stern. "It'll cool things off."

"It wasn't the rain," she said.

He knew it wasn't the rain. Rain never woke him once he'd got to sleep. But he didn't want to admit his worst fears. If there was another killing, the block associations were going to put vigilantes on the streets. It was the last thing Stern wanted. He'd seen self-appointed law enforcers going after the Jews in Cologne thirty-five years ago. Vigilantes wouldn't solve New York's problems.

He said, "I guess it was that dog of Mr. Burton's."

"I don't like that guy," she said.

As she spoke, the noise came again, piercing the slush of the rain, reverberating down the tunnels of the streets. It was scarcely human; yet, as he heard it, Stern knew that it *was* human.

"Stay here," he said. He went back to his bedroom and picked up the gun. His wife didn't stir. She lay curled in a ball under the sheet, like a hibernating squirrel. The noise rose up from the yards outside, with the continuous sizzle of falling rain behind it.

A voice from above him called into the night, "They're animals! You can't change them!"

It was McGlade's voice. Stern threw open the window, but there was nothing in sight. Far below, rain flooded the yard of the brownstone where four young gays had built a garden in the spring. Just as he was about to close the window, he heard somebody answer McGlade:

"I don't wanna change them! If a guy wants to knock the shit out of his woman, that's his affair. As long as he lets me sleep!"

Stern peered out again. On the deck that jutted out level with his room was a man in a T-shirt and white briefs. The light from the open window behind him lit up his back but left his face in shadow. It was Burton. He was leaning with his elbows on the frail wooden railing, looking away from Stern into the yards below. The rain poured down on him. The soaking T-shirt clung to his body. Stern could see the tautness of the muscle structure down Burton's back, and the heavily muscled legs.

"What about the woman?" McGlade called. "Hasn't she got a right to some protection?"

"Okay," called Burton, without turning to look in McGlade's direction. "Let her walk out on the guy.

Let her go to the cops. Shit, we pay enough in taxes. Why we gotta do everybody's job as well?"

Somewhere below, a woman was howling. The sound went on and on, a continuous series of uncontrolled sobs. It turned Stern's gut to hear it. He was going to have to do something.

Burton lifted his head and looked upward. He called, "Did you put some plastic sheeting over that bike?"

"The bike's okay," McGlade called back.

"No use letting it rust the first day you rent it," said Burton, turning away and climbing back into his apartment.

Stern called the police. The black guy he'd sold the liquor to had beaten up the woman before. The police never seemed to be around when it happened, and when they finally came, they never seemed to do anything. Burton was right this time: She ought to walk out on the bastard.

Officer Callaghan said over the phone, "We've already had a call, Tony. Two guys are investigating it. If it's another murder, we'll get to it."

"I didn't say it was a murder," said Stern. "But the woman's been screaming. The guy she's living with has beaten her up again. I sold him a pint of vodka just before midnight."

"Don't blame yourself," said Callaghan. "You're in business to sell vodka."

"I'm not blaming myself," said Stern. It was true. He didn't feel any guilt.

"That's fine," said Callaghan. "Leave it to us. We'll take care of it."

Stern went back and stood at the bedroom window. The rain fell in one continuous sheet. The lights that had gone on in the brownstones were out now. New York was a rain forest with a hundred different levels. You lived at second-floor level or twelfth-floor level or thirty-ninth-floor level. But there were no connections between the levels—no communication pathways, no ties of human responsibility, no love. From each level, you could look up or down on human agony without feeling guilt or pity or any kind of involvement.

If that was how God felt, living at the highest level of all, God help humanity, thought Stern.

CHAPTER 5

There was no carnival of sailing ships. It rained for four days without a break—four days in which eleven inches of rain fell on Manhattan. Thomas began to think it must be dryer at the bottom of the Hudson than it was on Columbus Avenue.

At first, New York sighed with relief. The temperature dropped, and a breeze began to filter down from the north. The rain swilled the trash off the sidewalks and carried the dog shit from under the parked cars down toward the gratings. The stink of urine disappeared from the steps of the Bethesda Fountain in Central Park.

But every day creates some new record in New York City. After the first hour, the system couldn't cope with so much water. The swirling garbage clogged the gratings. The rain built up behind, then crossed the roadways. By Saturday afternoon, the water had backed up onto the sidewalks and begun to pour down into the cellars through the gaps in the iron coverings. Everything Stern sold came wrapped in glass. But the storekeepers with perishables on the floor began to speculate about bankruptcy.

Late Sunday, statistics from the Belvedere weather station confirmed that if the rain continued to fall at the present rate, all records were going to be broken within forty-eight hours. The mayor's office refused to

confirm a press report that the city was making a plea
for federal aid. The Monday TV news shows focused
on the deluge that was inundating New York, only
incidentally mentioning hurricane Brenda, which was
battering Florida.

By Tuesday the rain had eased up. The water began
to drain away, leaving the garbage piled over the
gratings that covered the road drains. The "I-Love-a-
Clean-New-York" campaign put volunteers on the
streets. When Thomas got up on Wednesday, everything had changed. The trash had been stacked neatly
on the sidewalks in black plastic bags, ready for collection. There was sweet, clean air coming down from the
north. The sky was a cloudless blue. It could have been
an early spring morning.

Thomas hadn't spoken to his father about working
for Burton since their clash in the early hours of Saturday. There was a barrier between them now, and
Thomas didn't like that. He had always got on well
with his father. Now he wished he hadn't mentioned
Mr. Burton, though what his father had against the
man, he didn't know. Okay, he thought, if he couldn't
work for Mr. Burton, perhaps he could help his father.
He offered to mop out the cellar.

The steps into the cellar led down through a trap
in the floor of the store. Thomas had finished the job
and was climbing the steps with a bucket and mop
when the warning bell sounded and someone came into
the store. It was a woman. The sight of her brought
him to a stop with only his eye above floor level.

His father was standing behind the counter. The
woman walked straight up to him and called through
the glass, "Was it you told the cops about my man?"

Thomas found her speech difficult to understand.
She was the Hispanic who lived around the corner with
the big black guy. Obviously she'd been hit in the
mouth, because her bottom lip was split and puffed
outward, the skin taut and blue, like a bicycle inner

tube protruding through a split in the tire. She had a Band-Aid over her left eyebrow and another across the cheekbone. The bruises under her eye and down to the line of her jaw were yellow against the deep olive of her skin.

Stern reached behind him and slid a bottle toward her. He said, "I didn't get to the phone first. When I called, the police already knew."

She put her face right up to the glass and shouted, "Next time, mind your fuckin' business!"

Stern shrugged and put the bottle back. "Okay," he said, turning away from her and starting to rearrange the bottles behind him. "Let him kill you."

"What d'you mean, kill me?" she cried. "You think I can't take care of myself?"

"You were screaming the block down. It was four in the morning. What d'you expect me to think?"

"They took him away, the fuckin' cops! Broke the door down, dragged him outta bed. That's what you wanted, isn't it? You satisfied now? What am I gonna do without him?" When Stern didn't reply, she screamed, "Hey, punk, I'm talkin' to you! You hear me?"

Stern turned to her. "Okay, lady," he said. "I'll know next time."

"You better!" she screamed, glaring at him through the glass. Then she turned and walked toward the door.

Thomas was trembling. It was the sight of her face that disturbed him. The bruised flesh and broken skin took him straight back to the face he'd seen lying by the steps in the rotunda. He started to climb out of the cellar, when the woman suddenly turned from the door and screamed at Stern:

"Where were you the night that kid was strangled in the park? D'you try to help *her?* D'you get the cops in *then?* Shit no! You don' wanna help nobody. You just don' like livin' with blacks! Well, all right! I don' like livin' with you! An' lemme tell you this, man: They gonna let him out when they find out he didn't do nothin'. I'm gonna get him to pay you a visit then. An' man—Jesus Chris' help you!"

When the woman had gone, Thomas climbed into the store. He was going to walk straight out back as if nothing had happened, but Stern turned and saw him.

"You heard her?" Stern asked.

"Yes," said Thomas. He still had the bucket and mop in his hands.

"D'you think she was right? D'you think I called the police because the man was black?"

"I don't know, Pa," said Thomas.

"It's not easy, knowing what to do for the best," said Stern. "I guess I did the right thing, whatever she thinks. I've got nothing against blacks—just against bums."

Thomas felt uncomfortable. His father was speaking to him as an equal, just as if he was another man instead of a son. He'd never done that before. Thomas wasn't sure how to handle it. He said, "I've finished the cellar, Pa. I guess we ought to leave the flap open to let some air in."

Stern said, "I guess so." He came from behind the counter to where Thomas was standing by the open cellar flap. "Do you really want to help Mr. Burton?"

"That's okay, Pa." Thomas didn't want to add to his father's worries.

"If I said okay, would you still want to go?"

"D'you mean it, Pa?"

"Yeah, I mean it," said Stern. He put a hand on his son's shoulder. "In the old country, I did what my father told me. It's the way we were brought up. But that's a long time ago, and this is America. It's your vacation. I've no right to tell you how to spend it. If you want to work for Mr. Burton . . . okay. Go ahead."

Thomas rode his bike over right away. When he got to Burton's shop, he stood in the open doorway, the machine leaning against his body.

Burton was working at the bench, a mask over his mouth and nose. He was respraying a bike frame with an aerosol can of paint. The dog lay in the shadows beside him, his eyes fixed on Thomas. Thomas cleared his throat.

Burton put down the paint can, lifted the mask, and called out, "Yeah?" Still he didn't look up. He was examining the paintwork.

The sound of the big fan in the ceiling over Burton's head made the whole shop hum. Thomas called, "You need any help, Mr. Burton?"

Burton didn't answer. He was lifting the frame up toward the light so that he could see it better. He picked up the aerosol and gave the frame a quick squirt.

"Mr. Burton?" Thomas called again.

"What kind of help?"

"Cleaning. Lubrication."

"Can you weld?"

"No."

"Can you use a buffing machine?"

"No."

"What *can* you do?"

"I can use a wrench. I can take a wheel off. I can mend a puncture."

Burton looked at him for the first time. He said, "*Can* you, by Christ. Come on in."

Thomas chained his bike to the rack on the sidewalk and went inside. The dog lifted his head and gave a low growl. Burton snapped, "Blue! Damn you!"

Thomas looked at the racks of brand-new machines hanging from the walls. There were silver Fujis and pale-blue Panasonics and golden Motobecanes. Every one of them spelled freedom. You didn't need oil or gasoline. You didn't need insurance. You didn't need a license. Mounted on one of those, you could go all the way to the Pacific Ocean without asking anyone's permission. It must be the greatest thing on earth, he thought, to own a bike shop.

Burton watched him gazing at the machines. "You got seven hundred bucks?" he asked.

Thomas grinned and said, "No." He guessed that Burton knew what he'd been thinking.

"Well, okay," said Burton, wiping his hands on an oily rag, "let's see what you can do." He pointed to a wheel leaning against the counter. "Repair that flat," he said.

Thomas looked at the dog. He was watching every move Thomas made. Thomas screwed up his courage and asked, "What'll you pay?"

"What's that?" asked Burton.

"What'll you pay me?"

Burton looked him up and down, his eyes resting on Thomas's Snoopy T-shirt. "Pay you?" he said. "You oughta be paying me for the experience."

"I don't expect full rates," said Thomas.

"Well, that's nice," said Burton. "How do I know you're any good? If you make a mess of it, I've got to fix it. What happens then?"

"I'll give you the money back."

Burton dropped the mask on the bench and went to stand in front of Thomas, his hands in the back pockets of his jeans. Again he looked him up and down. At last he asked, "How old are you?"

"Eleven. Nearly."

"You been in business before?"

"No," said Thomas.

"You coulda fooled me. Does your pa know you're here?"

"Yes."

Burton thought for a moment. At last he nodded. "Okay. I'll give you a buck for every flat you repair. *After* I've inspected it."

Thomas stared at him. Was Burton really offering him a job in the bike shop?

Burton said, "Well? D'you want the job or not?"

"Sure, Mr. Burton," said Thomas. "A buck a flat —that's fine. When do I get to start?"

Burton picked up the wheel with the flat and handed it to Thomas. "You've started," he said. He pointed to the steel shelving on the back wall and said, "Third shelf down, left-hand side. You'll find tire irons, French chalk, patches. There's a bucket and some water in the bathroom, straight through that door there."

"Aren't you gonna watch me, Mr. Burton?" Thomas asked. He felt less confident, now that he was actually employed.

"Why should I watch you?" asked Burton, going back to the bench. "You say you can do it, I believe you. And stop calling me Mr. Burton, it makes me feel fifty."

"Okay," said Thomas.

He got the tire irons and lifted the inner tube off the wheel rim. The dog never took his eyes off him. He went to the bathroom and brought back a bucket of water. The animal growled as he passed him.

"Ignore him," said Burton. "He'll get used to you."

Thomas fed the inner tube through the water. The escaping stream of air bubbles showed him where the puncture was. He began to dry the tube with a wad of rag before using the marking pencil on it. "If I can't call you Mr. Burton," he suddenly asked, "what should I call you?"

"D'you have to call me anything? Can't you work without talking?" Burton snapped.

Thomas earned four bucks that first day. The next day, when it became clear that there weren't going to be enough flats to keep him fully occupied, Burton changed the arrangement. He said, "Let's do it right, kid. Say you come six hours a day—three in the morning, three in the afternoon. I'll pay you fifty cents an hour."

"That's only three bucks," said Thomas.

"Jesus!" cried Burton. "How'd I get into this? Okay —what'll you take?"

"A buck an hour?" Thomas wanted the job—he wanted to work with Burton in the shop—so he said it in such a way that it still left room for negotiation.

"Five bucks a day," said Burton. "But I wanna see results."

That afternoon Burton was called out. Someone had been going up Central Park West on one of his rental bikes and run into a downtown bus. The police wanted him to collect what was left of it.

"Have to go out." he told Thomas. "Blue'll keep an eye on the cash."

"How long will you be?" asked Thomas.

"Depends," said Burton. "Anybody calls, tell them to leave a phone number. I'll get back to them." He went over to the dog and gave him a couple of cuffs across the muzzle. "You behave yourself, now, you hear me? You do what Thomas tells you or I'll have the ASPCA pick you up."

Two blacks came and stood in the doorway when Burton had gone. They were tall and loose-limbed, and one wore a gold stud in his ear. He stood looking toward the cash register, while his buddy leaned with his back against the doorpost, eyeing the bikes in the wall racks. Blue bared his teeth and growled.

The black with the ear stud called, "Hey, boy, what about the five bucks you owe us?"

"What five bucks?" Thomas called back. They didn't bother him. He'd seen others like them come into the liquor store, and heard his father handle them.

"We did a job for the man. He said to come by and collect five bucks."

"Come back when he's here," said Thomas.

The black leaning against the doorpost straightened up and took a couple of steps into the shop. The warning buzzer bleeped. Blue got up and started toward him, and he retreated. The two men hung around on the sidewalk for a while, then finally drifted off downtown.

Thomas said, "Good boy, Blue," and slapped his thigh. The dog looked at him, then walked slowly over to where he was working at the bench and dropped down beside him.

Burton had been gone half an hour when Blue lifted his head and looked toward the doorway. Thomas caught sight of the movement and following the dog's gaze, he saw a woman standing in the doorway holding a bike. She was in her twenties, slim, about five feet seven, with shoulder-length blonde hair that glistened like gold in the sunlight.

"Mr. Burton around?" she called.

"He's out," said Thomas, coming forward. "Can I take a message?"

Blue had got to his feet. He was watching the woman, but he didn't make any threatening move.

"Are you his new partner?" the woman asked.

"I work for him," said Thomas.

"That's nice. How long will he be?"

"Not long."

"If I wait for him, will Blue let me in?"

"I guess so," said Thomas, turning to look at Blue, who was still standing by the bench.

She wheeled the bike into the shop and propped it on its stand. She was wearing a blue cotton shirt and jeans. "What's your name?" she asked.

"Thomas Stern."

"And how long have you been working for Mr. Burton?"

"Two days." He began to feel cornered. He said, "Do you want me to take a look at the bike?"

"You think you can fix it? The front wheel keeps jamming. Something's wrong with the brake."

The return spring had broken on the front caliper. Thomas got a screwdriver and removed it. "I expect

we have some new springs. I'll have to wait for Mr.
Burton. I don't know where we keep them yet."

"Hey, where did you learn to do this?" She was
bending down with her hands on her knees, watching
him working.

"I've got my own bike," said Thomas. "I learned
from that."

"You really know bikes, don't you. Mr. Burton's
lucky to have you."

For a moment, Thomas thought she was going to
muss up his hair with her hand. She didn't. All her
reactions seemed exaggerated to him. He said, "Do you
teach school?"

"Oh, Lord!" she cried. "Does it show that much?"
Her blue eyes were very serious.

"Not really," he said. "It was just a guess."

She looked as if she was going to say something else,
but at that moment Burton walked in with the remains
of the rental bike and threw it in the corner by the
door. The bus had gone over both wheels. He went
over to the counter and took an insurance-claim form
out of the drawer.

The woman waited. He ignored her and began to
fill in the form. She said, "Hi there. Remember me?"

When he didn't answer, she said, "I bought a bike
from you in the spring. I paid a hundred and eighty-
nine ninety-five, cash. It's broken. Your partner says
it's the brake spring. *Now* do you think you could take
your nose out of that paper?"

He turned to the metal shelving on the wall behind
the counter and took down a box. "Fix the lady's bike,"
he said to Thomas.

"Okay," said Thomas, catching the new spring Burton tossed to him.

Burton continued to fill in the form. When he'd
signed it, he folded it carefully into three, slipped it into an envelope, addressed it, and laid it in front of him

on the counter. At last he looked up. "I remember," he said. "Miss Coburn."

"*Miz* Coburn," she said.

"What does that mean—'*Miz*' Coburn? You're married but still available? Or you're unmarried but not in the market?" He pulled an order book from under the counter and began thumbing through it.

"Oh, I'm in the market," she said. "For the right customer."

Burton tapped the order book with a finger and said, "It's here. Sixty-seventh Street. *Fay* Coburn. I let you have ten percent off because you were a blonde."

Fay Coburn laughed. "Like hell you did. More like you *added* ten percent because I was a woman."

Both Thomas and Blue were watching them. She was standing square-on to Burton. Thomas didn't know whether they were mad at each other or just kidding.

"Can't say I've noticed you among the merchandise," said Burton.

"Maybe you don't get to the best class of markets," Ms. Coburn replied.

Burton came out from behind the counter and walked across to the girl. "I heard they were going to pull Sixty-seventh Street down. I heard ABC was going to put up some plush new studio block."

"Like hell they are," she said. "Didn't you sign the petition to City Hall?"

"Petition?" he asked, a little smile of amusement beginning to play around his lips. "What petition was that? I never sign petitions, and hell, that's thirty blocks away."

She looked directly at him, standing with her back to the open doorway, so that the brilliant afternoon light threw her into partial silhouette. "I might have guessed," she said at last, a slight touch of irritation in her voice. "There's a final hearing this afternoon. We'll know after that."

He took a step to his right so as to avoid the light

right in his eyes, and looked at her critically. He said, "You live by yourself, I guess. If you didn't, the guy wouldn't let you out alone, looking the way you do. You oughta move to the East Side."

She looked at him a moment longer, then turned to Thomas and asked, "Will it take much longer?"

"It's finished," said Thomas. He was putting the final drop of oil on the reassembled brake unit and easing the brake lever.

"Go easy on it in future," said Burton. "It's a machine. It's delicate. It's not like you were handling a man."

She watched him turn away and walk down the shop and switch on the buffing machine. After a moment she called, "What is it you don't like about women? Who is it I remind you of? What did she do to you?"

"Women are all right," he shouted over the hum of the machine. "You've just gotta watch they don't start running your life."

CHAPTER 6

The first day without Thomas, Rudi cycled up to the Cloisters and sat on the grass, overlooking the river, to eat his lunch. He was glad that Thomas was working for Mr. Burton. He didn't have to follow him everywhere now. He could do what he wanted. He didn't get home till four o'clock.

The next day he did two circuits of Central Park in the morning, and, in the afternoon, went to see the polar bear bathing in his concrete tub in the zoo.

On the third day he'd run out of ideas.

He was sitting in the back room, working at a jig-saw puzzle on the table, when the phone rang. Mrs. Stern answered it, shouting into the mouthpiece "Who?" the way she always did. In the end, she turned to Rudi and said, "Go tell Mr. McGlade his agent wants to speak to him."

McGlade answered Rudi's knock right away, but he didn't take the chain off the door and so only part of his face showed in the narrow opening. He hadn't shaved, and was wearing only a pair of cotton shorts. His chest was covered with hair. "Yeah?" he said, as if Rudi had disturbed him in the middle of something important.

"It's the phone, Duke."

"Okay," said McGlade. "Give me a second."

Rudi was back at the table when McGlade came into the back room and walked stiffly through to the phone in the hallway. He'd pulled on a pair of jeans and a T-shirt. Rudi thought he looked very old.

McGlade asked, "Who is this? Oh, Joey. Hey, where've you been? It's two weeks since I heard from you. I called your office. There was no answer. . . . Oh, vacation. St. Croix. That's nice. Who did you take with you—couple of Charlie's Angels?"

Rudi had done the puzzle ten times that morning. He didn't have to think about it anymore. His hands could pick up the necessary pieces and drop them into place automatically. He could make out the shape of Duke's back and head in the hallway as he stood leaning against the wall with the phone to his ear.

McGlade was saying, "Sure I'm taking a vacation, Joey . . . the minute you earn me some money. I figure I might take a month in Paramus water skiing." Suddenly his voice took on a serious tone: "Hey, Joey, what about this war film that Frankenheimer's doing?"

There was a silence. McGlade shifted his stance. His voice took on an edge. He snapped, "What d'you mean, to hell with the war film? Have you seen *Variety*? It says they're gonna need more stunt men than *A Bridge Too Far*. Now, I want a part of that!"

Rudi's fingers picked up another piece of the puzzle and dropped it into position. He wondered if he ought to be there. He thought about going upstairs, but he didn't want Duke to notice him. He didn't want him to know he'd been listening.

"What are you talking about?" McGlade cried. "It says in *Variety* they're still casting. Don't you read *Variety*? . . . No! You listen to me! Okay, so I've got this back trouble. High falls are out. But they're gonna need drivers, they're gonna need guys for the fire stunts. You remember the work I did on *Hot Night*?"

Rudi sat quite still, his hands flat on the table. He looked at the half-finished puzzle without seeing it.

McGlade shouted. "I worked with Frankenheimer on *The Train*. Remind him of that!"

There was a pause. Rudi thought that Duke had put the phone down. Then, suddenly, McGlade's voice broke and he was yelling, half hysterical, "What've I been paying you ten percent for all these years? Two, three thousand a year, just for taking phone calls? Well, get on the phone now. Talk to somebody. I wanna be on that picture!"

There was a long silence. Out of the corner of his eye, Rudi saw Duke take a handkerchief out of his pocket and mop his face. The window in the back room was wide open. Rudi wondered how many people in the brownstones had heard.

At last McGlade said quietly, "You still there, Joey? Joey, I'm sorry. You know what it's been like since spring. . . . Okay. Yeah, okay, Joey, I'm listening. . . . Larry Feinberg? Jesus! That fag with the college education. . . . Okay, Joey. You don't have to worry. I'm not gonna cause any trouble. I guess you can't move in the business nowadays without slipping on turds like that. . . . White shirt, light-colored pants, sure. I'm still drawing workmen's compensation, you know that? . . . Okay, so long as nobody talks to Social Security."

When McGlade came out of the hallway, Rudi asked, "You going out, Duke?"

"Yeah," said McGlade. "They're shooting a film on one of the piers."

"Can I come?" asked Rudi. "I never seen a film being shot."

McGlade considered for a moment. "Why not?" he said. "We'll take the bikes. I just gotta get a shave and change my duds."

They rode downtown as far as Thirty-Sixth Street, then turned west to Pier 76. A police towaway truck was hauling a blue Monte Carlo into the car pound. They followed it through the barrier.

McGlade said to the guard, "I'm with the film unit." The guard waved them through.

Beyond the rows of parked vehicles, a stretch of broken asphalt had been marked off with wooden barriers. Great pools of oily water covered the ground. A girl standing at a gap between two of the barriers said, "Yeah?"

"Duke McGlade," said McGlade. "Joey Feinstein sent me."

She turned without looking at him and pointed to a group of people over to her right. "See Larry," she said. "He's been expecting you."

McGlade chained the bikes to one of the barriers and walked through the gap past the girl. "Stay with me, buddy," he said to Rudi. "You'll be all right." He walked over to the group and said, "Hi, Larry."

Nobody looked at him. A bearded young man in a red-and-yellow-striped rugby shirt was watching the cameraman checking the camera motor.

Rudi whispered, "Is this the place, Duke?" He didn't know what film they were shooting, but he'd expected something a bit more spectacular.

"Yeah," said McGlade.

"I thought there'd be more people and cameras and things."

"They shoot it in bits," said McGlade. "Bit here, bit there. Then they put it all together in the lab. This is only one of the bits."

"What kind of a film is it?" asked Rudi.

"Just a commercial," said McGlade.

The trouble with the camera was sorted out, and the man with the beard turned to McGlade and stared at him the way he would have stared at a derelict. At last he asked, "You the guy from Feinstein's?"

"Hey, come on, Larry," said McGlade, "you know me. We worked together on *Shipwreck.*"

"I told them eleven," said Larry, looking at his watch.

"They told me half past."

"Christ!" Larry took a step toward McGlade and

felt the texture of his shirt between his middle finger and thumb. "That's nylon!" he snapped. "I said cotton!"

McGlade shrugged. "What's the job?" he asked.

"You're crossing the road," said Larry, indicating the puddled asphalt with a flap of his hand. "You get hit by a car. You go down in the water. Then I want you to roll. Quit rolling when I tell you. Think you can manage all that?"

"That's it?" asked McGlade.

"What did you expect? Anything bigger and I'd have flown in a pro from the Coast. Just make sure you finish up face down. That way I can cut in the actor."

"You oughta teach film school," said McGlade. "You're wasted doing this."

"You don't have to take the job," Larry snapped. "Feinstein said you needed the money. I didn't want to see one of the old silent stars on the streets."

McGlade swallowed. "What about the clothes?" he asked, looking down at the white shirt and cream slacks he was wearing.

"We'll pay for the cleaning. I told Feinstein."

"How do I get home?"

"How should *I* know?" Larry said, waving to someone to bring the car into position. "Didn't Feinstein tell you to bring a change of clothes?"

"No."

"He's *your* agent."

The guy made Rudi nervous. He didn't know where he ought to stand. He sure didn't want to get in anyone's way and cause more trouble for Duke. Quickly he took a step backward away from the group round the camera, and fell over a cable.

"For Christ's sake!" snapped Larry, turning on Rudi. "Who's the kid?"

"He's with me," said McGlade.

"Well, tell him to keep out of the way!"

McGlade gave Rudi a pained grin and said, "Just watch the cables, eh, buddy?"

Rudi moved back until he was leaning against one of the barriers. Larry and the crew were on his right. The car was way up on his left.

McGlade went up to the car and examined it. He called to Larry, "Suppose I see it just before it hits me?"

"No."

"That way I could turn into it and absorb some of the shock with my hands and roll over the hood."

"Roll over the hood?" yelled Larry, going toward McGlade. "What're you talking about? Have you any idea what we're paying in rentals? You put a scratch on that hood and you pay for it!"

"Then, what do you want?" asked McGlade. It seemed to Rudi that Duke had just about come to the end of his patience.

"I told you! I want you to get hit by the car and rolled into that water."

"If I can't use my hands, if I can't roll over the hood, how do I miss getting a broken pelvis?"

"Christ Almighty!" Larry shouted. "*You're* the stunt man. Figure it out!" He walked back to the camera crew, and Rudi heard him say, "Jesus wept! What've they sent me? Look at the way he moves! What's he think this is—a *Moulin Rouge* remake? The guy's a cripple! He oughta be in a home!"

Rudi could feel his face burning. He didn't know whether to shout or cry. Didn't they know this was Duke McGlade, the man who had worked with John Wayne on *The Alamo* and once doubled for Alan Ladd? Didn't they know he'd hurt his back and shouldn't be here at all? That he'd come to help them out only because he couldn't stand seeing anyone in a jam?

McGlade called, "I'm gonna walk it through."

Larry turned to the girl standing by him with a note-book and said, "What's he mean—'walk it through'? He'd do better on a skateboard." The girl giggled. Larry called, "Okay, let me know when you're ready."

McGlade spoke to the driver of the car. When he'd placed himself, he waved, and the car came slowly toward him. He walked toward Rudi, across the path of the car, letting the right wing catch him on the forearm and slipping clear of it before the full weight of the vehicle reached his body. He made two slow pirouettes as if he was rolling through the water, then called to Larry, "What d'you think?"

"Let's get it in the can," Larry said. He looked at his watch. "You know who we've got here? Nureyev's grandpa, just out of Cancer Ward Twelve."

A couple of the crew laughed.

The car gathered speed, throwing up water as it came. McGlade began to walk across its path. Rudi felt his heart beat faster. He expected to see some trickery. He couldn't believe that Duke was actually going to let the car hit him. When it did, he felt sick to the soul. There was a resounding clang of metal and the car braked and skidded to one side. McGlade bounced off it, shot forward, and fell into the water.

Larry said, "Let's see if the old bastard can swim." He shouted, "Keep rolling! Just keep rolling! I'll tell you when to quit!" He let McGlade roll four complete revolutions before he shouted, "That's it! Now, finish up face down. Hold it. Keep your face in the water! Okay—cut!"

McGlade lifted his head. Greasy water ran off his face and out of his ears. Rudi could see from his expression that he was having difficulty getting up. He wondered why Duke didn't give up stunting altogether and maybe teach. He'd make a great teacher. He always took so much trouble explaining things. He never rushed you.

McGlade got to his knees and finally stood up. He brushed the surplus water off his shirt and slacks and ran a comb through his hair.

"Get him a towel," Larry called. He was laughing. The girl with the notebook was still giggling.

McGlade walked up to Larry and said, "Okay?"

"Yeah, okay."

"Anything else you want done?"

"Not a thing."

"What's it for?" He was rubbing the towel over his head and round the back of his neck as he talked.

"It's a pilot for a new detergent commercial."

McGlade looked down at his grease-drenched shirt. "Must pack a punch," he said.

"It's a living." Larry had already turned away from McGlade and was talking to the cameraman.

"I hear you're lined up to direct the new Cubby Broccoli," said McGlade.

"I'll be in touch with Feinstein if I can use you," Larry said.

McGlade turned to Rudi and nodded. "Let's pick up the bikes," he said, dropping the towel on top of the barrier rail.

They rode side by side up Tenth Avenue, McGlade on the outside. The great stretches of oily water standing in the gutters over the blocked gratings steamed in the heat. New Yorkers had been hoping for another record: the first August in history when the humidity never came back once it had gone. But that would have been a miracle, not a record, and everybody knew it. It was already getting sticky again. The illuminated temperature reading on the top of the Mony Building was back in the nineties.

Rudi turned his head and looked at Duke. McGlade was riding stiffly, his face a little screwed up. His shirt and pants were steaming. There were streaks of oil where the sludge had trickled down his cheeks, then evaporated. Why did he let himself get pushed around as if he was a nobody? Why didn't he whip them? Rudi wondered.

It wasn't Duke Rudi was mad at; it was Larry, that man with the beard. It was that whole crowd around him who'd been laughing when he'd had to roll through the water. They didn't know who they were working with. This was *Duke McGlade,* the guy who'd once auditioned for Tarzan, the guy who could have whipped the lot of them with both hands tied behind his back, if he'd decided to.

He'd had a different image of Duke. Whenever they'd talked, in the back room of the liquor store or jogging side by side in the park, Duke had told him about the spectacular things: high falls into box rigs that had everybody on the set holding his breath; explosions that could put you in the hospital forever if you didn't get the timing just right; standing, back to camera, while some professional archer shot a cloth-yard arrow into a block of wood hidden under your costume, and praying to God that he was as good as the director said he was. He'd never mentioned having to roll through filth in a clean white shirt on some slime-covered pier while other people laughed at him.

Rudi asked, "You didn't hurt your back, did you, Duke?"

"No," said McGlade. He was staring straight ahead, toward the great white palace of Lincoln Center.

"I guess the grease'll come off in the wash, huh?"

"Sure."

"You didn't mind me coming?" Rudi didn't want anything that had happened to come between them.

Duke suddenly turned to him and grinned. "Hey, why don't I buy us a couple of ices when I get out of this stuff? You put the bikes away and dry this saddle. By the time you finish, I'll be out of the tub and changed. We'll go down to that new place on Broadway and get us a couple of big English toffees."

When McGlade came down into the Sterns' back room, where Rudi was waiting for him, he was transformed. He'd clipped his mustache and brushed his hair straight forward. Every thinning strand gleamed under the artificial light. He was wearing sandals and blue jeans and a navy cotton shirt with a little alligator stitched on the left breast. His cheeks looked as if they'd been polished.

He said to Rudi, "Okay, buddy, what about that ice you promised me?"

Elsa Stern was sitting by the window. She had a copy of *Movie Stars* on the table in front of her and a hair dryer in one hand. With the other, she was fanning out her long golden hair in the stream of the dryer. When it slipped through her fingers, it fell down her cheeks and onto her shoulders. As far as Rudi could tell, she hadn't noticed either him or Duke.

Mrs. Stern came in from the yard and said to Rudi, "You make sure you behave yourself. You do what you're told, now, you hear me?" She used exactly the same words to Rudi that she always did.

"Yeah, Mom," said Rudi. He was anxious to be outside again with Duke. He opened the door into the hallway that led to the side entrance and the street, then turned to Duke.

McGlade was looking at Elsa, his hands in the pockets of his jeans, his head cocked to one side. "You want an ice?" he asked.

She didn't reply. Rudi hoped she hadn't heard over the noise of the dryer. He didn't want her with them. Duke was asking only out of kindness.

Mrs. Stern snapped, "Didn't you hear Mr. McGlade? He said, do you want to go with him and Rudi for an ice? It'll do you good, getting out of the house."

"I'm doing my hair," said Elsa. She didn't look at any of them and she didn't switch off the machine.

"How can you use that machine in this heat?" Mrs. Stern asked. "You're going to scorch your hair one day."

"We can wait till you're finished," said McGlade.

"I don't want an ice," said Elsa.

"Don't you say 'please' or 'thank you' anymore?" snapped Mrs. Stern. Her face was round and hard. Her eyes were black as olives. "You want me to tell your father how you speak to Mr. McGlade? After all we owe him?"

"All right!" cried Elsa, lifting her head just enough to see her mother. "I know! You keep telling me all the time! Okay—please and thank you. There! No, I don't want an ice."

She made Rudi mad. He didn't know what it was she had against Duke. Duke was always kind to everybody; yet every time he spoke to her, she either ignored him or snapped in his face. The one time Rudi had asked her about it, all she'd said was, "You're a kid. You don't know what he's after. You keep your nose out of it."

McGlade said to Mrs. Stern, "That's okay, Maria. She's a young woman now. She knows her own mind."

Mrs. Stern glared at the girl, who had turned her head and was running the jet of the dryer under the hair at the back of her neck. "You men are all alike," she said. "You spoil her. She ought to have a job in the vacation. All this time on her hands, it'll only lead to trouble. When I was her age, there wasn't a second I could call my own."

"Elsa's okay," McGlade said. "And don't worry about Rudi. We'll pick up a couple of burgers and take a jog to the river."

He followed Rudi out of the door and down the hallway into the street. The freshness that the rain had brought had evaporated. The stoops facing north were littered with lounging bodies. A black kid on one of them lifted his hand. "Hi, Rudi," he called.

"Hi," said Rudi.

The ice cream parlor on Broadway was Rudi's favorite. It carried twenty more varieties than any other place he knew. He looked up at the big white plastic board on which they were listed.

McGlade said, "You *want* English toffee, don't you? I don't wanna force it on you if you'd rather have something else."

"Hey, I *like* English toffee, Duke."

McGlade got a couple of small sugar cones and they sat at one of the counters, facing their reflections in the long mirror covering the wall. Rudi was thinking about Elsa. She treated Duke the same way that that Larry guy had treated him: as if he didn't amount to anything. It made him mad as hell.

McGlade talked to Rudi's reflection in the mirror. He said, "I'll let you in on a secret, buddy. You know why I ask for English toffee? It reminds me of home."

Rudi thought of the room that Duke had over the liquor store. "Home?" he said.

"London," said McGlade. "You never forget where you were born, you know, where you've got roots. You'll be the same when you grow up. Doesn't matter where you move to. Everybody's like that. Hey, isn't that crazy? I come in here to lick English toffee to remind me of somewhere I haven't seen since I was your age. Younger, even. No more than six, I guess." He had his elbows on the counter and wasn't looking at Rudi's reflection anymore but at his own.

Rudi relaxed. When Duke was talking like this, everything was okay again. "Yeah, Duke," he said. "Crazy."

"I'll tell you what, buddy. One day we'll just pack a couple of bags and take a jet from Kennedy and fly to London. How 'bout that? Just the two of us. And we'll go and get a couple of rooms in one of those places overlooking Hyde Park. What d'you call that place? The Dorchester—that's where we'll go. And there'll be guys to carry our bags and clean our shoes and whistle for cabs for us. We'll go to Buckingham Palace and watch them changing the guard—all red and silver and big black horses. Buddy, you've never seen anything like it—all the parades on Fifth Avenue rolled into one! We might even catch sight of the queen. And you know what? We'll pick up one of those trams that cross the river and I'll show you the place where I was born, right around the corner from Charlie Chaplin's house. Hey, how 'bout that?"

Rudi said nothing. Duke still wasn't looking at him. He'd finished his cone and was examining his face in the mirror, fingering his heavy cheeks and the padded flesh under his eyes. He seemed to have forgotten what he'd been saying. Then he caught sight of Rudi's reflection watching him, and turned and grinned. He put an arm around Rudi's shoulder and slid off his stool. "Come on," he said. "Let's go grab a look at the river."

They crossed Sherman Square, picked up a couple of Big Macs from McDonald's, and walked down to the riverside. Steam rose from the surface of the water.

McGlade said, "Let's get out of the sun."

They sat on the grass under the trees and started to eat the burgers.

"I didn't know that's the way you worked, Duke," Rudi said between mouthfuls.

"How's that?" McGlade had his ankles crossed and his knees apart and was leaning forward so that the drippings from the burger didn't fall on his pants.

"You know—in the water," Rudi answered. "I thought they'd just get *anybody* to do that."

"That's what everybody thinks," said McGlade, his mouth full of bun and burger. He swallowed. "You know what? They'll probably process that film and cut it up into short lengths and slot it into half a dozen big pictures. You could be seeing clips from that on TV for months—years, maybe."

"Jeez!" said Rudi. Maybe he'd got the whole thing wrong. You had to believe Duke when he was being serious.

"Why not?" asked McGlade. "Okay, they *said* it was a commercial. That's what they always say when they want it cheap. But look how many times they got me to roll over. They wouldn't have wasted film if they weren't gonna use it, now, would they?"

"No," said Rudi, "I guess not." He began to feel easier about the way he'd seen Duke pushed around.

"It's like any other profession." McGlade pointed toward the river. There was a tug towing a barge upstream, moving very slowly through the haze. "Take the guy driving that tug. That guy could've been running the *Stattendam* last year, taking rich tourists all the way to Bermuda and back. Now he's hauling cement up to Poughkeepsie. Same with any profession. One day it's this, next day it's that. That guy could take any ship anywhere. Depends what's needed. Same thing with a stunt man. One day he's working in the car pound for Telly Savalas, next day he's . . . jumping off the Empire State Building for Roger Moore."

Rudi thought he was teasing. Sometimes he did that. He'd make some statement very seriously, then suddenly grin and muss up Rudi's hair and say, "Got you there, buddy!" But he wasn't grinning now. He was staring at the river, not even focusing on the tug anymore.

Rudi said, "Jumping off the Empire State Building? Nobody could do that. They'd kill themselves."

McGlade turned to him quickly. "I'm not talking about just *anybody*," he said. "I'm talking about a stunt artist. Nothing's impossible for a guy who knows his job."

Rudi only looked at him. It wasn't that he didn't believe him; he just didn't see how it could be done—even by Duke.

His uncertainty must have showed, because McGlade said, "Watch this." He opened out his empty Big Mac container into a flat cardboard sheet, then held it in the air and let go of it. Slowly it spun down onto the grass. McGlade picked it up. *"Now* watch," he said. He screwed it into a tight ball and again let it drop. It fell straight to the ground. "You get the point?" he asked.

Rudi wasn't sure what the point was, though he

could see there was a difference between the two ways the box had fallen. He nodded.

McGlade said, "You gotta juggle with gravity. That's all a pilot does with an aircraft. Look"—he picked up the cardboard ball and put it down between him and Rudi—"the Empire State, okay? Fifth Avenue here, Thirty-fourth Street here." He marked out the plan with his finger. "Now, I'd close Thirty-fourth Street for half a block west——"

"Close it?" Rudi said. "They wouldn't let you do that! All the stores are on Thirty-fourth Street—Macy's, Gimbels——"

"I don't mean *personally*," said McGlade. "I'd get the cops to do it. They closed Seventy-fifth when *Cherry Street* was being shot with Sinatra. They closed Columbus Circle for Faye Dunaway. C'mon—you remember."

It was true. Rudi remembered. They'd put barriers across Seventy-fifth Street, and he hadn't been able to see anything because of the crowds standing around watching. "Yeah, that's right, Duke," he said. "I remember."

"Well, then." McGlade looked down at the crushed container for a moment. "You'd have to figure out the rig, of course. I wouldn't use boxes, not from that height. I'd jam the street with air bags. Dar Robinson uses them out on the Coast, and he's as good as they come."

It began to sound possible to Rudi. It was great to see Duke's mind working, figuring every angle. He wondered if they'd let him stand on Ohrbach's roof and watch. He wondered if he wanted to. Could he stand the suspense? Suppose something went wrong. If anything happened to Duke . . .

McGlade was saying, "Now, the launching. I've given that a lotta thought. See, the Empire State isn't vertical. Most people don't notice that. It goes up in steps. You'd have to jump far enough out to clear every one of them, otherwise"—he brought his hands together in a sharp clap—"splat! But midtown's full of up currents this time of year, because of the heat. I'd make use of them, get some lift from them, like hang gliders do. That way I'd clear the steps and slow down the fall as well. There—how's that sound?"

It was pretty convincing, but this idea of being a hang glider bothered him. He asked, "How would you use the up currents, Duke? You mean . . . fly?"

McGlade looked at him for a moment; then he gave one of his slow, pained grins. "Hey, buddy," he said, "you think I'm some kind of nut? Nobody can *fly*. But you can control your fall. You've seen those free-fall boys on TV, turning, maneuvering in midair. It's a question of knowing how to handle your body." He half extended his arms and spread his fingers to show what he meant.

"Would you *really* try it, Duke?" Rudi asked.

"Damn right I'd try it! All they gotta do is ask me."

Three of Rudi's friends were passing. One of them called, "Hey, Rudi, you wanna play?" He was wearing a baseball hat and juggling with a ball.

"I'm busy," said Rudi.

"Aw, c'mon. You can bat first."

McGlade said, "That's okay, Rudi. I'll just be sitting here."

"You sure, Duke?"

"It's okay."

McGlade watched the kids walk off through the trees. Wouldn't it be nice, he thought, if he could take a baseball bat to that fucking faggot who'd made him roll through all that piss in front of the kid? What had gone wrong with the profession? Having to take that kind of crap just to stay alive! Joey Feinstein was an asshole. He'd have to get himself another agent—someone who'd get him some *real* work, so he wouldn't have to go smashing himself up anymore. He was really an actor. Christ, if his parents had never come over here, he'd be a star in London by now! He thought of the ads he'd seen on TV. It looked a great town still: cool, clean, civilized. They appreciated talent there. Was it too late to go back?

He picked up the crushed cardboard carton, walked over to a trash can, and tossed it in. His wrist was a bit sore. The car hood had caught him right on the bone. Then he dropped down again in the shade and rolled onto his stomach, propping himself up on his elbows. There were a couple of tall Hispanics in the distance, coming along the path that ran across the slope above him. A white woman was walking between them. They each had an arm around her and were leaning over her, giving her little kisses. She was giggling. Yeah, he thought, it would be great to get back to London. You wouldn't see an Englishwoman cuddling up to scum like that.

He was going to roll back and face the river again, but something about this woman caught his attention. Now she was closer, she looked more like a girl. The guys had to be in their thirties. Jesus, why did parents let their kids act this way? Decent white kids. They could all take a lesson from Tony.

Then suddenly, he recognized her—the way she carried herself, her long blonde hair. He'd been right. She *was* only a kid! He'd known her since she was ten —bought her presents for Christmas and her birthday. She was Tony's girl! What the Christ was she doing with those spics?

They passed within thirty feet of him and disappeared toward the Seventy-second Street exit. He wanted to throw up. Was it these scum bags she'd been doing her hair for? She thought she was grown up. She wasn't, whatever he'd told Maria. Should he go after her, tell her to remember who she was? Would she take any notice of him? She didn't take any notice of her mother. He'd have to tell Tony.

McGlade got to his feet and walked toward the boat basin, looking for Rudi. When he saw him, he called, "Hey, Rudi, we gotta get back!"

It was a minute to four when they crossed West End Avenue. The towaway trucks were parked in a row with their engines running, waiting like vultures for the stroke of four.

Beyond Broadway, a group of young kids, fully dressed, were soaking themselves in the gush of water from a fire hydrant. The spray attachment supplied by the fire department to save water was lying in the middle of the street. A light-colored Hispanic woman screamed from an upstairs window. None of the kids even looked up.

Nobody gives a fuck, thought McGlade. *Manhattan's a disease. Everyone's infected.* He detested what he'd seen by the river, but it shouldn't have surprised him. The girl had been exposed to the West Side all her life. What was the point of telling Tony now? Tony couldn't help her. He'd have to find some way himself.

Thomas worried him, too. Tony oughtn't to let him work for Burton. There was a *real* West Sider. It was guys like Burton who caused all the problems: never caring; never giving a damn. Why wouldn't a guy call the cops when he knew there'd been a killing? *Why?* He still couldn't figure it out.

He turned to Rudi. "How's Thomas making out with Mr. Burton?" he asked. "I never get to see him in the mornings now."

"He goes out as soon as he's had his breakfast. Sometimes he goes for a ride in the park before work. Mr. Burton's always riding there, every morning; sometimes at night."

"Is that right?" said McGlade. "At night?"

"Thomas told me."

▼▼▼▼▼▼▼▼▼▼▼▼▼▼▼▼

CHAPTER 7

▲▲▲▲▲▲▲▲▲▲▲▲▲▲▲▲

In the heat of summer, the trash cans in Central Park spill over with discarded junk food. During the day, squirrels slip out of the trees and ferret among the remains of hot dogs and half-chewed pretzels. Every bush covers a hundred empty cans of Budweiser. But at night, when the trash fades into the darkness and the trees stand black against the purple sky, everything changes. For Lora Zimmerman, sitting under the stars on the granite ridge at the north side of the Sheep Meadow, the sheer electrifying magic of the place made it one of the seven wonders of the world.

It was her first concert in the park. In front of her, filling the great bowl of the Sheep Meadow, a hundred thousand people watched and listened. Some lay face down with hands under their chins. Others lounged sideways, their heads propped up on elbows. Those at the front sat upright on chairs. Here and there, kids wore luminous necklaces that gleamed like strings of glowworms in the darkness. The air was full of smoke from the pretzel carts behind her.

A thousand floodlights lit the distant band shell. The conductor and the players, so bleached by the intensity of the illumination, were figures from a dream. Beyond them, in the far distance, the backdrop of Central Park South towered up into the night, a dazzling wall of lights. What would she ever see that could compare with this? she wondered. What was Rome, London, Paris compared with the great glittering jewel of Manhattan filled with music? How was she going to survive when she went upstate to college next year, away from the throbbing pulse of New York City?

She became aware of people clapping, and joined them automatically, without knowing why. They were getting up, but she'd no sense of being connected with them. If they wanted to go, let them.

A voice said, "Hey, Lora, snap out of it. You gonna spend the night here?"

Barbara was standing beside her with a hand out to help her up. The concert was over and Lora hadn't realized it. She got to her feet without speaking and turned east with the others toward the long line heading for Fifth Avenue. She could still hear the music reverberating somewhere in the night.

There were people beside her, people in front and behind. She moved with them without being part of them. Her friends were talking loudly and laughing to one another. She wasn't with them. Her spirit was still with the breathtaking experience she'd just been through. She'd seen new worlds.

They moved north, roughly following the East Drive, part of a long, straggling line of people making for the East Seventy-second Street exit. Lamps threw a soft yellow light onto the pathway. The night was hot and humid. The trees locked in the heat. Traffic moved steadily down Fifth Avenue, a background of moving lights through the black trees.

Suzie said, "We don't wanna be in that hassle. Let's go on as far as the museum."

"Will it be safe?" asked Barbara.

"With all these people? Hey, all that stuff's for the West Side. Jeez, who'd be dumb enough to do anything here? There must be a cop every fifty yards."

Just as they were passing the East Seventy-ninth Street exit, a cyclist came at them straight out of the darkness. He had a radio going but no lights and was shouting, "Move it! Move it!" People in front parted and let him through. He braked, swerved, then drove down on the pedals again. He made for the group of girls. They broke and scattered before him. A male voice screamed, "You bum!" Somebody grabbed Lora by the arm and pulled her to one side as the cyclist swept past.

When it was over, Lora looked up to find they'd already reached the back of the Metropolitan Museum of Art. She'd been too preoccupied with her own thoughts to notice what had happened. People were talking around her. She said, "Hey, suppose I could major in theater instead of English? What d'you think?"

No one answered her. She glanced at the people beside her. She didn't know them. She stopped and they walked past her. There were still other groups ahead of her, but none of them were her friends. She looked back. There was no one in sight. "Barbara? Suzie?" she called. There was no reply.

She hesitated. The night was full of strange sounds. The music had gone and she was suddenly scared. A police car cruised past on her left. She thought of calling out to it, but it had already slipped out of sight.

She was coming up to the East Eighty-fourth Street exit. She began to run. The Marymount School and the blazing lights of Fifth Avenue were less than two hundred yards away. The group ahead turned to look back at her. Then, suddenly, she saw her friends. They were crossing the underpass, making for the exit on the far side. The sense of relief almost choked her. She became aware of her heart pounding in her chest and the sweat trickling down her neck and into her T-shirt. She called their names and ran toward them.

When she reached the underpass, she saw that they weren't her friends but only tree shadows cast by the glaring sodium light that lit the road. She would have turned and run back, but as she hesitated she caught

sight of a car coming up the road toward her from behind. Its lights were out and it moved at a walking
pace, sliding through the pools of yellow lights and
into the deep shadows absolutely noiselessly. And suddenly she became aware of all the demons of the night
that lay around her. She ran on, forcing one foot after
the other, ignoring the pains of cramp in her stomach.
Even if she caught up with her friends now, she was
determined to get out of the park at the very next exit.
The children's playground at Eighty-fourth and Eighty-
fifth streets still lay between her and the glittering
lights. Fifth Avenue had never seemed so desperately
attractive, so secure and at the same time so unattain-
able. High above the park, influential New Yorkers
moved with martinis through their air-conditioned co-
coons, as far removed from the terrors of the night as
Martians.

She noticed two objects glittering in the bushes
ahead, one yellow, one red. They didn't immediately
register with her. The one thing uppermost in her mind
was getting onto Fifth as quickly as she could. But
they caught her eye again and suddenly she knew what
they were. Someone had propped a bicycle by the side
of the path, and the light from the sodium lamps was
catching the reflectors on the wheels. A paralyzing terror ran through her and she came to a stop. She was
caught between the car behind her and the bicycle in
front.

She was trying to figure out which way to run now,
but it was already too late. She heard a quick rustle of
leaves behind her, and before she could turn, something
had caught her around the throat and she was being
dragged into the bushes. She tried to scream, but nothing passed through her throat. She couldn't breathe.
She clawed with her hands but touched nothing. Her
head was bursting. Her heart drummed like a piston in
her chest. Her lungs gasped for air but found none.
There was a searing pain behind her eyes, and some-

thing finally ruptured in her brain. Gradually, the glittering lights of Fifth Avenue dimmed and went out.

Fay Coburn looked up. It was early morning, the only bearable part of the day during August, and she was coming down the East Drive on her bicycle, completing her first circuit of Central Park. Ahead and to her left, the spire of the Chrysler Building soared above the shadows of Central Park South. The sun struck the polished steel surfaces and fragmented. It was like a picture she'd once seen of Istanbul in a travel brochure. She made a mental note to use the example in class.

She was thinking about what Burton had said to her. If ABC really was going to pull down most of the block and build some kind of TV palace there, she would have to move. The problem was, where? She didn't want to live too far uptown and she couldn't stand the pretensions of the Village. She'd got attached to that part of the West Side between Seventy-second Street and Lincoln Center.

She rode past the Sheep Meadow and through the Sixty-sixth Street underpass. It was 6:46, according to the sign on the Mony Building, with the temperature already at 80°. On the pathway to her left, chugging determinedly northward, was a squat, overweight woman in the classic uniform of the jogger: T-shirt over bare breasts, white shorts, white Puma sneakers. The T-shirt carried the words "Polish is beautiful." Anyone who didn't know the ethnic structure of the West Side would have thought she was advertising furniture polish.

No matter that she was unattractive, the woman had courage jogging alone at this time of the morning, Fay thought. Courage was a West Side quality; so was excitement. Berlin must have been like that in the twenties—Paris, too—except that even in Europe there'd never been such a stewpot of ethnic types and eccentric temperaments as the West Side could show you. Good

God, if you looked hard enough you could find a colony of Eskimos carving walrus tusks in one of the brownstones on Seventy-fourth!

She left the road and turned east along one of the pedestrian pathways. Fifth Avenue lay ahead, the other side of the Conservatory Pond. On her right, the cliff face of Central Park South rose up out of the shadows into the bright sunlight. There were still pools of water left over from the rainstorm, standing in the hollows under the trees, and they steamed in the morning heat.

She considered the East Side, comparing the trimness of Madison with the sprawl of Broadway around Sherman Square. She could get a nice studio in Yorkville for about the same as she was paying for two rooms now. She could shop at the Gristede's on Lex without being touched for a quarter by some louse-hung derelict. At night, she could walk home after visiting friends without having some glue-high cowboy proposing a free blowjob. People over there had settled for things, the way people had done back home. They'd settled for being bankers or teachers or tycoons. The idea was attractive. But was it what she wanted?

She'd settled for nothing yet—not for teaching or marriage or having kids. All her options were open, and that's how she wanted to keep them. There wasn't an experience she was going to refuse if it came her way. How else could you develop except through experience? That's the way it was with everyone on the West Side. The future was wide open. You could still make president even if you were a woman. There was nothing you couldn't grab so long as you kept at it. That was what was finally going to keep her on the West Side. Nobody moved to the East Side unless they'd already said "Enough!" to life.

She skirted the zoo and kept to the pedestrian paths to avoid the traffic that was now beginning to build from the south. Two black guys raced toward her. They rode neck and neck, bodies forward over the handlebars, legs driving down on the pedals. Absolute concentration showed on their faces. In a moment they'd swept past her, leaving a faint smell of sweat in the air.

She was riding alone among the trees, with the pond on her right, when the sound of a radio began ripping the morning stillness. She tensed. God Almighty! she thought. How could they sound off about human rights in Washington, when any bum was free to invade your privacy with noise? If someone had flung a beer can at her, she could have called the cops. That was assault. Couldn't they make a law to cover assault by radio? She began to build up speed, treading down on the pedals with a steady increase in power.

The noise was still with her. She swung right toward the statue of the Mad Tea Party, then left and up the long straight that led to the kids' playground. Suddenly she became aware of a dark shape jogging alongside her. What had New York come to, she thought, when a guy couldn't jog in Central Park without the support of WABC?

She shouted, "Hey! Why don't you can that garbage?"

But the sound wasn't coming from alongside, it was coming from behind. She took a quick look back. A man was coming up the path toward her, crouched forward over a bicycle, driving his legs into the pedals in a continuous flow of powerful movement. She knew him at once from the red and yellow bars on his helmet and the steel blue of the Motobecane. Above all, she recognized the characteristic rhythmic sway he always developed when he was moving under full power. It was Burton. Her irritation dissolved and she felt a flutter of activity in her stomach, the way she always had when she'd seen him like this. She hesitated, easing up on the pedals. Then, suddenly, she changed her mind. *The hell with it,* she thought. *If he's after me again, let him work for it.*

She dropped down a gear and began to increase speed. She was back into top gear by the time she reached the playground. She ducked through the underpass and climbed out the other side, head down, ass barely touching the saddle. Okay, she couldn't beat him, but she was going to give him one hell of a run. It was different now from those early days. The best part of a summer had slipped by. She'd put in daily training and covered more than two thousand miles. Anyway, in those days she'd wanted him to catch up with her.

The shadow beyond the bushes was still loping alongside. She knew who it was now. She called "Blue!" and the big German shepherd swerved toward her and ran beside her on the path.

The long line of the Metropolitan Museum lay ahead of her through the trees. The sun glanced from the windows of the south wall. Behind, Burton was calling. She couldn't make out what he was saying. She tucked her head back toward her shoulder and caught sight of him out of the corner of her eye. He was coming up on her right, still thirty yards behind. His head was tilted up just enough for him to be able to keep her in sight.

She crossed the bridge and drove downhill. Blue stayed with her. For a second she thought of swinging right and giving Burton a jinking chase through the traffic all the way down Fifth, but she changed her mind and veered left toward the back of the museum. She took the bike so far over on the turn that she clipped the asphalt with the pedal. It checked her rhythm for a moment, and when she glanced to her right, she found that Burton was coming up fast on her shoulder. She grinned.

He shouted, "You crazy? D'you know what you're doing?"

She could hardly hear him above the noise of the radio. She had her head tucked in again and was driving down on the pedals with all the energy she had. Two police cars stood parked on the grass to her left. In the distance, where the bridge crossed the Eighty-fourth Street transverse, there were policemen standing around. She was only vaguely aware of them. All her attention was taken up by Burton. He was up on her shoulder now, shouting, "Come on! Quit fooling! Pull up!"

She didn't look at him. She wanted all her power to go into the pedals. But she couldn't stop grinning. She'd made him mad, giving him such a ride. She yelled, "I can't hear you!"

He dropped a hand and turned the radio off. When she still didn't stop, he pulled ahead of her and began to edge her onto the grass. She held her course for a moment. He was a foot ahead of her and edging in all the time. He'd never change. He just didn't give a damn. Another inch and he was going to touch her handlebars. At that speed it would be one hell of a pileup. As far as she was concerned, it was all a joke. She didn't want to carry it as far as the emergency room at Roosevelt.

She veered off the path and came to a stop. By the time he reached her, she was lying on her back on the grass with the sweat pouring off her, shaking with laughter.

Burton took off his helmet and tossed it down on the ground. He was shouting, "You some kind of nut? You saw me coming. Why didn't you stop? I oughta belt the shit out of you!"

She stopped laughing and looked up at him, eyes squinted against the sun. He was standing over her, a tall black silhouette against the sky. She couldn't see his expression, but the sound of his voice was enough. He really was mad at her. She sat up. "Now, hold it, Burton. If you think you've got any rights over me, you'd better forget it. All that finished weeks ago— the day you never showed."

He wasn't listening. He bent his knees and crouched beside her with his hands resting on his thighs. "You haven't heard the news? You don't know about the killing?"

"Killing?" she asked. She'd expected an explanation for why he'd been playing this crazy game with her, not some sick joke.

But Burton wasn't kidding. She'd never seen him so serious. The sweat was running down his cheeks and neck, soaking the neckband of his T-shirt. She could see the marks along his jawline where the helmet straps had been. He looked very powerful and very male. He nodded.

"Oh, God," she said. The flirtatious mood she'd been in evaporated. She felt a sudden need to be protected from the savagery of the city. She wanted to bury herself in his arms and have him look after her, though it went against everything she believed.

"Last night," he said. "The other side of the museum—where the cops are standing, I guess. Some security guard found her in the bushes. She'd been strangled like the others."

"Another woman?" she asked, trying to gather up her feelings again into some kind of equilibrium.

"Sure another woman," he snapped. "You think I'd come after you if the VC had knocked off a Cambodian?"

A cop was coming over to them from one of the police cars. Burton stood up and pulled on his helmet. "Come on," he said to her. "I don't wanna talk to any cops."

She got to her feet and picked up her bike. Burton threw a leg over his saddle and whistled. Blue came out of the bushes.

The cop called, "Hey, you!"

Burton turned to Fay. He was still mad. "Look what you've done now! If you'd stopped when I yelled, we coulda got out at Seventy-second." He turned to the cop and called, "Yeah?"

The cop came up to them and said, "This area's off limits."

"Yeah?"

The cop had his feet apart and his thumbs in his belt. His belly hung over his hands. He stared at Burton without any expression. "D'you ride in the park every day?"

"Do I need a license?" Burton asked.

"You ride here yesterday?"

"Sure."

"How late?"

"How would I know? I don't time myself."

"You at the concert last night?"

"What concert?" snapped Burton.

"You got some identification?" asked the cop.

"Like what?"

"Driver's license."

"Look," said Burton, "I'm riding a bike in the park. Why would I wanna carry my driver's license?"

The cop said, "Lemme look at that bike." He took his thumbs out of his belt and did a deep knee-bend beside the machine. He took hold of the chain and felt the tension. There was half an inch of slack. It seemed to satisfy him. He looked at the oil on his finger and thumb and said, "You're the guy with the bike shop on Columbus, right?"

"Jesus Christ!" yelled Burton. "What is this?"

The cop wiped his hand on the grass and got to his feet. "Okay," he said. "You can go."

"Like that?" cried Burton. "No thumb screws? No water torture?"

"We know where to reach you," said the cop.

Fay had already mounted and turned away. When Burton caught up with her, she said, "What's the matter with you? He was only doing his job. What's the point of me teaching kids to be law-abiding when there are grown-ups around like you?"

He didn't say anything. They rode north along the reservoir. People jogged doggedly by the side of the wire fence, their eyes focused inward on themselves. Blue was way ahead, knowing the path that Burton would take.

Fay felt she'd handled the whole thing badly. Ever since June, she'd wondered if they'd get together again. One time, she thought she was over it. She'd gone to the shop to prove it, only to discover that she wasn't. Now all she'd done was make him mad. There was something she had to know, but his head was down over the handlebars and his eyes fixed on the pathway ahead, and she couldn't bring herself to break into his train of thought.

They turned west, then south, riding shoulder to shoulder. The breeze over their faces was too full of moisture to let the sweat evaporate. It ran down their cheeks and dripped off their noses and chins. Still neither of them spoke.

It was too much for Fay. She said at last, "Why *did* you come after me?"

"Don't go getting any ideas," said Burton.

They were passing the Museum of Natural History when he spoke again. He said, "Why did *you* come to the shop?"

"I had a brake problem. Weren't you listening?"

"Don't be smart. You can get a brake problem fixed anywhere. What did you come back to *me* for?"

"I was curious."

"There isn't a woman around, if that's what you were looking for."

She glanced at him. The anger hadn't left him. She felt that if she put out a hand to touch him, he'd give off sparks. She said, "Why didn't you turn up?"

"What are you talking about?"

"Hey, come on, Burton! It's me. Don't you remember? We had a nice thing going in the spring. What happened to it?"

"I guess it died. These things happen. Don't you go to the movies anymore?"

"I waited two hours in Battery Park. I saw six ferries leave for Staten Island and six come back. We weren't on any of them. A nice romantic experience for a girl just new in town. Were you sulking because I wouldn't move in with you? Is that why you never showed and never sent me any explanation?"

He didn't say anything for a while, only hissed a little through his teeth. At last he said, "It was getting too steamy. It had to go all the way or not at all. I was getting in too deep. I started thinking about you when you weren't there. So I cut it off."

It was too much for her. "God Almighty!" she cried. "I thought it *had* gone all the way! What's living together? How much further would that have gotten us? We don't owe anything to anybody, you and I. I told you that at the beginning. We're individuals. I'm just living my life the way I see it. You're doing the same. Let's make the most of it without getting too involved. One day we're all going to be blown away. We ought to make it easy on ourselves."

"Is that what you say to your kids?" he asked.

"Who's being smart now? What do you know about education?"

"Nothing, I guess. I never made City College. I'm just another one of your self-educated New Yorkers."

"You sure make it easy to resist you," she said.

They reached the traffic lights where the West Drive met the transverse road at Seventy-second Street. The lights showed red. Burton ignored them and swerved into the traffic moving from the left. Fay followed him. When she caught up with him, he'd turned off the road and onto the pedestrian pathway alongside it.

She said, "How did you know I'd be in the park at this time? We always came in later."

"I made it my business."

All the old feelings came back to her: the excitement, the quivering in the gut, the irritation, the slight fear she'd always had of him. Still she resisted. As lightly as she could manage, she said, "D'you want to start again—is that what you mean?"

"Oh, come on!" he snapped. "It's not up to me. *You're* the one that got stood up."

"Oh, I see," she said. "You mean if I go down on my knees and apologize for not understanding these male whims of yours, I might get to see you again? Maybe cook dinner for you, buy you a bottle of wine now and then?"

She could see the severe expression on his face begin to crack. He sat upright, let go the handlebars, and folded his arms across his chest. He gave her that devastating smile he could turn on when he wanted to, and she could feel her resistance finally beginning to crumble. He nodded. "Something like that," he said.

He manufactured charm the way he manufactured insulin: as if it was just another hormone. She'd always known that. It still didn't make it any easier for her. She said firmly, "I'm not moving in with you."

"Okay," he said. "But stay out of the park until they clear up this mess. You don't wanna tempt this guy."

She'd sworn never to get tied up with him again. Now she was right back where she'd started. Maybe this time it was going to be different. He *had* come looking for her. If he really was that concerned about her safety, it gave her some leverage over him.

"That kid you've got working for you," she said. "He's cute. What did he make of that scene we were playing?"

"I guess he believed it," said Burton.

"Really?"

"Why not? You were always a hell of a performer." He nodded to the dog, who was now running alongside. "I guess the only one who knew was Blue, but then he majored in psychology."

"City College?" she asked.

He looked at her for a moment, then dropped forward onto the handlebars again. "Come on," he said gruffly, driving down on the pedals. "Don't you teachers ever do any work?"

McGlade was standing in the liquor store watching the open trap. He had his hands in his pockets and his shoulders hunched. There was that look of discomfort on his face that he often wore, as if he was in pain. When Stern came through the trap carrying a case of Scotch, McGlade said, "Jeez, I feel terrible, Tony, watching you hump that stuff and not being able to give you a hand."

"You oughtn't to work at all," said Stern, putting the case on the floor and stacking the bottles on a shelf. He worked quickly, his hands reaching automatically for the necks of the bottles, his wrists giving a final little twist to place them base down exactly where he wanted them. "You ought to give that back a chance. What are they paying you workmen's compensation for, if you never give it a chance to heal?"

McGlade shrugged and turned away from him and stood looking beyond the display of bottles in the window to where the traffic was moving down the street. He said, "I gotta keep in touch, Tony. My agent gets me a little job, I can't afford to turn it down. You never know where it could lead."

"Well, it's crazy," said Stern, turning to the cellar steps again with the empty crate in his hand. "You never think of changing your job?"

"Yeah, I've thought," said McGlade.

In the street, a police car turned out of the stream of southbound traffic and pulled up outside the liquor store. Officer Callaghan got out and walked slowly across the sidewalk. He pushed the door without breaking his stride. It was locked. He began rapping on it steadily with the back of his hand, without looking through the glass.

"Who's that?" Stern shouted from below.

"Officer Callaghan," McGlade called, going to the door and unlocking it.

"When did you take to locking the door this time of day?" asked Callaghan. He was still holding it open against the tension of the spring that would have closed it.

"Tony's down in the cellar," McGlade explained.

Callaghan nodded. He walked in and stood in the blast from the air-conditioner, letting the chilly air hit him in the neck. He was a big man, solid as a tank. He stood with his feet apart and his regulation NYPD belly hanging loose, while the sweat poured off him and into his shirt. "Jesus!" he said. "It never lets up."

"You any nearer to catching this guy?" McGlade asked. He'd sunk back into his old posture, shoulders hunched, hands deep in his pockets.

There was no doubt who he was talking about: Every twenty-two minutes, Radio WINS was putting out bulletins about the latest killing, and ABC News had talked about "the West Side terror spreading east," and added $10,000 to the reward fund set up by the *Daily News*.

"Some," said Callaghan.

"You made an arrest yet?" called Stern, coming up through the trap with another case.

"Not yet," said the officer, turning to him.

"You got a suspect?"

"We got some names."

"What kind of a guy is this?" cried Stern. There was anger in his voice, and frustration. He was expressing what everyone in the neighborhood felt.

"Some psycho," said Callaghan. "We'll get to him. Now he's moving around, everybody's after him. He'll make a mistake soon. Maybe he's made one already."

"You think so?" McGlade asked.

"I said maybe." Callaghan came out of the blast from the air-conditioner and took a step toward Stern. "Where's that girl of yours, Tony?"

"Upstairs, I guess." Stern had put the case down on the floor and closed the trap, and now he was starting to stack the bottles on the shelf.

"For Christ's sake, keep an eye on her," said Callaghan. "She's a looker, you know that? All that beautiful hair. Don't let her out after dark."

"Okay," said Stern. He was shaken and it showed.

Callaghan took a fistful of damp handkerchief out of his hip pocket and patted the back of his neck. "That black guy you called us about," he said, "the one that beat up his woman. He's back on the street. The woman wouldn't testify. He's a mean bastard. If he comes in for liquor, don't serve him."

"Aw, come on!" said Stern. "Selling liquor's my business."

"You oughta get a dog," said Callaghan.

"There oughta be more cops on the streets, that's what!" Stern snapped.

"That's right," said Callaghan. "So why don't you call Gracie Mansion? Meantime, keep the door locked, like that store on Amsterdam. All the time, not just when you're down the hole. Put a bell push outside. That way, you don't let anyone in you don't want. Jesus, you know what this weather does to some guys."

Stern looked at him for a moment, then shrugged. What was one more hassle in a summer like this? "Okay," he said. "I'll think about it."

"Maybe it wasn't the same guy, this killer," said McGlade. "Everything's different, you said."

Callaghan thought for a moment; then he pushed his handkerchief back into his pocket and said, "Well, for one thing, he left us his card again. For another, the weapon was the same."

"Weapon?" said McGlade.

"A bicycle chain. But that information's not been in the papers yet. The department's only just released it. If it wasn't the same guy, how would he know?"

"God Almighty!" Stern cried, glancing toward the hallway on his right to make sure none of his family had heard.

"The kid's larynx was all caved in," said Callaghan, his voice quiet and confidential. "He must wear gloves made out of bull hide; otherwise his hands'd be like ground chuck, the kind of force he uses. Apart from his being into kids now, there's something else we know. He used a bike to get away. That soft ground under the trees shows up every mark."

"They oughta sweep the whole goddamned lot away!" McGlade snapped. "All these bums, these derelicts— they're animals! They oughta be branded and put in a cage. They're bleeding this city to death! It could've been that wino you just put back on the street. You thought of that?"

"Hey, hold it," said Callaghan. He looked surprised by the savagery behind McGlade's remarks. "That's where you're wrong. The way that guy drinks, he'd have a tough time standing to take a piss. How'd he ever stay on a bicycle?"

McGlade turned away from him.

"This guy we're after," explained Callaghan, "he could be any color. When we get to him, it'll turn out to be some loner, like the shrinks say: some guy who doesn't socialize, a guy without friends, a guy who doesn't like people. I've met the bastards."

"I guess so," said McGlade, shrugging. He knew that back of it all was the incurable disease of the city.

Callaghan turned to the door. "Don't forget what I said about Elsa, Tony. Let's keep her safe, if we can."

"Thanks," said Stern.

Callaghan wasn't dumb, McGlade thought. He knew

what the girl was up to and was trying to warn Tony. He was wasting his time.

Callaghan looked up at the air-conditioner and shivered. "Jesus," he said, "how do you guys live in here? It's better on the street. If I was you, I'd start worrying about pneumonia."

▼▼▼▼▼▼▼▼▼▼▼▼▼▼

CHAPTER 8

▲▲▲▲▲▲▲▲▲▲▲▲▲▲▲

For two days, Burton didn't call Fay Coburn. He knew what he was getting back into and it made him hesitate. She was *numero uno* in the bedroom. But orgasm wasn't enough for her. She wanted his balls as a trophy.

On the second night, it was too damned hot to sleep. He lay naked on his back with the sweat trickling down his flanks. He could feel her body under his fingertips and smell her hair the way it had smelled in the spring. He tried to kid himself that the only reason he hadn't had a woman since Fay Coburn was because he hadn't had time. It wasn't true and he knew it. He hadn't had a woman because since he'd been with her he couldn't look seriously at anyone else.

He got up next morning tired and drained. He had thought he'd cracked the problem. If he could do without her for the rest of the summer, the whole thing would have cooled. But he'd forgot about Manhattan, where the summers last forever and the hassles come when they're least expected.

Officer Callaghan came into the shop at 10:20 A.M. He wanted to see the bike that Burton rode. His partner was with him: a tall, lean guy with a heavy blond mustache. Callaghan examined the Motobecane while his partner nosed along the racks of new machines on the walls.

"What the Christ goes on here?" said Burton.

They ignored him. Callaghan's partner was checking the tires and chains of all the rental bikes. Outside, they'd left the red flasher spinning on the car roof. Anybody passing would know the cops were paying an official visit to Burton. It was what Callaghan called "the lean"—the psychological equivalent of belting a guy with a night stick.

"I said, what goes on?" Burton yelled. Blue growled. Thomas put out a hand to quiet him.

"Routine," said Callaghan. He was crouched beside the bike, comparing the tire tread with a photograph he'd taken out of his shirt pocket. Behind him, Thomas stood by the bench patting Blue on the head. The dog watched but didn't interfere.

"Well, just routine it out of here! I'm running a business. What d'you think it looks like, having you crawling around the place?"

"I'd say it gives it class," said Callaghan.

Callaghan's partner was now sorting through a pile of scrap in a corner by the bathroom door, picking out all the junked chains, and dropping them into a sack. All the time, his jaws kept working on the gum in his mouth. When he'd finished, he pushed a receipt form into Burton's hands and disappeared out to the car.

"What *is* this?" cried Burton. The paper was covered in black, oily thumbprints. "This signature coulda been done by a chimp!"

"Don't you never watch TV?" Callaghan asked, getting to his feet. "This kinda thing cuts right into whatever's on. Ask the kid. You could even make the ratings." He turned and walked out to the car.

Burton followed him onto the sidewalk. "What about my property?" he shouted. He knew there was nothing he could do about it and it made him mad as hell.

"You'll get it back if we can't use it," Callaghan called.

The car pulled into the traffic and rolled south, the red flasher turning all the way down Columbus. Burton watched it till it turned right on Eighty-Sixth. He'd been publicly screwed. He could see the guys in the Emerald Bar watching him from the other side of the street.

He went back into the shop and picked up a wrench. Thomas and Blue watched him as he toyed with it, assessing its weight, moving it from one hand to the other. And then his control snapped, and he spun around and flung the wrench at the back wall. It took a deep gouge out of the plaster, then clattered to the floor. Thomas ducked involuntarily, and Blue let out a long rattle of barks. Normally, Burton would have taken his bike and worked off the rest of the feeling with a couple of wild circuits of the park. This time it was different. He went to the phone and called Fay Coburn.

The minute she answered, he knew she'd been expecting the call. She sounded as if she'd won something. It figured. Okay, so here he was. He'd accepted her terms.

She said, "Where do we meet?"

"Where d'you wanna meet? Where'd be a nice place to pick up some food?"

"The Blue Max," she said, with not a moment's hesitation.

"Where's that?"

"Columbus and Seventy-first. It's a new French place."

Jesus, weren't they all. Did these guys always have to go back to Europe for their inspiration? Couldn't they look *ahead* for a change? "Okay," he said. "Around eight."

"Seven-thirty," she said.

She was laying it on. He wasn't going to argue over the phone, though. He could straighten her out when they met. It was summer, after all. It wouldn't do her any harm to sweat. "Okay," he said.

He got to the place at ten after eight. It was everything he'd expected. The minute he walked through the door, the icy air went straight through his denim jacket and began to raise goose bumps on his skin. What did these bums think New York was—Death Valley? Sure, it was a hot time of year, but Jesus, this was ridiculous!

He could just make her out in the dim lighting. She was sitting at the far end of the bar with her back to the entrance, part of an intimate little group chatting with the bartender. He could hear her voice as he walked toward her, and made out the words "block association" and "ABC." She was the center of attention, as usual.

"Gimme a Michelob," Burton said to the bartender.

The guy seated beyond her, in a T-shirt with "Monica" across the chest, glanced up at him; but Fay took no notice. The bartender was leaning on the bar with his elbows, looking at Fay. He had a heavy beard and a gold ring in his ear. If he heard what Burton said, he ignored him.

Burton shrugged. "Okay," he said. "If you've found some other way of earning a living, apart from serving customers, I'd be glad to have your secret."

He was going to turn and walk straight out of the place, but the sight of her in the mirror hit him where he couldn't resist. Jesus, she really was a looker, with her blonde hair set off against the black shawl over her shoulders. She was worth a little hassle—so long as he could get her to bed before the pair of them froze.

"A Michelob," he repeated.

The bartender pushed a glass under the pump without taking his eyes off Fay. She was talking about "building a community" and "getting a few creative people together." But, underneath, she was trailing the goods in front of that goggle-eyed group like any adolescent cockteaser in front of the high-school football team. Except she wasn't a cockteaser, and there wasn't a guy among that group who looked any more like a football player than Abe Beame did.

When the Michelob came, Burton said, "Put it on the lady's tab."

A guy started talking about the new season at ABC. Burton picked him up in the mirror. He was anywhere from forty to sixty-five, with corn-colored hair and that creamy skin that never wrinkles. His face was familiar. Sure, he was the macho bastard in the leather suit who appeared in the after-shave commercial in which a guy comes out of the bathroom dragging a couple of Dobermans. What the hell was she playing at? Couldn't she find better company than this?

There was a copy of the *Voice* on the bar to his left. He got up from his stool and took the paper over to a table. He knew damned well she'd be monitoring him through the mirror. "When you're through getting knighted by the queen, I'll be over here," he called.

He sat down facing the door. Beside him was a partition covered in pictures of aircraft from World War I. Directly above him a wooden propeller rotated slowly, blowing the icy air down onto his head and shoulders. He glanced at the headlines. It looked as if they were going to build West Way after all. *So surprise me,* he thought. He turned the page.

She came over at last and sat down facing him. "You call this seven-thirty?" she asked.

"I didn't call it anything," he said. He glanced at his watch. "Matter of fact, it's twenty after eight." He could feel her stiffen, and began to wonder whether it really was the air conditioning that was putting the ice into the place, or her.

"You are a first-rate bastard, Burton," she said.

"Yeah, so Blue tells me." He was still looking at the *Voice,* lying open on the table in front of him.

"What d'you think it looks like, a girl sitting alone in a West Side bar?"

"You picked the place."

"So that's it! You did it deliberately! I ought to walk straight out of here!"

"Sure, that's it," said Burton, closing the paper and pushing it away from him. "You wanna make some kind of monkey out of me? All this World War One flying crap and that Frog menu." He flicked a finger toward the blackboard standing at the entrance to the restaurant with the chef's recommendations chalked in French. "I don't like it. It's horseshit! I'm an American. Don't you recognize the accent, you teaching school and all that?"

"Screw you!" she snapped.

For a second he thought she might actually go for him, and he had a hand ready to parry the blow. There were little areas of high color over her cheekbones, and her eyes were like glass. When she did nothing, he began to feel easier. Maybe he'd gone too far. She didn't deserve it. He said gently, "You don't look like a whore, if that's what's bugging you."

"Don't give me the soft touch," she cried, throwing out her hands. "I'm a fool! Why did I let you talk me into getting together again? What made me think you might have changed?"

"Hey, hey," he said. He put out a hand to touch her, but she drew back. "I've had the cops all over me. I guess that threw me. I thought we said eight."

She gave a shrug. "That's a try. I guess I ought to be satisfied."

"It's true," he said. He turned and snapped his fingers. When a waiter came over, he said, "Lemme see the menu."

"Why can't you ever just apologize, like anyone else?" she asked.

She was looking directly at him, stiff and erect. Jesus, why couldn't she let up? She was liberated. What more was she trying to prove?

"Okay," he said. "I'm sorry." He couldn't help wondering if he was being a sucker all over again.

She didn't relax entirely, but she put a hand out to him and he took it. The waiter came with two menus, big as the Sunday *Times*. Burton ignored his. When Fay opened hers, it covered the table. It was in color, with little pictures of seafood and steak and game birds. "Well, now," she said, "let's see . . ."

He put his collar up deliberately. "That air-conditioner you talked about in the spring—did you ever get around to buying it?"

"No."

"You don't need one. Listen, I've lived through these summers all my life. They're not that bad. You've just gotta go with them. Everybody's sold on perfection, like they're sold on immortality. They oughta live in germ-proof greenhouses."

"It's better here than outside," she said. "I find it refreshing." She was still locked into the menu, not looking at him.

He shrugged. "Okay, so you find it refreshing. But lemme tell you this: If New Yorkers were polar bears, one of those newshounds from Channel Two would be screwing the ASPCA about this place."

She went through every entry on the menu. When Burton had got fed up watching the top of her head, he looked at the new customers who'd come into the bar. They fell into three categories: actors, wrestlers, and pansies. The actors sipped Martinis and Margaritas and presented everyone with a profile. The wrestlers clutched beer glasses in both hands and never took their eyes off one another in the mirror. The pansies drank Bloody Marys and looked confused about the choice between actors and wrestlers.

When the waiter came, Burton said, "Steak, medium rare; french fries; salad on the side."

"And madam?"

"What you gonna have?" Burton asked.

She looked up at last and said, "I don't think I want anything."

"What? We're supposed to be having dinner. What are we doing in here?"

"I think maybe you're right," she said. "It's too cold to sit. Let's go back to my place. I guess I can find something in the fridge."

Outside, he said, "You set me up! You never intended we should eat there! All you wanted to prove was you could get me to go anywhere you wanted!"

She took hold of his arm and walked beside him.

"That's not true," she protested. "They do a very good *steak au poivre*. I'd have stayed if you hadn't kicked up such a ruckus. I shouldn't be surprised if you turned up their air conditioning yourself just so you'd have an excuse to go to my place."

He wasn't mad, just amazed that she could get away with it. He strode down Columbus with his jacket over his shoulder and Fay hanging onto his arm, walking straight through anyone who got in his way, the way he rode a bicycle.

When they got to the corner of Sixty-seventh Street, she made a right toward Broadway, but he didn't turn with her, and her hand slid out of the crook of his arm. She stopped and turned back to look at him expectantly. He was standing with his hands in the back pockets of his jeans and his head in the air.

"What the hell is this?" he asked, nodding toward the dark, towering mass that rose up into the night sky immediately in back of her block. A vertical string of red lights marked its position.

She sighed. "It's a crane," she said, going to him and taking his arm again. "Do what the rest of us do: ignore it. Maybe it'll go away."

"Hey, wait a minute," he said, a mocking tone coming into his voice. "You mean . . . you never got anywhere? The petition, the protest to City Hall, the letters to *The Times*—nobody took any notice?"

"Drop it," she said. "Nobody's amused around here. People have got to move their homes. That's not funny."

He lowered his head and looked at her. People on the sidewalk brushed past him, but he didn't get out of their way. He behaved as if the pair of them were the only couple around. At last he said, "Honey, I'm not being funny; I'm just amazed at you. Where do you think you are? This is New York City. If it doesn't change, it'll die. That's the way of things. New business comes and eats up the old. Right this minute, ABC's on the crest. There'll come a time, though, when some bigger fish appears. It's life. It's progress. It's the way things are."

A guy with a brown bag lurched up the sidewalk from Broadway. He paused when he caught sight of Fay, five or six yards ahead of him, and a slow, crafty smile came over his face. He wiped his hand on his belly, then put it out as he approached her. "I need a quarter," he slurped, trying to get his tongue around the words.

"Get lost," said Burton. He spoke without anger, as if he was simply brushing aside some irritating insect.

The guy stood looking at him for a moment, swaying gently from side to side. Finally he got Burton into focus. He gave a slow, knowing grin, nodded, and moved on.

"What about the people?" asked Fay, picking up the earlier conversation and ignoring the incident with the brown bagger. "Don't they concern you?" It was the whole nub of the issue between them, this attitude of Burton's to the rest of mankind. She spoke very intensely.

"*You* do," he said. "Where you going to move to now?"

It wasn't enough for her. She expected him to show some concern for her, if only out of self-interest. It was the wider issue that bothered her. Was he really typical of New Yorkers, or was he simply a total egocentric? "Have you any idea how many lives this is going to affect? There are nine families in my building alone—

nine! And God knows how many buildings they'll finish up demolishing. What about the kids being dragged right out of the neighborhood? What about the folks in business here?" She turned and pointed to the Hispanic deli on the corner. "What about *them?* They're in their sixties. They've been there for thirty years. Don't you care about them?"

He shrugged. "I don't know them," he said. "How can I care about somebody I don't know? I care about you. I know you. Isn't that enough? Jesus, what do you want me to say? It's the truth. I can't force feelings I just don't have. You want me to lie to you?"

She let go of his arm and faced him. Suddenly he looked vulnerable to her, as if all this brash and independent behavior of his was simply a front. She got the impression that he made all these outrageous statements and all this noisy bluster to hide his loneliness and isolation. If this had been the first time she'd met him, she'd have thought he was no more than a grown kid whistling in the dark to keep the tigers at bay. Knowing him as she did, it was a completely new side of him and she softened to it, feeling oddly protective toward him, as if he was the stranger to Manhattan and she the native.

She took his arm again. "Come on," she said, humoring him.

Immediately inside her door, the cat was waiting for her. She came right up to Fay and arched her back and rubbed her cheek and neck against her pants.

"It's all right, Mr. Tibbs," Fay said. "This is Burton. He's an old friend. Come on, move and let us in." She pushed the cat clear of the doorway with the calf of her leg.

Burton bent down and put out a hand toward the animal. "Who's this you're living with, then?" he asked. "You didn't say anything about this guy. When'd you pick him up?"

"She's not a guy and I didn't pick her up. I got her from a friend a couple of weeks ago."

"If she's not a guy, how come you call her Mr. Tibbs?" Burton was still in a deep-knee-bend position, his hand out toward the cat.

"Because that's her name," said Fay, closing the door behind them and putting on the security chain. "Why do they call you Burton?"

He considered the question for a moment, as if it really merited some thought. Finally he nodded and said, "That's reasonable."

"I thought you'd think so," she said, snapping on the kitchen light. "Fix yourself a drink. You know where they are." She walked away from him down the little passage ahead and into the bedroom.

"C'mon, puss," said Burton, gently snapping his fingers.

The cat backed away, one foot moving carefully behind the other.

"Hey, what is this?" asked Burton. "What you backing up on me for? You think I eat pussies, hm? What kind of a guy d'you take me for?" He was angling his remarks more toward the bedroom door than toward the cat.

"I expect she can smell Blue on you," called Fay. "She's not too fond of dogs. I think she must have had some tough experiences. Just leave her. She'll get used to you."

He straightened up, went into the kitchen, and took a can of beer from the fridge. Mr. Tibbs followed him into the living room, at a discreet distance. The place was stifling, in spite of the decrepit extractor fan rattling away in the window. He dropped his jacket on one of the chairs and looked around. She'd changed things some since he'd last seen the room. There was a new stereo outfit by the wall to his left. She'd got rid of the drapes and the old iron lamp and had hung a couple of sketches of Lincoln Center on the wall facing the door. But there were still the same books in the book-case under the window, and the same battered green velvet couch and chairs.

"Pull the table in front of the fan," she called.

He lifted the table out of the corner and set a couple of dining chairs facing each other. He wondered if she'd changed the bedroom around as well. The bed had been a queen size, with a Posturepedic mattress. It would have been a pity to get rid of that. The noise of the fan began to jar on him and he switched it off. It gave a long, dying rattle of loose bearings and finally went quiet.

"What're you doing?" she yelled to him.

"You're better off without it," he yelled back. "All it does is drag soup in from the yard and dump it back on the street. No way you can breathe the air this time of year. You just gotta get used to it."

"Well, have you got gall!" she cried.

He heard her go into the kitchen. He went and stood in the doorway, leaning with his hands on the jambs. The place was the size of a cupboard. She'd taken off her street clothes and put on a thin cotton robe tied at the waist. He could see the rise of her breasts and the erect nipples through the thin material. It was good to see she was still the same woman behind that liberated exterior. He put a hand out and stroked her breast, but she lifted it off and jabbed him away with a fork.

"You're everything I detest," she said, handing him a bottle of wine from the fridge. "You're arrogant, you're overbearing, and you're a bully. You treat a woman as if she was some kind of commodity."

"I hate myself," he said.

She laughed. "Hate yourself? *You?* You've never been in love with anyone else."

He caught a whiff of the perfume she'd just been using in the bedroom. It came through the smell of garlic and herbs and got into his bloodstream. She sure knew how to get to a guy. Where had she learned it, spending all those years in the boonies? He bent to kiss her bare neck, but she snapped, "Come on, move it," and brushed past him with the plates.

She put out the main light and lit a couple of decorative candles. They sat down and Burton poured the wine. "Well, well," he said, "look what we just happened to have in the fridge—cold cuts from Zabar's, fresh tossed salad, bottle of Gallo's all the way from California. Like the president said to the Arabs, Ma'am, I sure was took in by y'all!"

"I thought you'd prefer something . . . intimate, seeing as how it's a reunion."

"Honey chil'l!"

"You're not mad?"

He thought about it for a moment; then he said, "I'm not mad."

"And you're not going to lean on me again, about living together?"

"Lover," he whispered, "what I have in mind couldn't be classified as leaning."

She smiled and they clinked glasses. "Nice to see you again," she said.

"Nice to be back."

"Just so we know where we stand."

"Well, I sure know where *I* stand," he said, "and it hurts like hell." Something brushed against his leg and he looked down. It was the cat. She looked up at him, large, steel-blue eyes reflecting the candlelight. "Well, look at that," he said. "Pussy and I are finally getting places."

The wine and the heat had started to get to Fay; it showed in her voice and in the line of her body. She had her elbows on the table and was looking straight into his eyes over the top of her glass. He had to face it: He hadn't felt like this about anyone for years. Under the table, she'd pushed her bare foot inside the leg of his jeans and was rubbing his shinbone with her toes. For a moment he thought it was the cat again, but the animal had already left him and was now lying asleep on the windowsill under the fan.

"You're not really a bastard," she said. "You just do it to keep people away. What d'you think they're going to do to you?"

She'd undone the knot of her belt without his noticing. Her robe had slipped open, exposing the fullness of her breasts but leaving the nipples still covered. He began to wish he was wearing something more roomy.

"What d'*you* wanna do?" he asked.

"I want to fuck," she whispered. Her lips were very full and she barely opened them as she spoke.

"You sure know how to dot the *i*'s," he said.

"And cross the *t*'s," she said.

He took her hand across the table. He got the feeling she was looking more into him than at him. Her eyes were dark blue in the low lighting, her cheeks full and bright with color. She was the most sensual thing he'd ever seen.

"Jesus," he said, "we're nothing but a bunch of wide-eyed innocents, us New Yorkers. Here we are, thinking we're the center of the Western world, believing that nothing worth reporting ever happens north of Harlem or west of Riverside Drive, and all the time, in one of them little white towns upstate, there's someone like you growing up! Honey, there are kids on Forty-second Street would give their Minnesota eyeteeth to have your touch."

She lifted his hand, put the tip of his index finger into her mouth, and, holding it between her teeth, rolled her tongue over it. He began to think his jeans were going to strangle him. There was only so much that ordinary cotton denim could take.

She got up at last and walked to the door into the little central hallway of the apartment. "Give me a minute," she whispered. "Blow out the candles before you come through."

When she'd turned down the little passage that led

to the bedroom, he got up. The relief was enormous. He heard her come out of the can and go into the bedroom. He gave her thirty seconds, then snuffed out the candles and followed her.

The light was out in the bedroom. The air was heavy with the smell of gasoline fumes. She was standing in front of the open window, silhouetted against the greenish glow from the streetlamps, her robe lying in a dark heap beside her. He went across to her and stood close behind her, slipping his hands around her waist and cupping her breasts. He trembled as he felt the nipples pressing against his fingers, firm as hazelnuts. He pushed his face into her hair and ran his tongue around the convolutions of her ear. The sweat ran down his back. He didn't give a damn about the heat. He could no longer smell the gasoline fumes and the rotting garbage outside, only the overpowering perfume of her flesh. She was warm and mobile and alive, pressing the whole line of her body backward into his, running the palms of her hands down his waist and thighs, rolling her bare ass over his clamoring erection. Jesus! Another second and the whole shooting match was going to pop. Pants or no pants, he was going to come, but he didn't want to—not yet.

He put a hand down to undo the fastening; but suddenly she turned to face him, never losing contact with his body. She put a hand around the back of his head and pulled his mouth over hers. Her lips were full and soft, working over his mouth as if she were feeding on him, opening wide to receive his tongue. With her free hand, she undid his belt, unzipped his fly, and began pushing his jeans down over his hips. He let them fall, stepping out of them and kicking them aside without breaking the lock she had on him. His rod had thrust itself out of the opening in his briefs, and she had her pelvis cocked forward, rubbing herself firmly against it.

He began to lose control. He was going to come right

there in front of the window, before he even got inside
her, if he didn't do something about it. He put his
hands under her ass and lifted her off the floor. She
lifted her legs and wound them around his body, locking her ankles behind him. He turned with her and
carried her the six feet to the bed. She clung to him,
arms hooked under his arms and around the back of
his shoulders, lips still devouring his mouth.

He fell forward with her on the bed. She eased her
hips forward, bringing the head of his penis out of the
mass of hairs where she'd held it and into the lips of
her cunt. He stabbed forward with his buttocks. She
gasped and screwed herself downward and began to
moan. The lips opened wide. He felt the head of his
penis slip farther inside her. He struck again, ramming
into her, pulling down on her with his hands, impaling
her on himself, riding up till he'd got the whole length
of his rod inside her.

"Jesus Christ!" she breathed. "Where've you been
all these weeks?"

He didn't want to come. He wanted to stay there
forever, suspended inside her, one minisecond on the
upbeat side of orgasm, but he couldn't. He tried to
distract himself by thinking of the street outside, the
garbage around the corner, the brown baggers lying in
the gutters on Columbus. It made no difference. She
was lying under him, writhing, moaning, smothered in
sweat. In the end, the climax came against his wishes
and he began to melt away.

He lay there on top of her, sweat pouring off his
body, running into his eyes and nostrils. Every mid-
summer tension had drained out of him and flowed into
her or over her. He had to have a woman; that's all
there was to it. It didn't necessarily tie him down. She
let out a long, low sigh, and as her body shifted, he slid
off her wet belly and rolled onto his back.

"Jeez, I was dumb," he said, when his heartbeat had
slowed some. "I should never have let you go."

"Forget it," she said softly. "It's over."

He lay there with his eyes open, staring up into the darkness. Outside, he could hear all the comforting night sounds he knew so well: the howl of a radio; a guy screaming somewhere below in Spanish; the clatter of a trash-can lid; and back of everything, the reverberating hum of the living city. Then the sound of a siren came out of the distance, rose to a crescendo, and faded into nothingness, and the sense of ecstasy and total relaxation gave way to a sense of uneasiness. He couldn't put his finger on it. Nothing left a guy so defenseless as getting in deep with a woman.

She turned toward him, put a hand on his chest, and ran her fingertips through the damp hairs. "Do you feel better?" she asked. Her voice was deep and very relaxed.

"Sure."

"What's really bothering you?"

"Nothing."

There was a scar high up on the left side of his chest, just above his collarbone. She couldn't see it in the darkness, but she knew exactly where it was. He'd never told her how he got it or whether it gave him any trouble. She slid her fingers up until she reached it. It was a deep depression in the flesh, a couple of inches long. She could feel the little scars left by the sutures that had been used to pull the torn flesh together.

"Does it hurt?" she asked.

"No."

She waited for him to say something more, but he didn't. He'd clammed up on her again. It was instinctive with him—the technique he'd evolved for keeping the world at bay. She didn't believe that long-term it was a useful technique. There came a time when the only way to crack a problem was to share it.

"Let me help you," she coaxed, still running her hand over his chest.

"You've helped me," he said. "Just leave it."

Something in his voice made her lift her head from the pillow and look at him. "Hey, what is it?" she asked. "You having second thoughts about us?"

"No."

"Well, then?"

He turned and looked at her. She had her head propped up on her elbow and was waiting for him to say something. "That bastard Callaghan," he muttered.

"Who's Callaghan?"

"He's a cop. He's been on my back for months."

"What for?"

"How would I know? They don't like independent guys. They wanna know where they stand with everybody. Maybe I didn't give to their orphan fund."

She took her hand off his chest and sat up. "What've you been doing?"

"What d'you mean?" he asked, hauling himself up. "You don't have to *do* anything around these parts to make the cops take notice. You just gotta *exist!* That way, if you don't fit into one of their slots, they wanna know why. And they wonder why they don't get cooperation. Jesus, I wouldn't lift a phone to call that bastard if I knew who put the finger on JFK!"

"What did this Callaghan say to you?"

The tightness was back across his gut, the way it had been earlier. He began to massage the back of his neck with his fingertips, trying to ease the growing tension. "He didn't say anything. He didn't have to. He had a partner with him. They went through everything in the shop. When they finally took off, they'd got a sack full of scrap from out back. All I got was shut mouths and a receipt."

"They can't do that. They've got to give some reason——"

"They can do anything! You saw them in the park. Jesus, you can't even ride a bike anymore!"

"Hey, Burton, be fair," she said. "A girl had just been murdered. A maniac's loose somewhere. There's a bike involved; they've been saying so on the radio all afternoon. You expect the police to ask questions. You weren't exactly cooperative. Four women have been killed since spring."

"So?" He got off the bed and went to the window. In the street below, a guy was poking inside one of the garbage cans that lined the sidewalk ready for collection. He knew she wouldn't stop there. She had to pursue everything to the bitter end, till it was all neatly explained in her head. He hoped she wouldn't push him too far. He had only so much endurance.

When she finally spoke, her voice was full of disbelief. *"Four women,"* she repeated. "Don't you *care?"*

"No."

"I don't believe you."

He shrugged. "Have it your way."

"Burton . . . tell me you don't mean it."

He turned to face her. "Listen," he said, "if I went around caring about every woman gets herself murdered in this city, I'd be in the nuthouse!"

She'd got to her knees and was poised on the edge of the bed, facing him, a lighter shape in the general darkness of the room. She cried, "Don't you feel pity? Don't you feel any kind of . . . social commitment?"

"What are you talking about?" he yelled. "What d'you mean, social commitment? For Christ's sake, what's *anyone* committed to?"

"Other people!" she screamed.

"People! I don't like people! They're nothing to me! That's it." He picked up his pants and pulled them on. He was praying she wouldn't press him any further.

After a moment, she said quietly, "Does that include me? I mean, if I was in danger and needed help, couldn't I turn to you?"

"Sure."

"And what would you do?"

"Nothing."

She gasped as if he'd hit her across the face. Then she said, "I don't believe bastards like you exist!"

He turned to her. "You're old enough to take care of yourself. You wouldn't have survived eight months in this city if you hadn't been. What kind of danger do you have in mind? Nothing happens to *nice* girls. Didn't they tell you that in Saratoga?"

"You're not human."

"I'm a New Yorker. What else did you expect?"

He stared at her for a moment. He thought she'd be in tears, but she wasn't. He bent and picked up the rest of his clothes and started to put them on. It was over. All he could do now was get the hell out. Why did she have to press everything to the nth degree? He carried his shoes over to the bed and sat down on the edge.

Fay studied his back as he leaned forward to tie his laces. He was the most goddamn stubborn bastard she'd ever met. He wouldn't give an inch. He was incapable of any kind of flexibility. It was up to her again. If she didn't make a move, he'd get up and walk right out because of some crazy male pride she didn't begin to understand. Was it worth the sacrifice? Was he worth hanging on to, considering all the effort that the relationship demanded from her? Maybe not, she concluded; yet there was more to him than this dumb defensive front he threw up whenever he felt threatened. Some deep intuition told her that despite everything, he *was* worth hanging on to. Whether he admitted it or not, he wanted her to stick around.

She crawled toward him, still on her knees, and put an arm around his shoulders. He tensed instinctively. "Hey, c'mon," she crooned, her voice soft and very comforting. "You don't have to compromise your independence. I'm not going to compromise mine. You like my body; I like yours. Okay. So what's bugging you? You can level with me."

He finally turned and looked at her. Her hair was

brushing his cheek and he could smell the heat of her body. He began to relax under the influence of her presence. "Listen," he muttered at last, "I've about had this up to here." He patted the top of his head to indicate that something was bugging him to the point where he might explode.

She stayed very still, not understanding what he was talking about but sensing that, with enough encouragement, he might say something that would clarify his attitude for her.

"When I was a kid," he went on at last, "we lived up on a Hundred and Tenth. Nice place. Riverside Drive one side, Columbia in back. I was your average kid—dumb, know-all, full of lip. But I'd been brought up right; my old man saw to that. Maybe I was spoiled, I don't know. I had a couple of sisters, but they were five, six years older. I never went with them and I never took much notice of them. I was friendly with a kid my own age, a kid by the name of Johnny O'Malley." He paused for a moment, then turned to her and asked, "You bored by this?"

"Oh, for God's sake," she said, trying to keep the exasperation out of her voice. "It's the first time you've ever talked about yourself. Do you know what it means to me? I'm just beginning to think that maybe there's a human being behind that front after all. No, I'm not bored."

For a moment she thought he was going to bring the discussion to a close. Her damned temperament had got in the way again. But after a pause he said, "Okay. I had to ask."

"So I've told you," she said.

He seemed easier again. He got up off the bed and went and sat on the windowsill, his back toward the street. "Jesus," he said, a touch of wry amusement in his voice, "I can see the poor little bastard now— squat, thickset, carrot hair, and those bent kinda legs kids get through living in the saddle or not getting the right things to eat. He was a kook about candy. I'd go in a store with him and he'd come out with his pockets loaded. He wasn't a thief; just he couldn't see a pile of candy in a store without his hand slipping away from him and lifting the stuff."

He paused for the sound of an ambulance siren to pass the window and fade into the distance. Fay had drawn her knees up and was sitting in the middle of the bed with her hands locked around them. She was aware of the dampness of her skin in the sticky heat.

"There was a drugstore around Broadway, down in the Nineties," he said crisply, as if the sound of the siren had focused his attention again on what he was trying to say. "We'd gone in for a soda. It was around this time of year and the place was cool. And suddenly I caught sight of three guys in the mirror. One had a gun. Johnny spotted them the same time. We sat side by side on those chrome-plated stools without moving a muscle. The guy behind the counter went white; then, like a dumb punk, he put his hand down like he was reaching for a gun. Maybe he was; we never knew. Before he'd got anywhere near it, the guy with the gun pistol-whipped him, and he sank down out of sight.

"When Johnny told me later that he knew where the bastard with the gun hung out, I told him we oughta go to the cops. It never occurred to me that we were doing the wrong thing. The cops—Jesus! We walked into the station house side by side, the most law-abiding goddamn dumbbells you've ever seen. I tell the cop what happened, and Johnny answers 'Yes sir, no sir' to all his questions!"

He went up to the window, a dark silhouette facing out toward the street. She could see from the line of his body and the movement of his shoulders the kind of tension he was under.

"The bastard took down everything—names, addresses, parents. You think once it was down on paper that's where it stayed? You think there's such a thing as confidentiality where the cops are concerned? The guy with the gun had a brother, and the brother had a friend. A couple of evenings later, Johnny and I are in Riverside Park. It's dusk—not that that bothered us. We knew the area, everybody knew us, we were street wise. But they were waiting for us back of Grant's Tomb. I was lucky. I took a knife in the neck and they figured I was dead. But they kicked the shit out of Johnny till his head was like raw liver. If I ever found that cop again I'd pull his tongue out with my bare hands! Don't ever talk to me about cops and duty!"

She was horrified, not so much by the story and the words he'd used as by the intensity of feeling with which he recalled the incident. "I'm . . . sorry," she stammered. "I didn't realize . . ." Then, by way of easing him out of the mood he'd got himself into, she asked, "Do you ever see him now—Johnny?"

He shrugged and said quietly, "No, I don't see him anymore. I figure he's still upstate in Grasslands. They turned him into a vegetable that night in Riverside Park. I saw him a couple of years ago. He couldn't even zip his fly."

She wanted to go to him and put her arms around him and comfort him, but she also began to feel an irritation creeping in. Everyone had rough experiences; that was pretty much what growing up was about. Maybe not as rough as this, but how rough is rough?

"Okay," she said, "but that's a long time ago. You're not ten anymore. You can't spend the rest of your life carrying that kind of chip on your shoulder. What brought all this up again now? I thought we'd got something creative going between us at last——"

"I'm trying to tell you!" he cut in, voice full of exasperation. "It's the cops again. They're trying to pin these murders on me. They figure I'm this Bald Eagle guy."

▼▼▼▼▼▼▼▼▼▼▼▼▼▼

CHAPTER 9

▲▲▲▲▲▲▲▲▲▲▲▲▲▲

Rudi was right alongside McGlade, his sneakers padding on the asphalt path. "Come on, buddy," said McGlade, putting his hands on the sides of his chest. "Breathe! In . . . and let it go! In . . . and let it go!"

It sure was some morning. The sky was a light emerald, without a trace of a cloud. A little breeze was coming up from the south, fresh and clean. The limp leaves stirred overhead. The scorched grass covering the Sheep Meadow looked as though it might survive after all. Everything was in sharp focus again for the first time in weeks—the trees, the big rock outcrop on the other side of the meadow, the towers of midtown beyond.

McGlade's spirits began to lift. Maybe things weren't all that bad. Even his back felt good. "Jeez," he said, "this could be some town! Wouldn't it be something if you could tell the world you were a New Yorker without feeling you gotta apologize?"

"Why you gotta apologize, Duke?" panted Rudi.

"The filth," said McGlade. "All the filth. You can't be proud of that." As he spoke, he could feel the pulse in his right temple begin to throb. The vision of the city disappearing under one great heap of filth had become increasingly real to him recently. "Somebody's gotta do something about it. There's gotta be a great big cleanup; otherwise it's just gonna choke us all. But nobody takes any notice. What d'you have to *do* to get somebody to listen?"

"You mean, like garbage?" Rudi asked hesitantly.

"Yeah," said McGlade. "Garbage . . . and things. It's gonna take one big broom." Garbage! he thought. If only it was that simple. *People*—that was the real trouble. His head felt tight, as if he had a metal band around it that somebody kept tightening. He took a glance at Rudi, trotting beside him. The kid was beginning to flag. McGlade cut the pace when they'd crossed the road at the end of the mall, and made for the steps leading down to the zoo.

They passed a hot-dog cart and a couple of Hispanics selling beer out of a bucket full of ice. At the bottom of the steps, the polar bear was marching back and forth in his cage, right up against the bars the way he always did. It seemed tough on him, McGlade thought, stuck in there with a little tub of water and a couple of fake rocks. On a day like this, he should be roaming free.

In the plaza beyond, there were the usual crowds: camera-hung guys from out of town; kids with balloons and ice cream cones; old guys tossing nuts to the monkeys. The sharp smell of ammonia was everywhere. The breeze that was freshening the park hadn't got into the zoo.

"Let's go talk to Arthur," said McGlade, "see how he's getting along. Can you imagine—a guy wearing a fur coat in this weather?"

Arthur the badger was in the big shed. The door to his outside run was open, but he never went out there. Most of the time he just lay hidden inside his hollowed-out log. The shed was hot and fetid. The capybara was submerged in its tub, with just the tip of its nose breaking the surface. Across the way the ocelots lay draped along the dead branches in their cages, eyes half closed, looking like the stuffed animal McGlade had bought in Macy's and given to Tony's daughter last Christmas.

There were two black guys standing in front of Arthur's cage. They were giggling, slapping each other on the shoulders. One cried, "Hey, man! What kind o' animal's that? I don't see nothin' but eyes. Looks like he's crawled up his own ass!"

McGlade said, "Let's wait here, buddy. He'll come out when they've gone. They don't understand animals."

Rudi wasn't interested in the black guys. He was looking at Duke. At last he asked, "You okay, Duke?"

"Why not?" McGlade turned sharply to look at the boy.

There was a strange look in McGlade's eyes, as if he didn't see Rudi but was focusing on something far beyond him. It gave Rudi a shock. He'd seen the look before—the time they rode back from the car pound, and again when Duke talked about a fall from the top of the Empire State Building—but never this intense. He said tentatively, "It's hot, Duke. I figured you might have a headache again."

The focus came back into McGlade's eyes. He shrugged. "Maybe," he said. "Yeah . . . maybe."

"You want me to go get some aspirin?"

"Aspirin? No . . . no, thanks," said McGlade after a moment. Aspirin wouldn't touch it. Action was the only answer. He'd just have to . . . do something. Yet the thought of "doing something" only tightened the band around his head and filled him with a terrible sense of anxiety. Maybe he ought to call Joey Feinstein, try to fix up some more work.

When the black guys moved on, arms around each other's shoulders, long, thin bodies rippling like drapes in a light breeze, McGlade stood in front of the log and said, "Hello there, feller. Hey, Arthur, you gonna let me and my buddy take a look at you?" He could see the eyes shining deep inside the darkness of the log, but there was no movement. He put his hands on the guardrail and eased himself down until he was looking right up the inside of the log. He said, "Hey,

it's Duke—Duke and Rudi. Come on, pal, you remember. We were the ones used to come and see you
in the spring, when nobody else cared. You gonna
have a word with us?"

Arthur moved a couple of inches forward, nose
twitching, the wart and the big bare patch on his head
just coming into sight.

"He's coming, Duke!" Rudi whispered, bending forward beside McGlade.

"What about that promise you made"—McGlade
continued to talk to the log—"about taking us upstate,
showing us your home, introducing us to all your
relatives? C'mon, Arthur . . . you remember."

But Arthur didn't come any farther, and finally Mc-
Glade pushed himself upright and said, "Maybe we
oughtn't to bother him. I guess it's kinda hot still. They
oughta give him a bigger cage and a tub to play in, as
long as they're gonna keep him shut up."

"Shall we go take a look at the silver back?" asked
Rudi, pointing out the door toward the gorilla's cage.

McGlade shook his head. "Maybe next time," he
said. "I gotta get back now. I gotta call my agent."

As they were jogging back, Rudi asked, "Don't you
like seeing Arthur, Duke?"

"Sure I like seeing him," said McGlade. "Why
wouldn't I?" The sweat was really running now. There'd
been a change in the atmosphere. Breathing wasn't all
that easy anymore. He was pressing the back of his
neck with his hand to ease the pain in his head.

"You didn't like his cage. You never mentioned it
before."

"Once they're in a cage they're stuck. Nothing they
can do about it," said McGlade. "It's different for people. They don't have to stay put if they don't like it.
These guys in the park, jogging, dodging around on
bikes, if they don't like it here, all they gotta do is pull
up stakes and quit. A *guy* doesn't have to stick in Man-

hattan if he doesn't like it, but *Arthur*—that's different."

"*You* stick, Duke," said Rudi. "*You* don't quit."

The kid had something. "Hey, that's right," said McGlade. "Well, maybe I like it after all, or maybe me and Arthur, we've got a lot in common."

"Oh, no, Duke," Rudi protested. "Arthur's an animal; you're *someone*."

McGlade glanced down at him. He really was a great kid. He never got low. He never gave any trouble. Despite the heat and the hassle of summer, his eyes were bright and his face eager. McGlade gave a half-smile. "Hey," he said, "maybe *you* oughta be my agent."

"Wow! I wish I could!" said Rudi.

"Well, you think about it. You could do a lot worse than taking me on. Might even get you one or two other guys. How d'you think you could handle Sly Stallone?"

Rudi grinned. "Aw, c'mon, Duke."

"Crazier things have happened," said McGlade. "Hey, there's a parade of liners down at the piers. Might be worth looking at later."

"Okay!" said Rudi.

"You know where they're going? All the way down the coast, right to the islands. Now, how much d'you think that costs, seven days cruising the islands? Seven days—all them rich people, all that blue sea, all that beautiful cool air. Christ!"

That word—"Christ"—threw Rudi. Sure, he'd heard it often, on the streets, in school—he even used it himself when he wanted to make an impression—but he'd never heard Duke use it, not in front of him. Duke was very strict about what he said in front of kids. He began to worry about Duke. He had said some odd things recently. Maybe he wasn't as well as he made out. Maybe he'd hurt himself doing that stunt in the car pound and was keeping quiet about it. That could account for his headaches.

"I guess millions," said Rudi at last.

"Maybe one day," said McGlade. He winked and tapped the side of his nose. "One day, buddy."

They crossed Central Park West at Seventy-second Street, jogged down to Columbus, then turned uptown. It got more difficult to stay together. There were people all over the sidewalk, hauling dogs along, shoving shopping carts. As he passed the Wrangler House, McGlade said, "Remember the T-shirt I got for your birthday, the one with the picture of Yak Canutt on the front? That's where I picked it up."

Rudi didn't answer.

McGlade glanced to his side. Rudi wasn't there. He checked his pace and looked back over his shoulder. As he did so, he became aware of a radio blaring above the clatter of the traffic. For a moment he couldn't figure it out. Where had the kid got to? Then the pattern of people behind him on the sidewalk broke apart to make room for a guy riding a delivery bike. He was a big guy, bare to the waist, carrying a trunk-sized radio under one arm. When he spotted McGlade he made straight for him, the big aluminum box attached to the front of the bike rattling over the broken sidewalk.

McGlade hesitated. The summer had driven the whole goddamn world crazy. In the end, he jinked to his left. But the guy didn't leave him. McGlade opened up his stride and swerved right. The guy swerved with him, leaning back in the saddle, free arm straight out grasping the handlebar, as if he was riding a steer. It began to look serious. Was the nut going to let up at the last second, or was he going to go all the way?

It wasn't worth taking any chances, not in this town. McGlade checked his stride and took a couple of quick steps left, putting a parking meter between them. Still the guy came at him. Then, with only a yard to spare, he wrenched the machine to his right, swerved around the meter, and hurtled past McGlade.

McGlade rested a hand on top of the meter. He was breathing heavily and his heart was pounding in his throat. The guy had taken the bike straight off the sidewalk and was working his way north against the solid stream of southbound traffic, head flung back in a great cackling laugh.

Rudi came up from behind, blond hair dark with sweat. "You okay, Duke?" he asked.

"Where the hell'd you get to?" gasped McGlade, still leaning on the parking meter and grabbing air into his lungs in great gulps. His head was on the point of splitting wide open, and objects at the periphery of his field of vision were blurred. "D'you see what that bum did? If there was any justice in this city, that guy with the big Mack truck there would go right over him, squash him like a roach. Everyone's too soft. There's not one guy in a million ready to make a stand!"

Rudi hardly recognized his friend. Was this the same Duke McGlade who'd taken him up to West Point last summer and out to Shea Stadium to see the Mets play? "What happened, Duke?" he asked at last.

"Shut up!" snapped McGlade. He wasn't looking up Columbus anymore but directly across the street through the torrent of moving traffic. His eyes had picked up a movement on the cross street opposite and now he'd got it into focus. There was a massive black guy coming up Eighty-first with a pump shotgun in his hands. It was the wino Tony Stern had called the cops about, the one Callaghan had said was back on the street.

Right away, McGlade could see what was going to happen. The guy was out of his mind with booze. The Hispanic woman clinging to his arm and screaming at him wasn't going to be able to stop him. Nothing was going to stop him till he'd blown somebody away. There wasn't a doubt in McGlade's mind who that somebody was going to be. He stepped off the side-walk and began working his way across the traffic flow.

"What is it, Duke?" called Rudi.

"Stay on that side!" McGlade snapped. "You hear me?"

He had to get to the store. No one in there would be expecting anything. The bum could walk straight in and start blasting. All around McGlade, the air was solid with the honking of horns. Brakes howled. Drivers screamed. He ignored it all, never taking his eyes off the black guy.

He got to the sidewalk before the guy had reached Columbus, and began to run north, dodging through the slow-moving shoppers ahead of him. He was planning the line of action the way he planned a stunt. The store was still half a block away. If he put the squeeze on his body, he might give Tony a clear thirty seconds' warning. Once he was in the store, he had to lock the door; that was priority number one. Then he had to call the cops and get the gun from behind the counter.

He started checking through Tony's family in his mind. Rudi was out of it, waiting for him on the opposite sidewalk. Thomas was up with Burton. Maria would be in back, and Tony would be in the store. This time of the morning, Elsa would still be in her bedroom. He ran through the priorities again: lock the door; call the cops; get the gun. Maybe once he'd got the door locked, it would be better to go straight for the gun and leave Tony to call the cops. But, if it came to it, was Tony going to be able to use the gun? He'd been in the war, but had he ever killed anybody—up close, face to face, the way somebody was going to have to now?

He turned off the sidewalk onto the entrance step and hit the wooden frame of the door with his hand. He expected it to give at once, and he'd already decided what he was going to shout to Tony the second he got inside; but it didn't work out like that. He'd overlooked one possibility. The door was locked, and he came to an abrupt stop, with his face smacked into the glass.

It took him a moment to clear his head. He gave a couple of loud raps on the glass with the flat of his hand and yelled, "Tony!" There was no movement inside. Puzzled, he dropped back onto the sidewalk.

People were watching him, curious, apprehensive, the way they always behaved when anything unusual happened. He shoved past them. They didn't resist. Maybe it wasn't a bad thing the door was locked. It took care of one of his problems. All he had to do now was go in the side door, grab the gun, and get Tony to call the cops.

Once inside the entrance, he turned and dropped the latch and rammed the bolts home top and bottom. Again he yelled, "Tony!" Still there was no answer.

When he got into the back room, Maria Stern was standing in the kichen doorway, her hands covered with flour.

"Where's Tony?" McGlade cried. The sweat was in his eyes. He mopped them with the sleeve of his sweat shirt.

"In the store. Why? What's———"

"He's not in the store!" How could anyone be so dumb?

She hesitated. "Sure he's in the store," she said. "He's just come out of the bathroom."

Tony's voice came from the hallway leading into the store. "That you calling, Maria?"

It was going to be all right; McGlade suddenly knew it. He'd got there in time. He went into the hallway and walked right past Tony and into the store. He said, "Call the cops."

"The cops?" asked Stern.

McGlade was behind the counter. He reached underneath and took the gun from the shelf. It was working out fine. "That nigger's on the street again," he called.

"He's coming this way with a pump shotgun. Where's the girl? Keep Maria in back."

Tony hesitated. Then he yelled, "The door!" He rushed back into the store and flung himself down the narrow aisle between the wall shelves and one of the floor racks.

"It's okay," said McGlade. "It's locked."

"What d'you mean?" Tony screamed. "I just opened it!"

McGlade felt his guts drop out. While he'd been slamming the bolts home on the side entrance, Tony had come down from the bathroom and unlocked the front door. He muttered, "Oh, Jesus Christ!"

It was too late. The black guy had shaken his woman loose and was walking right at the door as if he didn't see it. It flung open under his weight. Tony was still ten feet away from it.

"Tony, get down!" snapped McGlade, cocking the pistol with his thumb. He didn't take his eyes off the black guy. He wasn't having difficulty focusing anymore. His eyes had cleared. He was going to kill the bastard. There was no place in a civilized society for a slab of sweat-hung crap like this. He'd be saving the sanitation department money. But he had to do it right. The only thing that made him hesitate was the fear that he might miss. The first shot had to count.

The black guy looked around, swiveling his head like a periscope, ignoring the pistol McGlade had pointing at him. "Where's the . . . the guy called the cops?" he said thickly.

"He's not here," said McGlade. "You'd better come back later." He was calculating the distance between them: maybe twenty feet. It was a 9-mm Browning Hi-Power he was holding. It would take a guy out, all right, but you still had to hit him square. At that range, even with a bum this size, he couldn't be certain. He needed to narrow the odds. He started to edge forward, both hands gripping the pistol, the way he always did when he was doubling for a star performer.

The black guy swayed, dribbling from a half-open mouth, eyes like bloody sockets under the thick-boned brow. He was trying to get Tony into focus, and finally he took a couple of shaky steps toward him.

As the guy cleared the door, McGlade caught sight of Rudi out of the corner of his eye. He was standing in the entrance, trying to see through the glass. McGlade wanted to scream, "Get the hell away from here!" But the black guy was waving his gun like a flag. Christ knew what he'd do if anything spooked him. McGlade couldn't take his eyes off him, but he took his left hand off the pistol and slowly raised it, palm open toward Rudi, to indicate that he should stay where he was. Either the kid didn't see him or he didn't understand, because a second later he came into the store and closed the door behind him.

"Somebody must've locked the side door," Rudi said. "I couldn't—— Hey, Duke, what is it?"

The black guy began to swing around toward Rudi, a top-heavy, uncoordinated mountain of sweating flesh.

"Get down, you dumb kid! Drop!" screamed McGlade.

He had wanted to wait until he had the bum sitting right on his foresight. But now the guy swung back toward him, guided more by hearing than by sight, and the muzzle of the pump gun was aimed directly at McGlade's gut.

McGlade fired twice. The explosions ripped the air. A hunk of loose plaster fell from the ceiling and dropped in front of him. The shots took the guy in the right side of the chest, and he spun around fast, but he didn't drop. The release of tension in McGlade was exquisite. He fired two more shots. They pushed the black guy into the wall shelves, and bottles began to fall around him as the woodwork splintered under his weight, but *still* he didn't drop.

Tony had got to the phone in the hallway. McGlade could hear him yelling to the cops. In back, Maria was screaming. McGlade wondered which side of the central floor rack to move around, to put in the next shots. His head was clear, his judgment cool as ice. Then the black guy recovered his balance, pushed himself forward out of the shattered wall rack, and took a single heavy step forward. The rest of the bottles behind him slid to the floor and smashed. That same moment, the shotgun went off. Something pounded into the wall on McGlade's left, and pellets clinked around the glassware.

McGlade stepped straight out from the cover of the floor rack and pumped the remaining slugs point-blank into the black guy's chest. Blood welled out of the wounds and began to run down his sweat-soaked T-shirt into the waistband of the pajama trousers he was wearing. His jaw moved, his mouth frothed, but he didn't speak. Finally, his red eyes glazed and his legs buckled. He dropped to his knees, head lolling forward, spewing blood over McGlade's sneakers.

McGlade kicked the shotgun out of his hands, then put a foot on his neck and gave him a shove. The bum was an animal—a hulk of moving garbage. The black guy swayed for a moment, then rolled to his right and hit the floor.

McGlade watched him till he was certain the guy wasn't going to move anymore. Then he turned to look for Rudi, and found him sitting on the floor with his back against the left-hand wall. "I told you to stay out of it!" McGlade cried. "You could've gotten us all killed." He was beginning to shake, now that the tension had snapped. He didn't want the kid to get too close. The black guy was a mess. He said, "Get in back. And *stay* there this time!"

He stepped between Rudi and the body of the black guy and dropped the latch on the door. There were people standing on the sidewalk staring into the store, but nobody made a move to come in. Thank Christ he hadn't needed to call on them for help.

Tony came out from the hallway. "You okay?" he asked McGlade. His voice was shrill with tension.

"Yeah." The chilly air from the conditioner was beginning to get to McGlade, despite his sense of elation. He felt as though the sweat was freezing on him. The place stank of gun smoke and spilled liquor.

"Christ Almighty! Thank God you were around. I . . . I don't know what I would have done."

"You'd better get something to cover this bum up," said McGlade.

"Yeah," said Tony.

"You get through to the cops?"

"They're on their way."

McGlade returned the pistol to its place behind the counter.

"Where's Rudi?" asked Tony.

"I sent him in back," said McGlade. "The dumb kid . . . I told him to stay out of it. He could've gotten himself killed. That boozed-up bastard!"

Tony nodded. "I'll go see to Maria and get a sheet to cover . . . You'll let the cops in, eh?"

"Yeah, sure."

McGlade was starting to shiver. Couldn't they ever get these air-conditioners right? They oughta close the whole town down for the summer, evacuate everybody, the way they would if there was any other kind of plague. The city would never be bearable, in summer— except for the rats and roaches—whatever gimmicks they invented.

Someone started kicking at the doorframe and slamming at the glass. The sound got through to McGlade, and, his heart pounding again, he reached instinctively for the pistol. He relaxed when he saw that it was the Hispanic woman, and went to the door and waved her away.

She ignored the gesture. "Lemme in! I wanna see

my man! What've you done to him?" All the time, she kept beating at the glass with her clenched fists.

She looked a mess. She had a raw patch of flesh on her scalp where someone had yanked out a handful of hair. There was a deep purple bruise over her right cheekbone, and the stream of tears running down her face had carried mascara onto her chin. McGlade pulled down the shade. She couldn't break the glass. The cops would yell when they wanted in.

He turned and put the main light on, and it was then that he saw something bundled up against the wall. McGlade felt a sudden stab of anger. It was Rudi, sitting exactly where he'd been before. What the hell was the matter with the kid? "Okay, stay there if that's what you want, but don't ask me to take you to see Arthur again!" McGlade yelled. "Don't ask me to do *anything* for you! You damn near got me killed, coming in the way you did. I said stay out of it! Didn't I say that?" He was trying to remember exactly what had happened. He had an odd sense of having missed something.

Rudi was looking straight at McGlade, but he didn't move and he didn't say anything. He had a crazy expression on his face, as though he'd just seen something wonderful. Jesus, hadn't he heard the shots? Hadn't he seen the slobbering ape fall?

Something was wrong. What had happened to the kid? Had he knocked his head when he went down to get out of the line of fire? Maybe he'd been hit by a stray pellet ricocheting from a bottle. McGlade went to him and asked, "You okay, Rudi?"

Rudi still didn't speak.

McGlade dropped down beside him and took the boy's head in his hands. "Hey, buddy, what's the matter?"

Rudi *looked* all right, just somehow vacant, as if he didn't know where he was or who it was kneeling beside him. He was still staring straight at McGlade, eyes wide open, lips parted a little.

Suddenly McGlade realized that his knees were wet. He was kneeling in a puddle of spilled liquor. Except it didn't feel like liquor. Liquor wasn't warm; liquor wasn't sticky. He put his hand on Rudi's chest, hoping that it was all in his imagination. The kid *felt* okay. He was breathing quickly, but that was only shock because of what he'd seen. McGlade's own breathing wasn't any too easy. He slipped his hand lower, down onto Rudi's stomach.

It was worse than his wildest fears. Rudi's pants were soaked in blood. The shot the black guy had let loose had taken the kid straight in the gut. He was a mess of mangled flesh and clothing. McGlade's heart died.

"I guess you cut yourself a bit as you went down, buddy," said McGlade, trying to keep an upward lift in his voice. He wiped his hand on his pants, then took a handkerchief out of his back pocket and mopped Rudi's forehead. "You're gonna be okay, partner. Pay no attention to what I said. You were doing what you thought was right, I know that. We'll have somebody take a look at you. You just hang on." He turned, still kneeling beside the boy, and called, "Tony! Hey, Tony!"

"Yeah?" called Tony, coming back through the hallway with the sheet.

"Better call an ambulance," said McGlade softly. "This buddy of mine's taken a fall. He's gonna need a bit of help."

"Oh, my God!" gasped Tony, tossing the sheet toward the black guy and racing over.

"Tony, the phone!" McGlade growled. He was having difficulty controlling his voice. He looked back at Rudi. The kid was grinning.

"Hey, Duke," he whispered.

McGlade bent forward. It wasn't too easy to see the

kid anymore. The tears were welling up in his eyes; some of them fell on Rudi's bare arm. "What is it, partner?" he asked, his voice cracking.

"Duke," murmured Rudi, "you were great, just great!"

CHAPTER 10

The waiting was a long, slow crucifixion for Mc-
Glade. The breeze that had lifted his spirits during the
morning jog through the park had died. He felt as if
someone had staked him out in the desert and left him
to bake to death.

Why had it happened? If somebody had to get shot,
why Rudi? Why not the Hispanic woman or Tony?
Why not McGlade? He was going through the whole
thing once more: the ambulance wailing; the stretchers
—the black guy on one of them, feet sticking over the
end and a blanket covering his face, Rudi on the other,
looking very small and frail—the Hispanic woman
screaming on the sidewalk. Now the kid was lying somewhere in the Roosevelt emergency ward, and Tony was
waiting in a bare room somewhere to hear what the
doctors had to say. It had been a terrible wound. Suppose Rudi couldn't walk again? Never jog through the
park, never ride his bike?

McGlade was sitting on the stairs, halfway between
the Sterns' bedrooms and his own room above. He had
his head in his hands and his elbows resting on his
knees. In front of him, the stairs dropped down, then
took a turn to the right. The wallpaper was worn and
grubby there, where he put his hand on it every time
he passed. He stared right through it.

He could see Officer Callaghan's face again as he'd

gone through the questioning. The cop had taken it badly. He had kids of his own. His cheeks were puffed, his eyes red, and he was having to swallow every now and then to keep his voice steady. He said to McGlade, "The fucking job's a waste of time. They kick up shit about the garbage. Then, the minute we clear it up, they shove it right back on the streets! That bastard should never have been released. If anybody's to blame, it's the courts."

"You taking me in?" McGlade asked.

"We'll get around to that," Callaghan replied. "I guess you'll be in the clear."

Then there were the television crews swarming over the sidewalk, and the reporters inside the store. They were picking at every irrelevant detail: How did Mc-Glade hold the pistol when he fired—one hand or two? When the pump went off, did the black guy intend to pull the trigger or was it an accident? Somebody said, "Hey, you're a hero, Mac! Standing up to a guy with a shotgun. So tell us how you felt when you saw that the kid was shot."

McGlade had faced cameras before, but this was for real. Christ Almighty, how did they *think* he felt? He'd turned away and gone through the hallway and up the stairs. Just let the kid get well again. Never mind how long it took or how much it cost, just let him walk again. Then, oh boy, they'd have some times together! There wasn't anything McGlade wouldn't do to make it up to Rudi.

He wondered if they were still hanging about outside with their cameras and notebooks, waiting for the phone call. He looked at his watch. It was nearly twelve. What was happening? Were the neighbors still downstairs with Maria? Maybe he ought to go and check.

He'd just passed the turn in the stairs when he heard the phone. He stopped. His heart began to pound. Sweat trickled into his eyes and fell off the tip of his nose. Two floors below, someone picked up the receiver. He strained to hear, but he couldn't make out anything beyond the distant echo of a voice. After that, silence.

He thought of turning back and locking himself in his room and dropping the blinds. He wanted to shut the whole stinking world out of his life, to resign from it, to say, "Leave me out of it! I don't belong! I didn't help make it the way it is! I'm not part of anything that goes on out there!" But, Jesus, wasn't that just what everybody else was doing? Putting barricades around themselves, pretending that whatever went on wasn't their concern? People had to be made to *care*. If he himself quit caring now, he'd be no better than they. No, he did care! He cared about the world, he cared about people, he cared about Rudi!

He was taking the last turn in the stairs when he heard the long, piercing howl from below. He stiffened. It was what he'd been expecting, however much he'd been trying to fool himself. *Okay,* he thought as he reached the bottom of the stairs, *if that's the way it is, let's take it from there.* He opened the door into the Sterns' back room.

The place was full of women. Maria was sitting at the table sobbing, her head lying forward on her arms. The Italian woman from the grocery next door stood watching her, tight-faced, hands clasped. Tony's girl was standing by the open kitchen door with another neighbor, her face entirely blank.

"Was that Tony who called?" McGlade asked, turning to the Italian woman.

She didn't look at him, but she nodded.

"Rudi?"

He knew what the answer was going to be before he asked the question. He'd known the truth the minute he'd seen the kid propped up against the wall, but as long as there'd been some hope, he'd gone along with it. If you didn't have hope, how were you going to survive? He'd built the whole of his life on that belief.

The Italian woman nodded again.

"How could God let it happen?" Maria moaned. "Oh, my lovely little boy!"

What a crazy question, thought McGlade. What was she talking about God for? This was Manhattan! God had lost interest. What He'd done for Sodom, He wasn't going to trouble to do for New York City. If it was ever going to drag itself out of the shit hole, it was going to have to do it by itself. It was every guy's responsibility to help. And if people got hurt in the process, that was all part of the necessary sacrifice.

"Anything I can do?" McGlade asked.

The Italian woman spoke to him at last. "Ain't you done enough?" she spat. "We're taking Maria and the girl outta here. You can tell Mr. Stern they're next door with me. Okay. Can you do that?"

"Yeah," he said. "I can do that."

He went back upstairs and into the boys' bedroom. Rudi's bed was made the way you'd expect a kid to make it, still full of lumps and wrinkles. The pictures on the wall behind it were of Telly Savalas and Sylvester Stallone. They'd been clipped out of film mags and stuck up with Scotch tape. There was a still of McGlade among them, doing a high fall. He couldn't remember when he'd given it to Rudi, but as he looked at it, the throb in his temple started up again and he felt a sense of being stifled by the heat, the room, the whole city. It was the stunt that had started all his back trouble. He remembered it as though it was yesterday. . . .

Joey Feinstein had called him right out of the blue, sounding real excited, as if he'd pulled something off for McGlade. "Listen, Duke," he'd said, "this may be the breakthrough we been waiting for. This new guy Patronelli—everybody loves him. He's about the most bankable thing on the scene right now. Well, he's doing

a special in New York—TV movie for Columbia—
and he wants the best, and I mean the *best,* high-fall
man he can get."

"The best?" McGlade asked. High falls weren't exactly his specialty. He'd never been a Dar Robinson or
an Alf Joint. Those guys didn't fall; they *swam.* They
could use the air as if it was water, controlling their
flight, slowing their fall by changing the surfaces they
were exposing, turning on their backs at the last possible moment for the actual landing. Why would they
want McGlade when there were guys like that around?
He asked, "Joey, you leveling with me? You know
that high falls——"

Joey cut in with that hurt quality he could put into
his telephone voice. It was as much a part of his office
equipment as the phone itself. "Duke, would I lie to
you? I went right to them the minute I got wind of it
and laid it on the line. There was nobody over in the
East with your track record. Now, don't let me down,
Duke. I'm counting on you to come through."

"What do I have to do?" McGlade asked, the way
he always did. He figured there was no point in putting
anybody to unnecessary trouble if he couldn't do it.

"They'll tell you when you get there," Joey said
matter-of-factly, as though that was something Mc-
Glade could take in his stride. "Ask for a guy called
Steiner."

"You said Patronelli," McGlade interrupted. For
Christ's sake, why had he stuck with this bum agent
all this time? There was always something!

"Duke," sobbed Joey, his voice crooning out of the
receiver, "d'you have any idea how many guys'll see
this thing? You know what we're talking here: twenty
million, fifty million, a hundred million . . . I mean, for
Christ's sake, how many people do we have in the
world? Take it from me, it's a big, big break! Now, just
tell me you'll do it."

"What kinda money we talking?" McGlade asked.

Exasperation oozed out of the phone. "The money's okay, believe me," Joey said.

They were shooting up in Yonkers, just in back of Getty Square. They'd built out a wooden terrace from the fifth floor of an old apartment house, and it was that that McGlade had to drop from. The minute he saw it his spirits lifted. Fifty feet—what was that to a guy with his experience? The way Joey had been talking, he'd figured they were going to push him off the moon.

Steiner turned out to be the second-unit director. McGlade had worked with him a couple of times before, out on the Coast. He was one of the old school. He'd worked with Breezy Eason in the days before the A.H.A. had started hollering about the rights of animals in pictures, and he was a whiz with horses. Now he was in his sixties and bald and chewed on the butt of a cigar that had once been a proud handmade Jamaica. The sight of him gave McGlade back his confidence in Joey Feinstein.

McGlade had plenty of time to set up the stunt. Steiner knew how important that was and had figured on it. There was really nothing to it. It was the kind of thing McGlade had done a hundred times. He was doubling for the madam of a New Orleans whorehouse around the turn of the century, and they'd given him a wig and a long satin dress. He was to run out of the building onto the terrace, looking for a woman who'd just ripped off the takings, and when he saw her, he was to run toward her and make a grab for her. She was to dodge left, and McGlade was to go through the parapet and drop into the street below.

"Any problems?" Steiner asked.

"None I can't take care of," McGlade answered.

He was going to rely on a box rig instead of one of the new air bags that Dar Robinson had used in his fall from the top of the Houston Astrodome. They were cheap, easy to get hold of, simple to stack and rope. They were stout cardboard and measured around four feet long and two feet square—the kind of thing that any supermarket has by the hundred. McGlade figured that a ten-foot-high stack would be enough to produce the necessary controlled collapse he was aiming at, and break his fall. He began to figure the logistics: forty-foot-square rig, five boxes high—that was a total of a thousand boxes. He'd need help opening them out, stacking them, roping them together, but the final approval would be his.

There was one nagging problem: He'd be leaving the terrace, fifty feet above the street, with a lot of forward movement. A straight fall was nothing. You built your rig directly under the takeoff point and fell into it. But, with a running fall, you 'had to figure exactly how far your run would carry you through the air. If you overshot or undershot the rig, you were crippled for life. He figured that with the check he'd get from the terrace rail as he broke through it, his forward movement would carry him only fifteen or twenty feet, and made that point the center of the rig.

Once he'd begun to wind up to a stunt, he liked to follow through without any holdups. He didn't want to have the rhythm broken. It was like getting ready for any other kind of physical contest. You had the peak moment clearly in your head, and you planned all your preparation and training to lead you smoothly up to it. You saw it with boxers and with distance runners. It was the same with McGlade.

The hassle began the minute he got out on the terrace. He was wearing the wig and the dress. Since his face wasn't going to be in frame, only his back, makeup had concentrated only on giving him the body of a portly, middle-aged madam. Props had prepared the terrace rail with saw cuts so that it would snap the minute he hit it. Everybody was waiting. There had to be a couple of walk-throughs with the actress who was playing the thief, so that McGlade could plot his steps before the actual "take." That's when the hassle set in.

Steiner had put chalk marks across the terrace floor to show McGlade when he'd be in frame. McGlade checked his takeoff point. At last he was ready.

Steiner called, "Okay, sweetie, let's do a walk-through."

McGlade waited, standing in the doorway with his hands on his hips. The cameraman had his eye to the camera, checking the shot. A couple of props men leaned against the wall of the building, waiting to make any adjustments to the terrace rail. But nobody moved.

Steiner was standing with his back to the street and his hands resting on the rail behind him. After a moment he yelled, "Valerie!"

There was no reply. McGlade began to feel the tension build inside him. It wasn't a tough stunt in itself, but any stunt that required split-time cooperation was never simple. And he had this deep-seated reluctance to working with women—ever since that terrible night. As the memories began to come into focus, he made a deliberate effort to force them out of his mind. A moment later they'd sunk back deep into his unconscious, and he was left with nothing but a little tremble in his hands. It was then that he noticed the gentle ache beginning to pulse through his temples. It was the first of the headaches that were to trouble him through the long, hot summer.

Steiner exploded. "Jesus H. Christ!" he bellowed, pushing himself forward from the rail and striding through the doorway past the waiting crew. "Where is that fucking hooker?"

He was gone three or four minutes. McGlade could hear his voice rumbling around somewhere inside the building, while all the time the tension continued to wind him up. He began to get bad vibes—a premonition that something was going to go wrong. It was crazy, he argued with himself. He was a specialist in this kind of thing. He'd checked everything: the rig, the rig's position in the street below, the run-up, the preparation of the rail. A kid could do what this actress had to do: step to the left at the final moment. A kid, yeah, he thought, but she wasn't a kid; she was a woman. He hadn't seen her yet, but he felt the same about women as superstitious sailors feel: Women were great for the things God had created them for, but in critical situations they could be a disaster.

McGlade left the doorway and walked to the rail and looked down into the street below, turning his mind away from his memories once more.

It was an hour before the actress appeared. When she did, she flounced onto the balcony as if she expected the rest of the company to drop to its knees. Everybody knew that the only reason she'd got the part was for the services she was rendering the backer. Nobody mentioned it. There was something about her that was terribly disturbing to McGlade. He couldn't put his finger on it. It had something to do with her name and her blonde hair and the way she carried her head. . . .

And then he remembered. It came back to him as a fully realized vision before he could do anything to exclude it: that woman standing in the center of the ring, looking upward, the lights catching the yellow of her hair and giving it a burnished touch; the breathless silence of the packed audience; the figure poised eighty feet above her . . . McGlade felt the scream rising in his throat. *"Pa!"* he called. And then suddenly a voice broke into his vision and someone tugged at his elbow.

"Hey, Duke!" Steiner snapped, standing right beside him. "You okay?"

It took McGlade a moment to collect himself. He'd been elsewhere, at some other moment in time, and he had to get his bearings. Something had happened to him, he knew, but he couldn't figure out what. "Sure," he said at last.

"Okay," yelled Steiner to the crew, "let's walk it through!"

The actress took up her position by the door. Only when Steiner yelled, "Well, whatta ya waiting for?" did she turn and half run toward the rail at the far end of the terrace. McGlade followed her, gradually gaining on her, and finally lunged at her. She stepped aside a second before he touched her, and McGlade came to a stop a couple of inches from the rail.

"Okay?" McGlade asked, turning to face Steiner.

Steiner came forward from behind the camera. "I dunno," he said. "I figure she'd better move right of you when you lunge. Makes a better picture."

"Right?" McGlade asked. He figured the adjustments that that would mean in his approach run.

"Any problems?" Steiner asked.

"I guess not," said McGlade.

"You got that, Valerie?" Steiner called to the actress. "Right, not left."

She nodded. She looked bored, as if the whole thing was beneath her talents. McGlade went up to her and said soothingly, "There's nothing to it. Just . . . when I lunge, you move right, not left. You'll be okay." He wanted to reassure her. Even on a simple stunt like this, things could go wrong. "You got that?"

"Well, of course I've got that," she snapped. "Right, not left."

"You want to walk it through again?" McGlade asked.

"What for?" she sneered. "So you can figure out what *you're* supposed to do?"

"Then, let's get it in the can," Steiner cut in. He was numb with anger. He passed his tension on to the entire unit.

Extras got out of the way. The makeup girl made a final adjustment to McGlade's wig. The crew took up their positions.

"Okay, roll it!" Steiner snapped.

The actress looked at McGlade. He nodded. She didn't give him any confidence at all. There was something about her whole manner that was irritating and offensive, not only in itself but because of the memories it disturbed. At moments like this he wanted to be right on top of the situation, and he wasn't on top of this one.

She turned and began to run, picking up speed as she went, making right for the far corner of the terrace rail. He followed her. He really had to move in order to start gaining on her. She was putting everything she had into it. He began to wonder if he was going to catch up with her before she reached the corner. He couldn't break into too free a run without coming right out of character. He was supposed to be an overweight, middle-aged madam. That put severe restrictions on his movement.

Finally he began to gain on her. A couple of yards before she reached the rail, he was within grabbing distance of her. Everything was working out fine. She'd break in a second, and the momentum he'd built up would carry him past her and through the rail. Once he was in the air, the camera in the street below would pick him up. He'd hold his line of fall till the very last second, then flip onto his back, spread-eagle himself to distribute his weight, and let the box rig do a controlled collapse under him. He figured he'd come to rest a clear four feet above the surface of the pavement.

She was a yard from the rail when suddenly she slowed and took a sharp step to her left. McGlade was right behind her. Was she crazy? She was supposed to go right—right! Everything depended on it! McGlade had a split second to make up his mind. If he stuck to Steiner's directions, he'd hit her in the back and the pair of them would go through the rail. Not that he was thinking about the actress. At moments like this, he was concerned only about himself. But if he took her with him, God knew how they'd land. The rig was built with only one person's weight in mind; two might collapse it completely. He checked fractionally, spun to his right to avoid her, and struck the rail with the small of his back.

He felt nothing at the time. The rail gave under his weight, and he was falling head first toward the rig below. His mental focus was sharp and cold. He had the rig clearly in view. He was going to hit it smack where he'd figured. He was dimly aware of the camera, and the little group of onlookers at the periphery of his vision, and the pavement beyond the rig. But all his concentration was on the gray tarp that covered the layer of mattresses on top of the rig itself.

Another ten feet and the stunt was over. He flexed his back and started to snatch his body from vertical to the horizontal for the landing. It was then that he became aware that something was wrong. Still he felt no pain, but the muscles didn't react as he'd expected, and instead of hitting the rig square on with his back, he struck it with his shoulders. All five layers of boxes collapsed under him, and only the four-inch pad of mattress saved him from hitting the pavement.

He began to claw his way out of the debris. He was in a ten-foot hole surrounded by tarpaulin sheet. From somewhere above he could hear Steiner's voice hollering, "Hey, McGlade, you okay down there?"

"I'm okay," he called, but even as he said it, he knew he wasn't. He didn't know what had gone wrong with him, but he couldn't get his legs to work properly.

"Left, right—for Christ's sake, what difference does it make? He jumped, didn't he? You got it in the can!"

McGlade looked up from the darkness of the hole. He could see the actress pacing the terrace high above him. She was screaming and waving her arms around. Her long hair hung in loose curls down to her shoulders. She'd damn near killed him. Had it been deliberate? As the thought occurred to him, his mind went back to that dreadful night in Pittsburgh all those years earlier. Maybe *that* had been deliberate, too. The horror he'd been a part of then—was it the accident everybody thought?

He began to drag himself slowly out of the hole. His back ached with every movement, but the worst pain wasn't in his back; it was in his head.

The insistent wowing of an ambulance siren down Columbus pulled McGlade's mind back into the present. He became aware of the room again, the kids' beds. He turned to the window in time to see the ambulance howl past, lights flashing like a mobile discotheque. He loathed everything he saw down there in the street: the cars and trucks rattling downtown, the bums littering the sidewalks, the kooks on bikes, the dogs. They'd killed Rudi, all of them. They'd killed him by not caring, the way they were killing every decent thing in town. They didn't deserve to live.

The outdoor broadcast truck from ABC was still parked below. The bastards never gave up. There was a guy with a hand-held camera leaning against the truck, and a couple of young women talking to him. He spotted McGlade standing at the open window and pushed himself upright. "Mr. McGlade?" he called, narrowing his eyes against the brilliant sunlight.

The women turned and looked up. McGlade recognized one of them from the news spot he'd seen her do on Channel 7. She called, "We'd like to talk to you, Mr. McGlade. Can you come down for a minute, or can we come up?"

He didn't say anything. They were vultures, the whole lot of them. They claimed to be after the truth, but all they were after was Barbara Walters's job. That's as near the truth as they'd ever get.

"You're a hero, Mr. McGlade, don't you know that? Folks want to meet with you. Why don't you come on down and tell us what happened? It might save some other kid's life."

You shit gobbler, thought McGlade. *What do you care about saving kids' lives? There was a kid who lived here, a great kid. If you backed the police when they tried to clean up the place, he'd still be alive. But no, you've gotta parade your liberal ideas. You've gotta be yelling about injustice the minute the police do anything, because that's what sells programs. It was you who put that nigger bum back on the streets. Don't talk to me about saving kids!*

"You want to save some other kid's life, don't you, Mr. McGlade?" the woman called.

"Go home," said McGlade. "Get that truck outta here. Go cover a fashion show on Rikers Island." He didn't feel mad, just tired.

"I understand how you feel, Mr. McGlade," she called. The cameraman was starting to film. People on the sidewalks were stopping and looking up.

"My ass you understand!" McGlade called. "And get that camera off me!"

He picked up the first thing that came to his hand and flung it into the street. The crew ducked, and it hit the truck and rolled out of sight. It was the baseball Rudi had picked up at Shea that last time Tom Seaver pitched for the Mets. McGlade could see the kid again, standing on his seat with his arms in the air among a forest of groping hands. The ball soared high in the air, hit foul, spinning right back off the bat. For a moment it hung like a bird in the bright-blue sky, then plummeted into the stands. Rudi was the first to drop down on his hands and knees and crawl between the trampling feet without a trace of fear. When at last he reappeared, face glowing, eyes bright, he had the ball clutched firmly in his hands. "How about that, Duke?" he'd cried. "Straight from Tom Seaver to me!" Jesus, how many lifetimes ago was that? Now the same ball was lying with the dog shit on Columbus. What the fuck! Nothing mattered anymore.

McGlade went out onto the landing and climbed to his room. It was suffocating. He was still wearing the sweat shirt and sneakers he'd put on to jog with Rudi. He went and stood at the open window, but it made no difference. The air was the same outside as in.

He looked down at the two guys on the flat roof next to Burton's place. They were stripped to the waist, very bronzed, sitting in canvas director's chairs and sipping from cans of beer. One of them caught sight of McGlade and spoke to his friend. Both turned to look up. The first one waved. McGlade ignored him. The second one blew him a kiss. When there was no response from McGlade, they began giggling to each other in high-pitched, reedy voices.

McGlade turned back into the room. He felt sick. What more did a guy have to do to bring this disease called Manhattan under control? Carter yapped about human rights when he should have been talking about human duty. Nobody could give you rights—not the president, not the UN, not God himself. Rights you had to fight for, every day of your life; otherwise you'd drown.

He lay on the bed. Christ it was hot! The sweat came out of him like water from a squeezed sponge. He considered taking a shower. No, that wouldn't help. You had to go through with it, get used to it, educate your body to take it, the way you got it used to jogging. There were times when you had to punish yourself. Summer was a time for suffering.

Maybe he wouldn't feel so sick if he ate something. The thought, though, of going into the kitchenette made him want to throw up. There wasn't even a window in there. The walls would still smell from the fish he'd cooked the day before. Every summer it stank of cooking smells. The smells had got into the walls. There was no way you could get a flow of air through it to freshen it up. All you could do was hang room deodorizers around to mask the stink.

What the hell, he thought, he'd pick up a sandwich from the deli. If he took a walk by the river, it might help. He sat up. It was after two o'clock. Jesus, what had he been doing for two hours? Were the women still down there?

He went downstairs. The place was empty. They'd gone without telling him, and Tony wasn't back yet. What kind of a state was he going to be in? One of his sons murdered! McGlade wondered whether he shouldn't stay after all, seeing as he was the only person there. That's what Tony would expect.

He went into Maria's kitchen, fixed himself a cheese sandwich and a glass of milk, and went to sit at the table in the back room. The milk was icy cold. He could have poured it over his head and let it run all the way down his back. How long, he thought, before Tony got back?

The phone rang as he was finishing the sandwich. Taking a final mouthful of milk he went into the hallway and picked it up.

"Yeah?" he said.

"Lemme talk to the kid," a voice snapped.

"Who is this?" asked McGlade.

"Is this Stern's liquor store?"

"Yeah."

"Then, lemme talk to the kid."

"The kid's dead. Who is this?"

"You gotta be kidding! He was in here just a couple of hours ago."

"I said, who is this?" McGlade snapped back. "You want me to hang up?"

"Burton—the bike shop. Quit assin' around. Lemme talk to the kid."

McGlade tried to visualize the bike shop and Burton with the phone to his ear; he said, "You mean Thomas. He's not here."

"Well, where is he?" Burton shouted. "He got this phone call and walked straight out. I wanna know when he's gonna show again. I'm *paying* that kid!"

McGlade could feel his gut beginning to churn. Every time he talked to Burton he felt he was being screwed. It was going to be tough to control himself if the guy went on this way. He said, "What's the matter with you? Didn't you hear me? His brother's been shot. He's dead! Can't you get it into your head?"

"So I'm sorry," Burton said. "I'll send flowers. Now, lemme speak with the kid!"

Something snapped in McGlade. He knew now where the Manhattan disease lay. It lay in this freewheeling cowboy and everybody like him—all the anarchists, all the self-interest bums, all the uncommitted, quick-buck boys. The energy churned inside him, twisting his gut, pounding his rib cage. But he was going to ride it. He was going to turn it to good use. He was going to find some crack in Burton's shell, some little chink through which he could corrode the bastard inside. He yelled, "You go fuck yourself, Burton! You hear me? You go ram your bike shop up your ass! Maybe you don't give a damn now, but one of these days you're gonna sob yourself to sleep!"

"Who is this?" Burton shouted. "Who *is* this?"

McGlade looked at the phone for a moment, then hung up. "Yeah," he muttered out loud. "One of these days you're gonna care so much!"

As he left the hallway and started up the stairs, he was still trying to figure out Burton's soft spot. Was there *anything* the bastard gave a damn about? There was the bike shop; he cared about that, but did he care enough? There was that bike he rode, loaded with three hundred bucks' worth of special equipment. Was there a way in through that? Then, of course, there was the dog. Maybe . . . Maybe he had a woman . . .

The minute he reached his room, he went over to the desk and looked at the print of the bald eagle hanging above it. It was a copy of the Audubon drawing, majestic with its great hooked beak and talons and its proud head lifted.

"We're a dying species, you and me," he said to it, "d'you know that? The air you breathe's poisoned. The meat you eat's full of weed killer. A couple of conservation orders aren't gonna save you. Everything that's worth anything gets killed in this place. Why don't you put out your wings, head up to Canada? Or go south, get up into the Andes, maybe, where there's no people yet? Me, I'm stuck. Look!" He spread out his arms. "Look," he sobbed, the tears rolling down his cheeks, "all I've got are arms. You, you're an eagle! You can fly!"

▼▼▼▼▼▼▼▼▼▼▼▼▼▼▼▼▼

CHAPTER 11

▲▲▲▲▲▲▲▲▲▲▲▲▲▲▲▲▲

All his life, Burton had accepted things the way they were. Life was just another situation he found himself in; he'd never questioned it. The future wasn't worth considering, and the past was dead the minute it ceased to be the present. He'd taken the same view of business. If he broke even at the end of a week, no problem; if he didn't, he wasn't going to find himself on the street.

It had been that way with women as well. He'd taken what he could when it was available. If he didn't get on with a woman, he let her go. He knew he couldn't change her, any more than she could change him. He'd never even tried. But Fay . . . Fay was something else. She'd got to him the way no other woman ever had. She was deep in his guts. Sometimes, right in the middle of fixing a brake-transmission cable, he'd remember the way her flesh smelled, just as if she was standing right next to him in the shop. Old Blue understood. He'd lie in his usual place by the bench and watch Burton, head on one side, eyebrow cocked, as if figuring out what advice to give.

She was riding beside him now, keeping shoulder to shoulder, hair rippling back in the wind. In the distance, guys were putting up the orchestra stand again in the Sheep Meadow, setting up batteries of lights over the bridging framework and filling in the backdrop with twenty-foot-high flats. This was going to be the last concert of the summer, she'd told him. Well, maybe the weather would take the hint and ease up after that —not that Burton minded the heat. It was Manhattan weather. What else could you expect this time of year?

"Okay," she said, "so what is it?"

"Hmm?"

"Hey, snap out of it. D'you know the last time you opened your mouth? We were crossing the Ninety-seventh Street underpass. What's keeping you chattering like this?"

He glanced at her. She was bronzed now by the summer sun. When he'd met her in the spring she'd had skin the color of milk, and she'd worn blue mascara and highlighted her cheekbones with a blusher. Now she used no makeup except lipstick and maybe something to keep her skin supple. She'd picked up the West Side image as if she'd been born on Central Park West.

"The market's climbing," he said. "I can make something very nice out of the business in two, three more years, really become *the* classy bike shop on the West Side."

"So?"

She was going to blow a blood vessel with that much enthusiasm. "I'm gonna expand," he said, trying to keep the irritation out of his voice. "The way they're slamming down on midtown parking—making pollution worse than homicide—I got the only form of transportation that's gonna be legal."

"Great," she said.

Jesus, she really was laying it on! What was eating her? He said, "Couple of years from now, I'll be eating at the Twenty-one Club and picking up silk suits by Dunhill. I'll have the biggest two-wheel business this side of Tokyo."

She gave him a quick glance. "Another couple of years and you'll be thinking about your health, getting your blood pressure checked over on Park, talking to

some well-dressed little guy from Scarsdale about starting a pension plan."

"Jesus—you asked me," he said. "I'm only telling
you. Isn't that what you wanted?"

"What's all this leading up to?" she asked, very cool.

It was too much for him. "All right, I'll tell you," he
snapped. "I wanna know where I stand. I get sick in
the guts lying alone at night, thinking of you twenty
blocks away, wondering how you are, if you're safe. I
get worried. This is a rough town. There are some
rough guys out there. You're not so street wise, whatever you think. I'm trying to figure what makes you so
goddamn self-sufficient. Don't you want anything outta
life besides a pension?" When she didn't answer, he
yelled, "Look—do we have something going or don't
we? Jesus, d'you know what it's costing me to run
around with you?"

"Costing you?" she cried. "You hardly pass for a big
spender!"

He jammed on the brakes and came to a stop. She
continued on for a bit, then slowly turned and came
back to him, braking when their handlebars were par-
allel.

"I wasn't talking about money," he said. "I was talking about us making it, having some sort of future——"
What the hell was happening to him? He'd never used
the word "future" before in his life!

"Face it, Burton: Men don't run the world anymore,
just because they're men. You've got the sulks, that's
all—like a kid who doesn't get what Santa promised
him."

He shook his head. "No," he said. "You're wrong,
honey. You're so wrong."

He thought of just writing it off, not even saying
"Kiss my ass" but turning right out of the park and
leaving the fucking mess behind. There were other
scenes and other women. He'd done it before. This
time, though, with this woman . . .

"Do I get to see you tonight?" he asked, wanting to end the whole dumb conversation.

"I'm going to the concert," she said. "Maybe after that." She sounded bored by the prospect. Pushing down on the raised pedal, she began to draw away from him. He went after her. Blue loped out of the bushes.

"Well, that's great," said Burton when he came up alongside her. "I mean . . . *gracious*. Managing to fit me in among all your culture and yoga and transcendentalism. Jesus, the West Side Y must turn out more gurus than India."

"Okay," she said, "that's enough. It's over. *We're* over."

He let her pull away from him; then he turned right, away from the mall, Blue tagging a couple of feet behind. As he neared the shriveled bushes that lined the track, he took a quick glance over his right shoulder. It was just what he'd thought: The cyclist behind had been following them, riding the same pathway but keeping a couple of hundred yards back. *McGlade!* thought Burton. *That cripple who lives over the liquor store and peeks down on me when he thinks I'm not looking.*

Well, the guy had a choice now. He could turn after Burton or he could stay with Fay—not that there was any doubt in Burton's mind which course he'd take. For a couple of weeks, now, he'd been waiting for McGlade to discover Fay's existence and make a move like this.

Burton made for the tunnel that underpassed the East Drive. There in the shadows he waited, looking back toward the mall. When McGlade finally came into view, he didn't even glance in Burton's direction. He had his eyes fixed straight ahead. Burton was right: It was Fay he was after, the son of a bitch. Suddenly all the anger Burton had been feeling toward her, all the frustration, evaporated. Whatever she said, she belonged to him. He was going to look after his own.

He turned the bike around, rode back toward the mall, and picked up the original pathway again. Blue had dropped that casual lope he put on when they were just out for exercise, and was moving like a hunter, ears flat, lips drawn back. McGlade was a hundred yards ahead of them. A hundred yards beyond that, Burton could make out the gold of Fay's hair and the arch of her back over the handlebars. *When can I close in on the bastard?* Burton wondered. He didn't want too many people around. At this hour the place was loaded with joggers.

Beyond the Seventy-second Street transverse, Burton began to put on the pressure, forcing down the pedals with the balls of his feet. He figured there was no point in putting it off any longer.

McGlade hadn't glanced back once. Burton moved closer, legs moving smoothly up and down. He could take the guy now whenever he chose. Sixty yards, fifty . . . Then, suddenly, McGlade swung off to his left and Fay had disappeared. Burton felt his gut tense up. Instead of being cut and dried, it had suddenly taken on another dimension. She must have cut in toward the Ramble, around the back of the boathouse. The place was a jungle of overgrown pathways and dark little cuttings. At this time of the morning she was going to be the only one around. Even in midafternoon, some people thought twice about going in there. You had to know your way through. She could easily come back on her tracks and run smack into McGlade.

He hit the pedals harder. The growing sense of urgency knotted the muscles of his thighs and calves and brought a lather of sweat to his face. The bright sun filtered through the leaves, throwing mottled shadows over the pathways, pitching the more overgrown tracks into semidarkness. The tracks were narrow, some of them simply worn through the bare earth where years of short-cutting had created them in places never intended by the parks department. Blue kept right up alongside the rear wheel of the bike, his nose only a couple of inches clear of the rim.

McGlade came back into sight quite suddenly. Burton had climbed a rise on one of the tracks, and at the bottom of the sudden dip beyond, McGlade was crouched over his machine, his balding head picking up the intermittent sunlight. Blue edged forward. He'd taken a dislike to the guy that very first time they'd met in the shop. Blue never changed his opinion.

Six months ago, Burton would never have got into this kind of hassle. Look out for Number One—that was his philosophy. All that help-thy-neighbor crap they yapped about in school was garbage. Swallow that and you'd end up like all the other fucked-up zombies. He'd never done the cops' job for them, or anyone else's. He'd lived his own life, and it had worked out pretty well. Call it anarchy; blame it on Manhattan—that's the way it was.

But now there was Fay—Fay with the sun-bleached hair and the long and loving legs. She'd come out of nowhere in the springtime and tossed a hand grenade into his life. Now *she* was part of him. That made all the difference. What he owed to himself, he owed to her as well. He was racing after this cramp-back runt ahead of him because McGlade was threatening *him*. He had to put the bastard in the picture.

Burton had figured out the track McGlade was taking. There was a little bridge ahead, so insignificant that McGlade wouldn't even notice it, then the climb before the long drop down toward the Seventy-ninth Street transverse. Burton knew the Ramble as well as he knew his own deck. He'd played there as a kid, taken his first girl friend there before the city had got scared of the dark.

He swerved left past the black-rock outcrop covered in wild-colored graffiti, eased the bike over the stretch of ground ivy, and began to drop down through the trees. He was going to come across the far slope and head the bum off. He could ease up now. He'd plenty of time. There was no way out for McGlade.

A blue jay let out a long, yammering alarm cry. A squirrel took off ahead of him and flew into the tree-tops like some new invention of Freddy Laker's for terrorizing the airway tycoons. Christ, *there* was an in-dividualist! Why had every bastard got a down on individualism? This was America! Individualists had built it, made it great. So what was wrong with that? All this bullshit about looking for roots. What did America owe to Europe or Africa? America was America! Its roots went back as far as anybody's. Back to the first Indians. Not anywhere outside.

He knew now what he was going to do when he got to McGlade. He was going to exercise his individual rights.

McGlade still had the girl in sight. With that golden hair catching every sliver of sunlight slanting through the heavy foliage, she wasn't difficult to spot. He wasn't going to do anything, not here in the daytime when any minute some jogger might plod into his path from one of the dozens of intersecting tracks. He kept his dis-tance, just making sure that he didn't lose contact with her. He was researching her, getting to know her habits and the routes she took when she moved around the West Side. When the time was ripe, he knew what he was going to do. *She* was the chink in Burton's armor that he'd been looking for.

Blue came out from behind the rock outcrop to his left. McGlade gave him a quick glance, then ignored him. He didn't recognize the big shepherd, and his eyes went back to the girl. The next moment, the dog was ripping at his track-suit pants, and for a second he lost control of the bike. He yanked on the brakes and slued around at right angles on the gravelly surface of the path. When he recovered, he lashed out at Blue with his foot. Blue lost his hold and rolled away.

Everything was out of control, McGlade was thinking: dogs, kids, people. Next thing, you'd find Central Park back in the hands of the Indians. He still didn't recognize Blue. Until he caught sight of Burton coming up on his right shoulder, the shepherd was just another shit machine that spent most of its days shut up in some tenth-floor apartment on Central Park West. But the sight of Burton brought it all into focus. He yelled, "What're you trying to do—get me eaten alive? Keep that wolf under control or I'll go to the cops!"

Burton didn't answer. Blue was back on his feet, coming up again on McGlade's left, snarling, snapping at his leg, trying to get a grip on the track pants again. Once that happened, Christ knew how far Burton would let the monster go. What was it with the guy? Did he know something?

"Call him off!" McGlade screamed.

Again Burton said nothing, staying just back of McGlade's right shoulder.

The track ahead was opening up. McGlade banged down on the pedals, ass clear of the saddle, head forward over the handlebars. He ignored the stream of salty sweat pouring into his eyes. If there was any pain in his back, he wasn't aware of it. He could see the open area ahead, and beyond that, traffic moving along the West Drive. Once into that, he'd be safe.

The dog had apparently summed up the situation the same way, because he drove in again from the left, getting his teeth into McGlade's calf, losing his grip when McGlade lashed out, then coming in again. In the end, there was no choice for McGlade.

"You crazy?" he shouted. "Get him off me!"

His nerve gave and he let Blue turn him off the track and into one of the cross lanes. Within twenty yards he was back into the twisting pathways of the

Ramble, kicking out at Blue, trying to keep his left leg away from that snapping mouth.

The path dropped through deep shadow and close-knit tangles of dogwood, climbed steeply, then dropped again. McGlade still drove down on the pedals, but he was aware of his body now. It wasn't going to take much more. Every movement tested his back. His calves were cramping. His thighs ached. The sweat was clouding his vision. They were hunting him—the shepherd trying to grab him from the left, Burton crowding him from the right.

Then, suddenly, the dog slackened his pace. McGlade glanced down. For a second he thought they were letting up. But it was Burton's turn. He closed with McGlade and began to force him to the left. They were working him like cowboys with a steer. He had flashbacks of some of the Westerns he'd extraed in. What were they going to do when they finally threw him? Brand him? Castrate him? Panic cramped his throat.

They were touching shoulders now. Burton was leaning into him. McGlade had to pull ahead or ease farther left. He put the first thought out of his mind. He hadn't a chance of beating Burton in a straight-out race. He thought of cramming on the brakes and letting Burton overshoot. In the split second of relief, McGlade might turn back and get out in the open again—except the shepherd was waiting, ready to rip him apart. In the end, he gave to his left.

"What d'you want?" he howled. "What're you trying to do?"

"I'm putting you back in sixth grade," Burton said, never letting more than an inch of space come between his left shoulder and McGlade's right. "I figure you missed out on your education. I'm gonna teach you."

"What're you talking about? Teach me what?" The trees that lined the edge of the track on McGlade's left were getting closer every second. If Burton didn't let up, McGlade was going to ram right into them.

"I'm gonna teach you to leave my woman alone."

McGlade's heart missed a beat. "What woman?" he cried. Still Burton crowded him. McGlade could smell the sweat on the guy's body.

"You think I don't know who you are?" Burton asked. "Haven't suspected for weeks? I was the guy on the bicycle that night you ran out of Riverside Park. You telling me you didn't know that?"

"Sure I knew that! What about it? You crazy or something?"

"Aw, c'mon," snapped Burton. "We know who's crazy, don't we? What's it like living inside that head of yours? You oughta write a book: *Bald Eagle: My Life with a Bicycle Chain!*"

"Is *that* what you think?"

"Think? I *know!*" yelled Burton. "The minute I heard the guy was using a bicycle chain, I knew. You still had the marks on your hands that day you came into the shop. I wondered then how you'd got them when you didn't even have a bike."

"If you really believe that——"

"D'you think I haven't handled enough bicycle chains to know the marks they make?" Burton cut in.

"Then, why didn't you tell the cops?" McGlade struggled to keep his balance on the narrow, winding pathway.

"Why didn't *you?*" asked Burton. "If you saw me coming out of Riverside Park that night of the killing——"

"I *did* tell them, you dumb bastard! I told them about you, about the guy in the car . . ."

They climbed a little crest, McGlade laboring up it, half standing on the pedals, trying to get the last ounce of speed out of the machine. Burton stayed right on his shoulder.

"Don't give yourself a heart attack," he said, grinning.

The grin meant nothing. Behind it was pure savagery.

McGlade knew he was trapped. Burton was psyching him till he could hardly think straight.

"What kind of a bastard are you?" McGlade howled.

"That's what you're gonna find out." Burton smiled.

They topped the crest. Below lay a long, straight run through the trees and dense shrubbery. The light was dim, as the leaves formed a continuous roof of deep greenery over the path. For Christ's sake, McGlade was thinking, where were the joggers this morning? Where were those plagues of guys on bikes who infested every other part of the park? Didn't anyone ever come this way?

Nobody came. His luck had run out. He got to wondering how it was all going to end. Was this bastard really going to turn him over to that slavering wolf of his?

A hundred yards ahead, the path turned right to avoid a black-rock outcrop and disappeared into darkness. McGlade could see at once what Burton had in mind. A romp in the bushes with the shepherd would have been nothing by comparison. He'd planned stunts like this himself for more than twenty-five years. If he was going to survive, he had to get clear of that rock face. It meant getting on the other side of Burton.

He dragged the last reserves of strength out of his legs and his aching back. There was a time when he might have done it—back in the fifties, when his muscles were piano wires and his body was spring steel —but he'd taken too many falls since then. It had already given him all he could ever expect from it. "For Christ's sake, let up! You can't do it!"

He was wrong. Burton had him boxed in, keeping him so far over to the left of the track that he barely missed the trees.

"You don't understand," McGlade gasped. "Somebody's gotta clean up the city. Somebody's gotta care. You want us all to go back to the swamp?"

"Better keep your eyes on the path," said Burton.

McGlade braked. The dog was into his calf again, and Burton had edged him an inch closer to the trees. It wasn't going to work. He'd have more chance with the rock face than with a tree. If he could catch it at an angle, he might slide along it instead of taking the full impact. Going into a tree at this speed would be like riding into Reggie Jackson's baseball bat.

He let go the brakes and shook the dog and drove down on the pedals again, standing right over the crank, head down over the handlebars. Burton stayed with him. Twenty yards before the turn right, McGlade resigned himself. He got ready for the fall, easing up on the pedals, relaxing his muscles the way that years of experience had taught him. But he was going to take Burton with him. When it came to taking a tumble, he had more chance of coming out of it whole than Burton. He'd think about the dog after that.

The black rock loomed. The path swung right. McGlade was going to drop over the back wheel, the way he'd dropped over the ass of galloping horses. At the same time, he was going to give the bike a twist to the right to get it to foul up Burton's machine. Burton could go ass over tit straight into the rock. With luck, the bastard would break his neck. All McGlade asked was to at least cripple him. Burton had asked for it right from the start. Now was the moment.

But he hadn't counted on Burton. The second McGlade slid his hands back and grasped the crossbar, Burton drove his left elbow straight into McGlade's ribs. McGlade lost balance at once. He tried to get his hands back on the handlebars, missed, and slued around sideways into the rock face. His left elbow and shoulder took the first impact, then his face. The bike hit the rock and bounced clear, while McGlade rolled across the surface and finally dropped to his knees on the path. Burton had taken the right at the last second. When McGlade got his vision together again, he could make out Burton riding back toward him with the dog trotting behind.

Burton came to a stop in front of McGlade. "You beginning to catch on?" he asked, resting one foot on the ground and looking down at him. "Leave her alone. Don't go near her. If I see you even look at her, I'll kill you."

McGlade got to his feet. His pants were ripped, and there was blood running down the left side of his face from a deep gash on his forehead. He nodded, expressionlessly, nursing his injured left arm with his right hand.

"I figure you're not gonna give me any more trouble," said Burton. He nodded toward McGlade's bike. The front wheel was buckled and the frame had been twisted out of shape. "Looks like you've lost your deposit. When you've fixed up your head with a Band-Aid, bring the bike in. I'll give you an estimate for the damage."

Riding back home down West Seventy-ninth, Burton felt good. He'd achieved something: made his point with McGlade; protected his woman. That's the way things ought to be done. You've got a problem, get up and solve it. Take the rap if you have to. That's the American way. Always had been; always would be. The buck didn't stop on some little guy's desk in Washington; it stopped on every guy's doorstep from Montauk Point to L.A.

He'd forgotten the hassle with Fay. Women were like that; you had to accept it. And, by Jesus, she was a woman! He thought of turning down Columbus and stopping by her place. He'd even tell her he was sorry, if that's what she wanted to hear. Let her think she'd won; what did it matter to him? They both of them knew the *real* truth. He was a man and she was a woman, and it didn't matter how they amended the

Constitution, nothing was going to change the course of nature.

In the end he changed his mind. Why give her the satisfaction of seeing him run after her? She'd only draw the wrong conclusions. Give her time and she'd come around of her own accord. Women had to go through these moods. It gave them a sense of importance to think they'd got a guy on a string. He'd call her later, maybe take her to the Ginger Man and soften her up with some of that French food she was so crazy about. Okay, he was in love with her. He didn't deny it. But, Christ . . . she was still a woman. He'd never had any trouble getting around women.

▼▼▼▼▼▼▼▼▼▼▼▼▼▼▼

CHAPTER 12

▲▲▲▲▲▲▲▲▲▲▲▲▲▲▲

Callaghan said, "Christ Almighty, I loved that kid. I'd give my right hand to see him around again. The way he used to ride that bike, the way he'd always give me a wave when he was out jogging with Duke McGlade . . . That fucking lawyer who let that nigger go —you think he lies awake nights worrying? Sure he does! He's figuring how to get tickets for the World Series and lay it off as tax deductible!"

He was sitting with Stern in the back room. The store had been closed since the shooting, and the shade on the entrance door was pulled all the way down. The air conditioner had been switched off, too, and the room was like a sauna. He could feel the sweat soaking into his shirt and trickling down his back into the waistband of his pants.

He had a glass of bourbon and ice in his hand. He took a sip, peering over the rim at Stern. The guy looked in rough shape.

"Anything I can do, Tony?" he asked. It was a crazy question and he knew it, but he wanted to help. What else could he say?

Stern was hanging onto a glass of iced tea. He stared at it. "You know how I feel?" he asked. "The way I felt after Alamein."

Callaghan nodded. He'd been too young for Stern's war, but he'd been through Korea.

"Dead," said Stern.

He was talking more to himself than to Callaghan. *Fine,* thought Callaghan. *If it helps, let him talk.* He nodded again.

"We'd pushed all the way east from Tobruk. Everything looked great. The night was warm—not this stinking heat, just beautiful. Stars wherever you looked. We were a mile or two back, dug in behind an eighty-eight-millimeter. All we were waiting for was fresh supplies to reach us. They kept telling us the war was won. Another week and we'd be in Alexandria. The British would just run away and we could all go home. I had a beer with a kid I'd known since school. It must have been eleven when I turned in. I went to sleep the minute I hit the pillow. The next thing, the world went crazy! I was buried under sandbags. Guys were screaming. The ground was giving way. Jesus, the noise! Christ knows how long it went on. I guess all the others were killed. I never met up with them again. The kid from back home—they didn't even find a fingernail."

Callaghan asked softly, "Is that when they took you prisoner?"

"That's what they told me," said Stern. "I don't remember. I had no sense of time, no sense of place. I remember the sand and the wire fence, the bedbugs —little, crazy things—but no people, no faces, no conversations."

"I guess you were shell-shocked," said Callaghan.

"I forgot about the folks back home, about the farm," Stern went on. "I never opened letters. I never wrote. I was dead without being buried."

"But you came through, Tony; don't forget that."

"Sure," said Stern. "One day I began to climb out of it, like crawling out of a hole in the ground. I remember starting to cry and not being able to stop. Then, gradually, I got things together again. I began to see some kind of future. You've got to. I guess it'll be the same this time. But just now . . ."

"Of course," said Callaghan. "Time, Tony—that's what you need." Jesus, what a fucking smart thing to say. What a gift he had. He should have been a priest, tossing out comfort like peanuts to squirrels. But what else did you say to a guy whose kid was lying dead in Park West Funeral Parlor and whose wife had walked out on him?

"I guess so," said Stern.

"Is Elsa still here?" Callaghan asked.

Stern shook his head. "She changed her mind," he said. "She's over in Queens with her mother. They're staying with Maria's sister."

"That's good," said Callaghan. "She shouldn't be around here by herself. It's getting to be too rough."

Maybe there was a chance for her after all, Callaghan thought, but without much conviction. By the time a kid had reached Elsa's age, the town had got into her too deep. He wondered if Stern had begun to catch on to what was happening to the girl, how she was developing. Callaghan had thought a dozen times of bringing it out into the open and asking Tony if he knew what was going on. But would any father take that kind of stuff, believe that his daughter was on her way to the screw house when she'd only just started growing tits?

Stern was back somewhere inside his own head. He looked lifeless. *He* was the one they ought to be burying.

"Why not put in a manager, Tony?" Callaghan asked. "Just temporary. Or shut the place up for a couple of weeks? You never take a vacation. It's not right. It's gonna catch up with you in the end."

Stern didn't answer. He was still staring into his glass.

Callaghan leaned forward and took it out of his hand. "C'mon," he said, "you'll get frostbite if you keep hanging on to that. Get out of town for a while. I'll keep an eye on the store. You don't have to worry about getting ripped off."

They sat for a moment in silence. The only sound was the hum of traffic from the street outside—distant and unreal. Then Callaghan asked casually, "You figure Duke's okay, Tony?"

Stern lifted his head. He looked puzzled. "How do you mean?"

"I just wondered," said Callaghan, a troubled look on his face. When Stern didn't press his question, Callaghan leaned forward and said confidentially, "Jesus, Tony, he put thirteen shots into that wino—the whole magazine! You know the kinda mess that made? That's a nine-millimeter pistol you got there. I figure a couple of slugs from that oughta be enough to take an elephant out, but thirteen! That kinda violence—that's scary."

"Scary?" Stern protested. "You any idea what it was like in here? The black guy just about filled the place. He was waving that shotgun around like a flag. McGlade did what he had to. Sure it was violent. But the guy saved my life, and he would have saved Rudi's if only . . ." He began to break up. Tears welled in his eyes and he sniffed them back.

"Yeah, I know that," said Callaghan quickly. He shouldn't have brought it up, except everyone at the station house was saying the same. He glanced at the clock on the wall. He ought to get back on the street. It might even be cooler out there. They weren't going to get any further just rapping. He drank the last drop of the bourbon and pushed back his chair. "Maria and Thomas—they okay?" he asked, putting his cap on.

"Thomas is back here. He wouldn't stay away from the bike shop. Maria won't come back," said Stern.

The poor guy sure looked desperate for a life belt. Callaghan nodded. The street would have to wait.

"I called her this morning," Stern continued. "She won't even let Rudi be buried from here. They're taking him over to someplace in Queens today for the funeral tomorrow. If she had her way, she'd have him buried back home. She sure hates this place. She's never gonna see it again, she tells me." He was getting pretty emotional. "All these years," he cried, "trying to run a business, bringing up kids, trying to see they grow up right . . ."

Callaghan just sat. What else could he do?

"She wants to go home," said Stern. "Back to Germany."

"Well, that might not be a bad idea," said Callaghan. "Long vacation, get away from everything, give her time to get over it."

Stern shook his head.

"So what's the problem?" Callaghan asked. "Money?"

"She doesn't mean a vacation; she means for good, to live there."

"Permanent?"

"Yes!"

"After all these years?" Callaghan couldn't believe it.

"I guess you never forget the place you were born. It'll be different for the kids. They'll be Americans. They were born here. This'll be their country."

Callaghan saw that the dead look had gone out of Stern's face, and there was animation in his voice. It was a hopeful sign. "What the hell is an American if it doesn't include you and Maria?" he said. He couldn't figure the woman out. "You're naturalized. You've built up a business, had kids, got friends. So you're German. I'm Irish. I had a grandfather came over from County Cork way back in ninety-nine, but let any bum try telling him he wasn't an American!"

"I tried to explain to her," Stern said.

"Will you go back, then?"

Stern shook his head. "She thinks it'll still be the way she remembers it. She forgets that everything changes. It'd be like emigrating all over again. No. If I can get rid of the business, I'll move west. She'll come with me."

"West?" Callaghan had never been west of the Henry Hudson Parkway in his life. "You mean like Chicago?"

"No," said Stern. "We're not big-city people. We wouldn't have settled in New York, except at that time we couldn't make it any farther. We'll find some little place nobody's ever heard of. A German community would make Maria feel happier. We'll open a store, work hard. It's not the money I want. I'd settle for just a decent living, security, a few friends to drop in now and then, but somewhere safe to bring up the kids. It's the kids that count, particularly now there's just the two of them."

Callaghan nodded in sympathy.

"I've got a cousin out in Mankato. I've called him. He's gonna look around."

"In *where?*"

"Mankato," Stern said. "Southern Minnesota."

Well, that was that, thought Callaghan. Funny old world. He'd been thinking that a move out of town might still save that girl of Tony's, and here was Tony going to take her out to Minnesota. How long would it be before she found her way up to Minneapolis and some brown-assed pimp picked her up and shipped her back east? Give her a couple of years and she'd be walking the "Minnesota Strip" with all the other blonde-haired Aryans, nipples erect, skirt halfway up her ass. Thank Christ by that time he'd be settled in Brighton Beach. He could forget the whole fucking shooting match!

He got to his feet and pulled his sunglasses out of his shirt pocket. "Take care, now, you hear?" he said, moving toward the passage that led to the side entrance.

"You going already?" Stern asked.

"I been here awhile," said Callaghan.

"Right, so you have," said Stern. "Nice of you to drop by."

"I'd stay longer, Tony, you know that, but there'll be some hassle or other going on out there that I gotta look into. You'd think in this heat, things would get easier—all the bums lay low for a couple of hours, take a siesta—but no. Never seems to make any difference."

"It's the same city," said Stern, "rain or shine, winter or summer. Always the same."

"You can say that again," said Callaghan.

Thomas got to the bike shop around eleven that morning. He was wheeling the wreckage of McGlade's bike. He didn't know what had happened to it, but he figured he'd try to repair it. He'd found it dumped in the yard out back when he'd gone to pick up his own machine. His aunt had tried to stop him leaving Queens, and even his pa didn't seem to want him back. He couldn't understand it. First you got treated like a grown-up; the next minute you were back to being a kid.

The warning buzzer bleeped as he walked through the shop doorway. Blue lifted his head, then got up and walked toward him, giving long, slow wags of his tail. Thomas put down a hand and patted him. It was nice to know *somebody* was glad to have him back.

Burton's voice called, "That you, Fay? Got yourself straightened out yet?"

Thomas didn't answer. He wasn't sure what to say. He knew he was late. He hoped Burton would understand.

Burton came out of the bathroom drying his hands. When he saw Thomas, his manner changed. "What the hell you doing, Blue, treating him like family!" he snapped. "The guy walked out on me." Blue turned and went back to his place.

Before Thomas could say anything, Burton had tossed aside the towel and come toward him. "Well, okay, say something. What d'you want?"

"I just got back," said Thomas.

"So?"

"I had to go with my mom to my aunt's house in Queens."

"What you trying to tell me?" asked Burton. "You looking for your job back or something?"

Thomas didn't know he'd *lost* his job. He said, "Well ... er ... I guess so."

"What's that you've got there?" Burton nodded toward the wrecked bike that Thomas was holding.

"It's Mr. McGlade's," said Thomas. "I thought maybe I'd fix it."

"You crazy or something? That's junk. Toss it with the other scrap."

Thomas dropped the bike among the rusting frames and chains.

Burton looked at him for a moment, as though considering what to do with him, and then sighed. "Next time let me know. Just tell me first. I like to know who I'm employing and who's just part of the furniture."

"Okay," said Thomas.

"Well, what're you waiting for? You figuring to do any work?"

It was all right. "Yeah!" cried Thomas. He walked down the shop past Burton. The wheel he'd been repairing was still hanging where he'd left it. He picked it up and reached for a wrench. Something was bugging Burton, he could tell that. He wasn't just mad at Thomas. Give the man time, he thought, and he'd come around. Grown-ups sure were strange.

Burton went to the counter and took a catalog from one of the shelves underneath. He thumbed through it, then started jotting things down on a sheet of paper. From time to time Thomas took a glance at him, but Burton seemed to have forgotten that Thomas had ever been away. Things looked right back to normal.

Thomas felt bad about walking out on his mom; but he'd have gone crazy just sitting in Queens, watching her cry all the time and listening to Aunt Lotti telling her that *that* wasn't going to do any good. He felt terrible about Rudi, somehow responsible. If he'd been around, maybe he could have done something. What was it going to be like, not having a little brother anymore? He thought of all the *good* times they'd had together and tried to forget the ones when Rudi had just been a drag. He'd have liked to take a look at him one last time, to see what he looked like dead. But nobody suggested taking him.

When he'd finished working on the wheel, he took it to Burton, the way he always did. Burton plucked the half-dozen new spokes with a thumbnail. Could he really tell they were okay just by the sound they made?

"They'll do," said Burton, handing the wheel back to Thomas. "Go ahead. Stick it back on the bike."

Thomas turned away.

"I heard about your brother. I'm sorry."

"It's okay," said Thomas.

"You want the rest of the day off?"

"No."

"You're right. It helps to stay busy."

Burton turned back to the catalog and the sheet of paper he'd been writing on. Thomas picked up the bike and turned it upside down on a couple of sacks on the floor, then began to fit the wheel. Blue lay with his head on his paws, watching him.

Thomas was doing the final balancing of the wheel in the fork when Burton called from the counter, "I figured that after what happened, I wouldn't be seeing you again."

"I don't like Queens," Thomas replied. "I thought you'd still need help."

"Damn right. We got an expanding business here. A decent mechanic makes a lot of difference."

That was nice; it made Thomas feel important. In Queens, he'd just felt in the way.

"How's your pa taking it?" Burton asked.

"I guess we're gonna move."

"Move? You mean outta Manhattan?"

"Pa says we're going west. We got relatives somewhere."

"Jesus," said Burton. Then he added, "Well, it might be an idea: change of scenery, fresh start. It'll help you get over it."

"I don't wanna go," said Thomas. "I wanna stay here. I wanna help with the bikes."

"I reckon Blue'll miss you," Burton admitted.

Thomas was still on his knees, trying to get the wheel balanced right. *Of course* Blue'd miss him; he knew that. It wasn't what he wanted to hear.

"You got good hands, you know that?" Burton said. "You'll make a good mechanic. You can start again, this new place you're going to—help somebody else."

Thomas said nothing. It sounded like a terrible idea. Could Burton really forget him that easily?

"Tell you what," said Burton, coming out from behind the counter to where Thomas was working. "Stay in touch. Couple of years and I might wanna open a branch office. Could be useful having a contact out west. We might work out a deal or something."

He really *did* care! It was just the way he talked that made you wonder. "Hey, thanks," said Thomas. He tried not to sound too enthusiastic. He was learning from Burton how to be a businessman. That was really going to pay off in time.

Blue let out a long, low growl. Thomas and Burton looked toward the door. A police car had pulled up outside, and Officer Callaghan was crossing the sidewalk with a sack over his shoulder.

"Hold it, Blue," said Burton, taking a couple of steps toward the door.

Callaghan came straight in. He walked over to Burton and, without a word, upended the sack. The bike chains he'd taken away earlier tumbled out over Burton's feet.

Thomas got up. He was sure Burton was going to hit Officer Callaghan, and when that happened, nothing would stop Blue going for the officer. It could end up with both Blue and Burton getting shot. "Here, Blue," he whispered. But the dog ignored him and stood poised, lips drawn back.

The two men stood square-on to each other for a long time. Finally Burton said, "Okay, you're a cop. Anyone else and you'd have had a boot in the nuts. But you're a cop, and cops don't have nuts—or anything else that's normal. Cops have lice between their legs. That's how they get to be so edgy. I'm not mad at you, Callaghan, just sorry. In the end, I might get to love you."

"You wanna count them?" Callaghan asked.

Burton stepped back, and the chains fell off his feet. He looked down at them. Blue watched. Thomas stopped chewing his lip. It might not come to anything after all.

"How come they got so rusty?" Burton asked. "You been pissing on them?"

"There's a kid in here," snapped Callaghan. "You watch your mouth!"

"It's not me that's gonna corrupt him," said Burton, "not when he's got guys like you to learn from. You find what you were looking for? Blood, skin, rabbit fur—like that?"

"I told you: Watch your mouth!"

Thomas saw Blue relax his lips, and wondered why. The atmosphere certainly didn't seem any less tense to him. But then Burton grinned—Blue had obviously understood the situation better than Thomas—and Thomas began to breathe again.

"Lemme be generous, Officer Callaghan," said Burton. "You got a job to do, despite the way it looks. I accept that. I guess you're under all kinds of terrible pressure: guys upstairs leaning on you to come up with something on Bald Eagle. Okay, come up with something, only don't look to me for help. I got my own problems. Find your killer the hard way. Walk some of that fat off ... or maybe get your palm read."

"Thanks," said Callaghan. "Glad to have your advice."

"I guess I'm off the hook."

"What's that mean?" Callaghan didn't look mad anymore, just tired. He'd taken his cap off and was mopping his big face with a handkerchief.

"You're not gonna hold me for murder."

Murder! thought Thomas. Were they still joshing?

"How d'you figure you're in the clear?" asked Callaghan. "Four women are dead. There's a guy with a bike involved. You've been seen riding around all hours of the night. I'd say you were the number-one suspect."

"C'mon," said Burton. "You wouldn't have brought back this stuff." He turned a couple of bike chains over with his toe. "I mean, that's what they call evidence —like exhibit A, exhibit B. Jesus, don't you watch *Kojak*?"

Officer Callaghan put his cap back on and slowly stuffed his handkerchief back into his pocket. "You're a bum," he said at last. "You think you can get to me like that? I take worse on the streets every day. I'll take it again. Part of the job. I can wait for you, Burton. You'll still be around. There'll come a time when you'll be screaming for the cops. That'll be when I get to thank you for all your cooperation."

He turned and walked to the door, moving heavily on flat feet, letting his belly hang loose. When he'd gone through the beam of the warning buzzer, he turned back and called to Thomas, "You oughta be with your sister and your ma in Queens, you know that? You're not gonna help your pa by staying here. Only gonna add to his worries. Think about it, son."

"Those goddamn bastards!" snapped Burton when the police car had driven off. "They've known all along they couldn't pin anything on me!" He turned to Thomas. "When you're in business, just remember: You can do without the cops sniffing through your garbage. Oh, they'll try. They'll ride you like they ride everybody who hasn't got his nose up his ass. The best-paid slobs on City Hall's payroll! They've gotta justify that some way."

There was only one thing Thomas wanted to know. Instead he asked. "Do you think Officer Callaghan was right? Do you think I shoulda stayed in Queens? I don't wanna worry my pa."

"Hell, no," said Burton. "You gotta figure it from Callaghan's point of view. As long as you're in Queens, that's one less kid he's gotta worry about. It makes his job that much easier. That's all that bothers a cop."

Thomas wasn't sure he understood. Officer Callaghan had always been nice to him and nice to Rudi. "Suppose you get into some kinda trouble," he said. "If you don't go to the cops, who do you go to?"

"Nobody," said Burton. "You handle it yourself, the way I do. Who else can you count on? If other guys did the same, there'd be no problems. You just seen what the cops do. Don't you ever learn? Listen: A guy's on his own—separate. You got a duty to look after number one, that's all. Cops are parasites. They feed on guys who won't take care of themselves. So we pay taxes to give them nice homes out of town, keep the courts turning, put color TV sets on Rikers Island. Cops, lawyers, warders—what *are* they? Only guys, the same as everyone else. They got their own interests to look after, their own nests to feather. Stay away from garbage like that."

Thomas had been only half listening. His mind was still on that terrifying question.

"You taken in anything I been sayin'?" Burton snapped.

"Sure," Thomas said.

"Then, snap out of it," said Burton. He took a kick

at the pile of bike chains on the floor. "Get this junk cleared up. Stick it back where it was before those slobs came for it. You still expect to be paid, don't you?"

Thomas didn't move. He *had* to ask. "You talked about . . . murder."

"So?"

He realized he'd made a mistake. Burton had just been telling him that a guy had to mind his own business, and here he was poking his nose in. It would serve him right if Burton got mad at him. "I . . . just wondered," he said.

Burton didn't get mad at him. Instead he said, "Well, okay, since you just wondered, lemme put your mind at rest. Callaghan knows that I'm Bald Eagle. So now you don't have to wonder anymore."

Panic hit Thomas. Why had Officer Callaghan left him? Burton was between him and the door. It was the one situation in which he couldn't count on Blue. His mind flashed back to that morning by the river. He could see the whole terrible scene again: Rudi standing by the steps of the rotunda, gaping; the upturned face of the dead woman, skin the color of an eggplant, flies swarming all over it.

"B-bald Eagle?" he stammered.

"Yeah," said Burton. "The guy's gotta be somewhere. Why not here? We sell bicycle chains. I strangled every one of those women. So now you know. Make you feel any better?"

Thomas couldn't answer. He couldn't get his mouth to move. He couldn't swallow. His heart was battering in his ears. In any case, what answer could he give?

"Well?" Burton asked.

Thomas still said nothing.

"D'you *believe* I did it?"

Thomas stared up at Burton towering above him. He remembered what his father had said about Burton.

Officer Callaghan had tried to warn him. *Did* he be-lieve that Burton was Bald Eagle? He didn't know what to say.

Burton's manner changed. "Hey, partner," he said gently, "I've gotta have an answer."

"No," said Thomas at last.

"No what?"

"No, I don't believe you're Bald Eagle."

"You gotta be sure," said Burton. "Otherwise how're we ever gonna do business when you open up the branch office out west?"

"I'm . . . sure," said Thomas. The relief was terrible. He could feel the tears well up in his eyes and start to roll down his cheeks. "I'm sure," he sobbed. He hated himself for ever having had doubts. He hated Officer Callaghan for thinking that Burton could ever kill any-one.

Burton ruffled his hair. "Hey, c'mon," he said, put-ting his hand in his back pocket and pulling out a five-dollar bill. "We've had a rough morning. Tell you what I want you to do: Go over to Sam's and pick up a couple of sausage wedges, plenty of peppers. I'll get some Cokes outa the fridge."

Thomas wiped his eyes and took the money. Being treated like a grown man wasn't all that easy. When he'd got to the door, Burton called, "Make that three. We don't want this wolf getting jealous."

It was six o'clock before Burton called Fay. Thomas had gone. Outside in the street, the last of the towaway trucks were dragging their victims downtown.

The phone rang half a dozen times. He began to think she wasn't home. A slight twinge of worry crept into his gut. Then, finally, she picked it up and said, "Yeah?" Great, he thought. She was still prepared to hang around for him.

He said, "You got over the little tantrum?"

"Who is this?" she asked.

"Come off it," he said. "How many guys've you given the brush-off to today?"

There was a long silence. Finally she said, "You do have a way with you, Burton." There was no warmth in her voice.

"Are you okay?" he asked.

"I was fine till you called."

"Hey, I can explain about this morning. You had a guy following you; did you know that?"

"It's been the story of my life," she said. "D'you know how boring it gets?"

Things weren't going the way he'd planned. He might have to climb all the way down. "Okay, I'm sorry. What more can I say?"

"You can say good-by," she said.

"I thought maybe we'd go see the new Stallone over at the Embassy, pick up a late dinner at the Ginger Man."

"Good-by sounds a nicer idea."

He began to think she meant it. "We don't have to *do* anything, if that's what's bothering you."

"I've already got a date."

"I've *said* I'm sorry. Okay . . . I get edgy. I've got things on my mind." He was trying to stay cool.

"I thought I made it clear in the park," she answered. "It's finished. I don't want to see you again."

"For Christ's sake, why?"

"You're no fun anymore," she said, her voice very flat. "If you want it straight, you're getting to bore me."

"Well, then, fuck you!" he snapped.

"No," she said. "Not anymore." She hung up.

He stared at the instrument in his hand, then rammed it back on the wall hook. He picked up his bike from against the wall and yelled at Blue, "Come on, you dumb fool dog! You wanna spend the night in here?

Jesus, why do I keep you? What d'you ever do for me?"

The confrontation in the Ramble with Burton had brought McGlade's mind into sharp, clear focus. Burton didn't give a damn about anything, and that attitude epitomized the cancer that was gnawing away the guts of the city. Nobody cared. They had to be made to. They had to be touched in some vulnerable spot that wasn't protected. And that spot, as far as Burton was concerned, seemed to McGlade to be Fay Coburn.

Yet, as McGlade stood in front of the mirror in his tiny bathroom bathing the deep abrasion on his left temple, Fay became more than simply a tool to use against Burton. She took on significance in her own right. It had something to do with her hair. It was beautiful—so yellow, so long. He could see it again floating behind her as he'd followed her through the park toward the Ramble. The image disturbed him. He remembered the actress on the terrace in the spring— the same kind of hair, the same arrogant carriage of her head. And then the two images fused and became one, and he was back in the big top at Pittsburgh and the heat was suffocating and the insistent reverberation of the bass drum from the band pounded in his head.

He threw water on his face, then filled the wash basin with cold water and plunged his face beneath the surface. He opened his eyes under the water and let the cool water bathe them. When he lifted his head, water ran off his mustache and out of his thinning hair.

He dried himself and put on sneakers and a dark-colored sweat suit, then went out into the evening. It was dark already, the air motionless and oppressive. Columbus was full of people—late shoppers, guys and girls on their way to and from restaurants. A cop stood alone on the corner of Seventy-sixth Street, glazed-eyed, loose-bellied, ignoring the woman asleep in the doorway behind him, all her worldly possessions stuffed into a couple of brown Macy's Cellar bags. A tourist came out of the new Copacabana and stood looking around him, hands on his hips. "Jesus Christ!" he muttered, gazing at the steady stream of traffic and the crush of sweating humanity crowding the sidewalks under the green glow of the streetlights. "Manhattan!" He might as easily have said, "Mars!" For him, another planet couldn't have been more strange.

McGlade saw none of it. His head was as clear as if he'd just snorted cocaine. Everything had suddenly become quite simple. The problem that had been recurring in his mind since spring had evaporated. He wondered how he'd ever seen it as a problem at all. He caught himself actually smiling. For the first time in days, he hadn't a trace of a headache. He broke into a gentle jog, and the sweat began to roll down his cheeks and neck.

He knew where Fay lived. He knew everything about her. Since he'd discovered her existence, he'd watched her. He'd followed her home. He'd seen Burton ring the top bell of the bank of six that was fixed to the wall outside the building, and he'd learned her name from the little printed tag beside it. He even knew her phone number. He'd looked her up in the book and put a big red cross beside her name.

She was on the top floor—exactly as he was himself. He'd never gone inside the building, but he had a clear picture in his mind of what he'd find when he did.

Somewhere in the roof there would be a skylight to give some natural illumination to the stairwell beneath. There was never a lock on such things. Anyone ripping off a building like that was going to look for some easier way in than from the roof. But McGlade was getting satisfaction from trying to figure out the least obvious way. He was a stunt man, and he was going to make the city marvel at his skill. It was going to take notice of him at last. It was going to listen and be disturbed. In the end, it was going to care.

He turned right when he got to Sixty-seventh Street and slowed to a walk. The apartment house was across the street. Behind him was the ABC Studio building. He stopped and leaned his back against the wall, looking across to where Fay lived. The building was one of half a dozen still left standing. It was tall and narrow, with a five-step stoop and a solid, impressive wooden door. Behind it, a crane jib was outlined in red lights. The place stood isolated now in the sea of surrounding rubble caused by the rebuilding project. It looked as if the city had passed it by, forgotten it. Garbage lay along the sidewalk in plastic bags that glistened under the streetlamps as if they'd been drenched with water. Here and there a bag had been ripped by a passing dog, and the contents spewed out into the street.

There was no way up the front of the building. The nearest rainwater pipe ran down the face of the next building. Even if it had been possible to get across from there to Fay Coburn's open window, he'd never have risked it. Instinct and long experience told him what was possible and what wasn't. Metal piping rotted; fixtures came away from the wall. He didn't plan on a fifty-foot fall onto bare sidewalk—not at this stage in his career. He turned and walked around the corner and came to the edge of the demolition area.

The demolition gangs had gone in from Sixty-sixth Street, nibbling their way northward. They'd got halfway through the block, so that nothing was left standing on the Sixty-sixth Street side, and the backs of the remaining property on Sixty-seventh were exposed to the night. The site had been wired off and warning notices posted. He figured if he decided to go in that way, the wire and the notices would help him. They'd guarantee that for the time he was working, there'd be no accidental interruptions. Concentration was the essence of pulling off a stunt—and what he had in mind was going to demand all his concentration.

He stood right up to the wire, fingers hooked through the diamond-shaped meshes, and surveyed the site. It was a rough rectangle, well lit by the streetlights in places, deep in shadow in others. Most of the rubble had already been removed and the surface rolled flat. What was left had been piled high by bulldozers, ready for the trucks to haul it away. On the far side from where he stood, the back of Fay Coburn's apartment house rose like a sheer cliff into the air. The wall had no windows; it was an internal wall, never intended for this kind of exposure.

He could guess the kind of surface that the demolition had left, though he couldn't see it from where he was standing: rough, unpointed brickwork. A skilled rock-climber might have made it up that surface, finding little irregularities here and there that could be turned into hand or foot holds. But McGlade wasn't a rock-climber, and he wasn't about to start learning now. In any case, a climb up the wall didn't give him the chance to display his skills, and that was crucial to him. He wanted to show this city that a single-minded citizen could do anything he put his mind to —despite cops, press, TV, whatever. More important, he wanted to prove that whatever rumors the film world was spreading about him, he was far from being washed up as an artist. And he wanted to show Rudi.

He turned at last to the crane, standing in the middle of the site with its jib reared up into the sky. He knew as he looked at it that that was the answer. It wasn't going to be a climbing job at all. It was going to be a high-wire job—the kind of thing his dad might have done.

He figured the distance between the crane jib and Fay Coburn's building. It would have made the whole thing easy if the jib had been over the building—he could have hung a rope from the jib and simply slid down it—but it wasn't. The crane had been parked clear of the building, with the jib at an angle of thirty degrees. McGlade was glad about that. He didn't want the thing made easy. He didn't want it to look as though just anybody could have got into the building. He wanted the cops and the media to respect him—after they'd figured it out.

He turned and got back onto Columbus and began to jog easily back to his room. He knew what he needed. It made him feel buoyant and clear-headed. It was as if twenty years had fallen away from him and he was back at the height of his powers. The stunt demanded ingenuity, and he'd always had that. Hadn't he come up with that reinforced umbrella handle that they'd used for the spectacular slide-for-life in *The Kingmaker*? It demanded dedication, and he'd had a reputation for that all his life. He'd never married and never, as far as he knew, sired a single kid. Why? *Dedication*—dedication to perfecting his art. Well, now he'd perfected it.

There was something else it demanded—courage. As he considered the word, he hesitated—not because he thought he lacked courage; only because he knew what this stunt meant. He knew who he was going to meet again when he started to swing from the jib. Could he face his dad after all these years? Could he meet him eyeball to eyeball and say, "I don't care what you think, it wasn't my fault"? He couldn't answer the question, not yet. But he'd know the answer when the time came. Until then, there were preparations to make.

CHAPTER 13

It was another long, hot night. Burton lay on his back on the bed, wearing a T-shirt and a pair of briefs. Outside, he could hear the hum of air-conditioners in the yards. Those guys were crazy. They'd wake up with heads full of buzz saws. When they'd put in forty years cussing the city for its climate, they'd pick up some concrete condominium in Fort Lauderdale and spend the rest of their lives breathing filtered air.

August was always like this. You had to go with it. In the end it would pass, nothing more certain. The leaves in the park would turn red and spin to the ground. The squirrels would hole up. The snow would fall, and Santa Claus and his couple of hundred clones would jingle their bells down Fifth Avenue and chink their collecting cans outside Saks and Macy's. It had been like that with the Indians. It'd be like that when the Martians landed. It was just a matter of waiting.

How long could he wait for Fay? He didn't believe it was over between them; he'd never accept that. He didn't believe she had another date. It was all part of her female dumbness. It wasn't him she was getting at; it was herself. She had to have some constant reassurance that she really was wanted. Well, all right, she was wanted! Christ, if she didn't know that by now . . .

Wanted? *Needed*—that was closer to it. He needed her the way he needed air to breathe and blood to carry oxygen to his muscles. He didn't think he'd survive without her, and this fighting they did together was all part of it. When he was with her, he felt free to say whatever came into his head. That was love. The *things* he said didn't matter a damn; but the freedom to say them—that was everything.

It wasn't any use. He couldn't get his mind off her. He got up and climbed out of the open window and onto the deck. Blue was lying out there. He lifted his head for a moment, then dropped it back onto his paws.

"She's gotta make the first move, Blue," said Burton. "You know that, don't you? That's where we left it. It's up to her."

The air was stagnant, breathed over and over again by a couple of million people and never renewed. Below, a couple of yards were still lit up with colored lanterns. He could see the glow from the dying charcoal in the hibachis and smell the smoke.

"What d'you make of it, Blue?" he asked. "All this cookout crap we're into. What do we think we are— pioneers tracking the source of the Yellowstone? Living off the land like there was still a West to be opened up? I mean, tell me. You got relatives in that kinda country. Are we in Montana or New York City?"

Blue didn't stir.

"Well, can't you say something, 'stead of lying there as if you weren't even listening? This city's a Hollywood set, I'm telling you. You meet a guy jogging in the park, you don't know anymore whether he's for real or just part of a new Scorsese movie!"

Something disturbed Blue. He suddenly got to his feet and padded a couple of times around the deck before dropping down again. He didn't settle. He had his head back on his paws, but his eyes were open and his ears cocked.

Burton turned and looked up at the window of McGlade's room. It was open and the light was on. "What d'you figure he does up there by himself?" Burton asked. "What goes on in that crazy head?"

He couldn't just hang around waiting. He'd have to get into the park and run off some of the tension. The minute he turned to go back into the room, Blue got up and followed him.

McGlade snapped off the light and walked carefully downstairs in his sneakers. Tony and Thomas were asleep. The place seemed vast and empty. He could almost hear the silence echoing through it. It was as if the house itself had died.

Outside, he turned down Columbus and broke into an easy jog. He didn't care if anyone saw him. It didn't occur to him that even on Columbus, a jogger carrying a coil of rope and a duffel bag looked a little out of place at two-thirty in the morning. He didn't feel part of the scene anymore. It wasn't that he was invisible. Sure, people could see him. But he didn't belong to their world. They were functioning in different realities, and that put him beyond their reach.

Physically, he felt reborn. For the first time in months, his back was giving him no trouble and the pain in his head was gone. He'd slammed into that rock in the Ramble so damned hard he'd thought at the time he'd smashed his left elbow and shoulder. Yet now all he could feel was stiffness. He'd made some great discovery, he knew that. He'd unearthed a truth that nobody else had stumbled on, and it gave him a strength and assurance he'd never in his life had before. He'd always lacked confidence; he could see that now. God Almighty, who'd ever have thought it, considering some of the things he'd done? But he didn't lack it anymore. He knew now exactly where he was going, exactly what he was going to do. Most important, he knew exactly how he was going to do it.

As he crossed Seventy-second Street, ignoring the lights and the couple of taxis bouncing over the broken surface toward him, he began to go over the plan in detail. It was like any other stunt, except that the reward at the end wouldn't be some measly check handed to him by Joey Feinstein. It would be the greatest achievement of his life. It would be his contribution to this city. It would turn the whole thing around, beginning with Burton and gradually spreading out through Manhattan until all five boroughs had been included. He felt like John the Baptist standing up to his thighs in the Jordan and cleansing the world. He had that power in his hands. He was a healer. He began to appreciate the vision the early English settlers had brought from the Old World into the wilderness that had been America. City of Brotherly Love—that's what he'd create out of New York City!

First he had to get through the mesh fence; for that he'd brought the wire cutters. Then he had to climb the crane jib—a simple matter of putting one foot in front of the other. Next he had to tie the rope to the jib. Finally he had to attach the grab swivel to the free end of the rope. That was the crucial element. This time he had to check it thoroughly. When he took hold of the grab swivel and let himself swing out from the jib into the darkness, he didn't want any repetition of that night in Pittsburgh.

He cut through the wire where a couple of rolls had been overlapped, and made his way gingerly over the uneven surface of the ground and through the piles of rubble. He knew what he had to face once he'd climbed the jib. He had to face that night of horror and he had to conquer it. If he managed that, it would be behind him forever. It would never lie waiting for him in the dark corner of the bedroom, never watch from the dense shrubbery of the Ramble, never stare accusingly at him through the eyes of the badger in the zoo. The dreadful guilt would be gone, and he'd be free to begin again.

Close up, the crane was enormous. It was mounted

on tracks, and massive screw legs had been lowered to the ground to give it stability. For a while it looked as if he'd never get onto the first platform. There was nothing but the tracks or the screw legs to go up, and neither gave him any secure grip for either hands or feet. He had eight feet to climb and he wasn't going to make it. The screw legs were solid with grease, and he couldn't make more than a foot up them without slipping back. Grease covered his hands and arms and the inside of his pant legs before he gave up. He was almost sobbing with frustration. He saw himself jogging back to his room, tossing the duffel bag and the rope into a corner, and lying on his bed choking with anger.

There had to be some way up, else how did the operator reach the cab? But there was nothing—no ladder, no set of steps. It was crazy! Had he come all this way, got everything worked out, to be stymied by some dumb mechanical obstacle like this? He looked around the site. The glowing remains of a fire still smoked. Ends of burnt lumber stuck out of it. They were the remains of beams and door frames that couldn't be reclaimed. Any one of them might have been useful to him in its original state, but now there was nothing longer than a couple of feet.

A police car raced along Broadway coming south, screamed its brakes, and made a left onto Sixty-sixth Street. He froze. Above him the giant jib of the crane, festooned with red lights, rose up into the night sky. On either side, the piles of rubble stood out a luminous green under the sodium lights and cast black shadows over the demolition site. Had someone seen him cut the wire? Had someone noticed him trying to climb to the cab of the crane? The car slowed, rolled along the street as if eyes were scouring every shadow, then finally slid away and crossed Columbus on its way east.

He moved again at last, heart still pounding. His confidence had been shaken by the frustration he felt. He was back to having doubts about himself that gnawed at his self-assurance. He was matching himself against a memory. Could he win such a confrontation?

He began to pick out bricks and slabs of smashed concrete from the nearest pile of rubble. Working at the back of the crane, between the massive tracks rising high on either side of him, he began to build. He built carefully so that there wouldn't be any slippage when he began to climb the crude steps he was constructing. Protected from view by the deep shadows cast by the body of the machine, he felt no need to work quickly. He could take his time. The sounds of the night were all around him: the distant howl of a chained dog going mad in the heat; the cacophony of a radio reverberating from the walls of some backyard. The air was full of the mingling smells of cooking coming from the blend of ethnic restaurants that crowded Columbus Avenue. And all the time, steadily, he built.

It took him ten or fifteen minutes to get the kind of secure structure he was after. He adjusted the rope around one shoulder, the duffel bag around the other, and began to climb. The structure held: a little shakily, but it held. It lifted him five feet from the ground, and from there he could reach up and get a grip on the raised lip of the platform above him and haul himself up. The instant he did so, however, he realized that he'd made a miscalculation. In the euphoria of planning and figuring every angle, he'd overlooked the one thing that mattered most: the condition of his own body. The climb over the lip of the platform showed him that his left arm had been more damaged than he'd thought in the tumble in the Ramble. The elbow was giving him pain. More important, the joint of the shoulder had been wrenched in its socket. It wouldn't stand any unusual strain without giving way altogether. He cast these thoughts aside. It was too late now to consider such things. Time would tell—the next twenty minutes.

The jib looked bigger than ever, now that he stood

at the foot of it, his eyes directed toward the cluster of red lights that marked the top. From the ground, it had looked as if he could use the zigzag tensioning struts as steps to climb on; but he saw now that they were too far apart. He was going to have to use both hands and make use of the main members as well as the cross struts, the way kids used climbing frames in the parks. Every strut was going to mean a pull on his shoulders, and the final part of the plan demanded all the strength they could give him.

He climbed steadily, establishing a pattern. Long experience had taught him economy, and part of economy was rhythm. He stood on each cross strut, balancing himself with his hands on the strut above, then climbed up the main jib-member, using the sides of his sneakers and relying on the rubber soles to give him traction. Halfway up to the next cross strut, he let go his grip with his left hand and took hold of the main member above him. From there he could swing his right leg high enough to get a footing on the next cross strut, and from there it required only pressure with that foot to drive him upward. Once established on the next cross strut he began the process over again. That way he was using his legs to climb and his arms mainly to balance with. He'd have plenty of strength left in his shoulders by the time he reached the top.

Long before, when he was still back in his room preparing his equipment, he'd realized that the point at which he was going to attach the rope was crucial. It was all eye judgment. He couldn't ask any of the questions he'd have asked if this had been a routine stunt: "How high's the roof of the building from the ground?" "How far's the base of the crane from the building?" "What angle's the jib at?" He'd have had answers to these and other questions, and it would have been a matter of minutes to calculate exactly the point at which to attach the rope. But now he had to guess. The only thing he knew was the length of the rope—fifty feet—and he knew that because the rope was part of his basic equipment. He'd bought it himself and used it in a couple of dozen stunts.

He'd reckoned it this way: The roof of the building was fifty feet high—based on a five-story structure with each floor ten feet high. He could go fifty feet above that to attach the rope, but no higher or he wouldn't be within safe dropping distance of the roof. And that dropping distance was the crunch of the whole stunt, because he was going to drop directly onto the roof, not into any kind of rig that would absorb his fall. His knees and his own flexibility were going to take the whole of the shock.

The question was, how far could he afford to drop without hurting himself? Ten feet? Fifteen? No, ten feet would be about it. It wasn't a simple drop. There would be some movement as well—forward or backward, depending on exactly when he released himself. Ideally, he wanted to release at that split second of his swing when he was stationary right over the roof. But that was the ideal, and experience had taught him that the ideal had no part in stunting. There'd be some movement however precise his release. He'd be crazy not to plan for it.

He continued to climb, keeping the same steady rhythm: left hand up the jib support, right foot up onto the cross strut, push upward with the right thigh and calf muscles, both hands on the next cross strut, and pause; then the whole process over again.

He was on a level with the roof of the building now and thirty feet to the side of it. A few red lights were already below him on the jib structure. He'd been right about the skylight. There it was in the middle of the roof, a beam of yellow light shining upward through it. He felt a slight easing of the tension in him. He could get in through there.

But as he climbed higher, a new worry struck him. He was used to aiming at rigs that were anything up to sixty feet square. The roof was no more than thirty-five by forty feet, and right in the middle of it was a glass skylight of around six by four. He had to miss that at all costs. If he landed on it, he'd fall a clear five floors down the stairwell before he came to a stop. There was going to be nothing routine about this. It was going to stretch him—imaginatively and physically—to the extremes of his power.

The scene below expanded the higher he climbed. He could see the façades on the north side of Sixty-seventh Street now, windows wide open to catch any little breeze that might come in from the river, and beyond them the skylights of the apartment houses farther north, yellow against the blackness of the roofs. To his right, Columbus opened like a brightly lit chasm slashed right through the West Side, traffic pouring down in half a dozen columns, an endless, interweaving stream moving south. To his left, Broadway cut toward him across Amsterdam. Farther over, he could see the triangular shape of Sherman Square, with its bag ladies and winos, and in the distance the black cleavage of the river and the high-rises on the Jersey shore beyond. He felt like an eagle soaring over the city, waiting to strike at the evil that was engulfing it.

By his calculation, the cross struts were six feet apart. He checked them off automatically as he climbed. Experience with stunting problems had taught him how to count unconsciously without the process disturbing his conscious train of thought. When he'd reached the fifteenth strut, he came to a stop. He was ninety feet up the jib, and the jib was set on a platform eight feet above the ground. That put him around a hundred feet up—fifty feet above the roof. If he tied his rope off here, his swing ought to carry him just above the roof of the building. It was better to be on the high side than on the low. He could handle an extra five feet of fall—even an extra ten, if necessary—but he couldn't afford to swing into the side of the building instead of over the top of it.

He tied off the rope and began to descend the jib, letting the slack run easily through his hand. When he'd reached the free end of the rope, he looked across to the building. He could just see the yellow glow from the skylight. He'd planned the thing just about right. He unfastened the duffel bag and took out the grab swivel.

At the sight of it, the doubts began to crowd in again. It was the one his dad had used that night in Pittsburgh. No one had used it since. McGlade had checked the swivel a score of times. He'd never been able to figure out what had gone wrong, not for certain. Val had handed it to McGlade. It was his job to give it to his father just before the final act. Afterward, Val had blamed McGlade. She swore he hadn't checked the thing. Maybe he hadn't. He'd never allowed himself to remember. Well, he was going to check it now —the only way that mattered. He'd find out at last whether it had been his fault or not.

The scene that night in Pittsburgh had never left McGlade. Like some old film, it was always being re-shown someplace at the back of his mind, ready to crowd out the present with renewed urgency. And now it was rolling again now, superimposing itself on the reality of the crane and the demolition site and the lights of Columbus beyond. He was there in the big top again. The pungent stink of ammonia from the animal cages surrounded him. From beyond the tunnel, he could hear the roll of the kettledrums building up the tension. . . .

Val was leaving them. She was always threatening to do so, saying she was fed up with looking after a kid who wasn't hers, complaining that some of the other guys around could give her more of the things she wanted. But this time she meant it. This latest quarrel had burst the thing wide open, and she'd packed her bags and cleared all her belongings out of the trailer. She'd made one concession: She'd see the act through this one last time.

It didn't bother McGlade. He'd never liked the woman. He didn't think she behaved right to his dad, always looking at the other men around the circus, always teasing him with talk of running off to the Coast or Europe with someone or other. He figured his dad stayed with her as much for Duke's sake as for his own. He needn't have bothered. She could never replace his mom. Nobody could.

But it bothered his dad. He was still pleading with Val even as she stood in the ring, her gold-sequinned outfit glittering under the lights, and introduced him to the audience. McGlade, standing in the darkness of the tunnel waiting for his cue, saw it all. His dad hadn't even been able to raise a smile at the mention of his name, and as he turned to the ladder that ran up the main pole and began to climb, a voice in the audience called out sarcastically, "Hey, Mac! You figure you can make it up there without taking a snooze?"

The first part of the act was a combination of flying rope tricks and hype. The hype was done by Val, standing below in the light of a single spot with a mike in her hand. McGlade's father did all the flying by himself. Ever since McGlade's mother had been killed, he never seemed to trust anybody else up there with him. He always said he didn't need anyone else; he could keep it going by doing everything himself. Women, he told McGlade, were trouble. Yet he took up with Val right after his wife had gone. It seemed he could never leave women alone.

The high point of the act was what McGlade's dad called the "Flying Bomb." It was crazy. Everybody who saw it knew that someday something would go wrong. Some towns wouldn't let him perform it, and he would come forward into the audience before going up the ladder and make a speech about it. "These gentlemen have got a real responsibility," he'd say, standing in the full beam of a spot poised high up on one of the flying lighting barrels. He used to stand with arms thrown wide and his eyes focused just above the level of the back row of the audience. "But it seems to me that no law ought to prevent you seeing the most amazing, the most spectacular, the most stupendous aerial act the world has ever known! But I'm not the man to break the law, however crazy that law may seem. And believe me, when I get up there"—McGlade could still see the finger pointed dramatically toward the top of the marquee—"I'll put all my skill and all my experience into showing you what the law *will* let me do!" Then he'd bow slowly—right, left, and finally center—and turn out of the spot and begin to climb the ladder.

An ambulance careering down Columbus dragged McGlade back into the present. He took hold of the end of the nylon rope. It was lashed around a pressed-metal eye and spliced back into itself. McGlade had done the splicing himself. The accident to his father had taught him never to trust anyone else when it came to checking equipment. He attached the eye to the swivel hook on his grab and locked the safety bar into position. Then he pulled on the grab, snatching it a couple of times to make sure it would hold.

Turning so as to squarely face the building where Fay Coburn lived, he grasped the grab swivel with both hands, bringing the rope into tension. He was going to put his life on the line. He was going to pit himself against the image of his father. He was going to do the Flying Bomb; but *he* was going to do it right! And he was going to show this goddamn town that he wasn't finished, that it couldn't pass him over.

He had his hands together at the level of his chest, and gradually he let them take his weight. The tension came out of his legs, and finally his feet lifted clear of the metal strut that had been supporting him. He swung out from the jib in a long, slow arc. As he did so, passing slowly over the piles of smashed bricks and broken concrete below, he could feel the weakness in his left shoulder and elbow again. Burton had really beat him up. The arm would never support his weight alone.

The swing took him twenty feet forward, held him for a moment, then began to carry him back. He realized his position more clearly. The building was farther from him than he'd figured, and the arc of his swing carried him too far to the east. He was going to have to not only increase his swing, to cover something like thirty-five feet, but also change its direction. There was one other problem: He could see right away that he was going to pass twenty feet above the roof—ten feet higher than he'd planned on.

He began to work first on the direction of the swing. He let himself move forward again, but as he did so he swung his legs to the right. A few years ago he could have taken his body out at right angles to the rope, but he'd lost that degree of flexibility in his back. It was a case of taking it patiently. As long as he could stay on the rope, he'd make the position he wanted in time. He began to sweat a little more.

As he worked, he thought of the times his dad had refused to let him even try to do the Flying Bomb routine. At first he'd thought it was to protect him. Later he knew it was because his dad didn't want a kid—even his own—taking any of the thunder. Well, he was taking it now. Sure, there was nobody watching. But they'd figure it out in time, once they'd spotted the rope dangling from the jib and seen the open skylight.

The more he swung toward Fay Coburn's building, the closer he got to the black nightmare of guilt that had plagued him all his adult life. The answer to it lay there in the past, high in the big top beside his father. He was eight years old again, standing beside Val at the foot of the ladder. She was holding the grab swivel in the spotlight for the audience to see, and cooing throatily into the microphone, "And with this unique device, the Flying Bomb will defy death! From eighty feet above the ring, he will plunge through the air toward that target!" A wide, dramatic arm gesture indicated the circle of red lights surrounding the landing point, and a slow rattle of kettledrums heightened the effect. "And all without a safety net!"

Absolute silence fell on the audience. Val gave a last bravura wave of the grab swivel, then handed it to McGlade. As she did so, she growled under her breath, "Tell him I'll have gone by the time he gets through. And tell him don't come after me!"

McGlade began his climb with the grab swivel in his hand. His father claimed to have invented the device, but there was nothing to it, really. There was a hook to latch onto the rope, and a safety bar to stop the hook from coming unhitched in flight. The hook was on a swivel, below which was a bar bent in the shape of a triangle and covered with leather to give a better grip. The whole thing was worth maybe ten bucks, but it had always been given such a buildup that for the kid climbing the ladder it had near-magical properties. McGlade felt responsible for it. Val was supposed to check it, but he knew she never did, so it was left to him to see whether the safety bar needed a spot of oil or the swivel itself was showing signs of wear. This time she'd kept it from his sight, flaring up every time he mentioned it, making out she was still too mad with his father to think about it. Now it was too late. He climbed the ladder up the main tent-pole entirely by feel. There was no way he could check the grab in the darkness. He'd wait until he was up on the platform with his dad; then he'd look at it in the light of the tracking spot.

But when he got within three or four feet of the platform, his father muttered sharply, "For Christ's sake, gimme that thing. Let's get this goddamn act over!" and bent and took the grab from him. "Is she still mad?" he snapped, straightening up and unfastening the rope that was secured to the platform rail. The row with Val was still uppermost in his mind.

"She said she'd be gone before you're through. She doesn't want you to go after her," said McGlade, pulling himself onto the platform.

"The goddamn bitch!" his father fumed, snapping the grab onto the rope.

It was all done so quickly, McGlade didn't have a chance to ask his dad to let him check the grab. Even if he had, his dad was in no mood to listen. The quarrel had really got to him, and now he knew she wasn't going to wait for him, he was madder than ever. "Gimme room, boy, for Christ's sake!" he snapped, out of the side of his mouth.

McGlade had always had premonitions. He took after his mother that way. "Feelings," he called them when he was a kid. He'd had a "feeling" the day his mom was killed. He'd had a "feeling" that first time his dad introduced him to Val. He had a "feeling" now. He wanted to say to his father, "Dad, don't go this time. Make that speech about the law won't let you. Make out it's one of those towns." But he couldn't bring himself to. He was only a kid and his dad was a real professional. So he stood there with his mouth shut and watched his father get himself into the mood.

When he thought about the Flying Bomb later, he realized there wasn't all that much to it. It wasn't like being fired from a cannon, where you had to rely entirely on other guys to set up the stunt right. With the Flying Bomb, it was largely hype. You killed every light in the big top but the tracking spot that was going to follow your flight; the music, too, except for a faint rustle from the kettledrum until the last second. You made a big deal of your preparation—hesitating, half taking off, then retreating to the back of the platform before advancing again. After long deliberation, you finally took hold of the rope and settled your hands in

the grab. Then, flexing your muscles and swelling out
your chest in a final, dramatic intake of air, you
launched yourself into space from the platform and
swung out over the raised faces of the audience below.
The trick was to change your direction of flight just
enough to let you miss the takeoff platform on the
backswing.

McGlade always stood with his back to the pole and
put his hands around it behind him, as he'd been taught
to do. The platform wasn't all that stable, and his
father didn't want him falling off. He could feel the
pole pressing into his back again now, feel his hands
locked behind him, sense the electric charge that had
been built up in the audience, everyone wondering
whether the Flying Bomb was going to fall—"waiting
for the blood," as his dad put it. His father jokingly
referred to them not as the "audience" but as the
"ghouls." "They may be ghouls," he'd say, "but they're
our bread and butter."

The lights in the big top dimmed and went out. The
little circle of red lights that defined the "target" came
up on the far side of the big canvas structure. Up where
McGlade stood, the only illumination was from the
tracking spot that was going to follow the Flying
Bomb's flight through the air.

His father finally took off, letting gravity pull him
off the platform, rather than pushing with his legs. He
was dressed in a sequinned leotard, and the tracking
spot flashed and jinked from him as he cut a deep arc
through the air. His body made the little adjustment
necessary for him to miss the platform on his return
swing. At the same time, it began to build up the
necessary momentum for him to hit the target. He did
the stunt without a net, except in those towns that
compelled him to use one. He always remarked that
the ghouls in such places were gypped of their money.
"Where's the kick in watching a flyer who's not taking
a risk?" he used to say.

He came to the end of the first swing, hung in the air for a moment, then slowly started to return. As he did so, he flexed his back so as to increase the arc he was moving through. On the first return, he usually passed the takeoff platform by a clear ten feet. On the next couple of swings, he repeated the movement, so that, by the time of his third return, he'd added thirty feet to the length of his swing. That was enough for him to reach his target.

Whatever risks the Flying Bomb took with the rest of his equipment—such as leaving Val to supervise its condition—he always set the target personally. And when he'd set it, nobody was allowed near it. He regarded the positioning of it as the single most important factor in the stunt. "I'm a bomb, kid," he'd once explained to his son. "I lock onto that target the way a bomb aimer used to lock onto a factory during World War Two. Once I've got it in my sights, I stay with it. Everything goes out of my mind except that target. And when I'm set, I just let go and fire myself right at it. I've never missed yet."

McGlade, his back to the pole, watched his dad swing past him, slow toward the end of his backward swing, hang stationary for a moment in the tracking spot, then return. From where McGlade stood, he could hear the slight hiss of air as his dad built momentum and edged closer to his final trajectory. Apart from that, the big top was one enormous silence.

The flyer came back for the second time. As he did so, there was some commotion from way below. A resonant whisper broke from the audience. Their attention had been caught by something happening down there. A couple of spotlights had come on and were illuminating the ring. Standing in the blaze of light was Val, still in her sequinned costume, her arms held high. A wave of horror broke over McGlade. Why was she still here? What was she doing, breaking into his dad's act right in the middle of the most dangerous part?

Didn't she realize . . . ? He turned to look at his dad, hoping he hadn't noticed. But his dad was looking down at her. He'd lost concentration, and concentration was everything; he'd said so himself.

"Dad!" called McGlade. He wanted to bring the man's mind back to what he was doing, to warn him, to take his attention off the woman, maybe get him to call off the stunt, even at this late stage.

For a moment the man on the high wire lifted his head and looked at his son. McGlade could see the puzzled expression on his face in the spotlight. A second later, the forward movement had broken the eye contact and the man had swung horizontal. But instead of hanging momentarily in the air, then flicking back for the final swing, he continued forward.

McGlade let go his hold around the pole and took a quick couple of steps forward onto the platform. Before he grasped what had happened, he heard a prolonged scream from below and panicked cries from the audience. The tracking spot followed his dad's fall. It was a long fall, all done in slow motion. To McGlade, hanging onto the two suspension ropes that supported the platform, it took the whole of a lifetime for his dad to disappear out of the spotlight and into the darkness below.

Lights came up. They came up suddenly and in no particular order, and they lit up a scene of screams and jostling panic. McGlade couldn't see his father, though the rope he'd been on still swung back and forth beside him. And suddenly he realized it was over—the act, the way of life, everything! His dad was dead, lying somewhere down there under the trampling feet of that demented crowd. . . .

McGlade's shoulder was sending pain through his entire chest. It didn't bother him anymore. He'd finally got everything straight. The sense of elation was intense. He became aware of his present situation again, swinging through the darkness over the demolition site.

He hadn't killed his dad; *Val* had done that. She'd blamed McGlade, of course—said it was his job to check the grab swivel; said he'd killed his own father just as certainly as if he'd murdered him. But there had been nothing wrong with the grab; he was proving that now. She'd set up the quarrel beforehand and given McGlade that final message to carry to his father waiting up there on the platform. The state his father had been in after that, he'd never noticed that the safety bar hadn't locked in position. How could it? She'd stuck a strip of cellophane in the spring to make sure that it wouldn't. It was an old trick in the profession. He couldn't prove it in a court of law, of course, but then he didn't have to; he could handle it himself.

And finally she'd tried to cover it up by that dumb last entrance of hers. She could apologize for that and drop a few tears, and everyone would believe that her dumbness in mistiming an entrance had caused the flyer to lose concentration and fall to his death. McGlade knew better.

He put his finger on the safety bar of the grab swivel. It was securely in place.

The air was hot, heavy with the smells of gas fumes and the sweet putrefaction of garbage. Life all around him was dying. He was witnessing the death of the whole West Side. He was an instrument of God's—an avenging angel destroying the filth of the city, cleansing, purging! The sense of power was intoxicating. He was a bearer of thunderbolts that he could launch with a glance. He thought of the target his father used to aim at—a net measuring twenty feet in diameter and marked by a perimeter of little red lights. That wasn't McGlade's target. McGlade's target was the whole of Manhattan.

He began to think of Burton's woman, lying asleep in the building beneath him. What was she dreaming

of—Burton? What did any of these women dream of—
men they could corrupt, the way his dad had been
corrupted? As he thought of them all—Val, Fay Coburn, the others he'd known—their images coalesced
and he couldn't tell them apart. They'd killed his dad
and put the blame on a kid. Left unpunished, they'd
kill the whole city. That's what it had all been about—
avenging his dad's death, clearing himself in his dad's
eyes, getting the city to *care*. . . .

The roof was sliding toward him now. All the fears
he'd had about his ability to reach it and land on it
safely without plunging through the skylight had gone.
Nothing was beyond him, now he'd cleared his head
of what had been troubling him.

He needed one more swing before he released himself. He was over the roof now, slowing as he neared
the end of the swing, coming to a complete stop and
hanging there, suspended high above the steaming
city, before starting his flight backward. Below him lay
the demolished buildings, homes that had been bull-
dozed into rubble in the name of progress. Then gradually the lights of Sixty-sixth Street came into view
below him, and he was flying over the honking cabs
and the winos. This time was the last. At the end of
the next swing he'd make the leap.

The final swing began. He flexed his knees in the air
and gave a flick forward to keep the momentum going.
Dimly, he was aware that his body was protesting.
Euphoria had distracted his attention from his back
and arm. But now that he'd geared himself to this one
last swing, the pain in his shoulder broke into his consciousness, and suddenly his confidence, the soaring
sense of power, dissipated.

Yet there was no choice for him. It would take him
longer to slow his movement down than it would to
complete the leap. And if he slowed it down, where
would that leave him? There was no way now that he
could ever get back onto the jib. If he came to a stop,

he'd be dangling in midair, sixty feet above the ground. Either way he was going to kill himself. The knowledge made him summon up the last physical energy he could muster. He focused on the roof ahead of him, concentrating on the skylight, pushing the pain in his body as far back into unconsciousness as he could manage. His shoulder was part of him; so was his back. If he fell, so would they. Whatever they had to endure in the next few seconds was nothing compared with the damage they'd suffer if he fell. The thought made it easier for him to bear the pain they were giving him.

He began to slow. Ahead, the skylight grew in size as he approached it. He'd planned the landing half a dozen swings earlier, and changed the direction of his movement accordingly. He was going to aim a fraction to the right of the shaft of light streaming upward through the glass. That way he'd land as near the middle of the room as possible. There was plenty of time. Experience had taught him that if you knew what you were doing, time was never a problem. In fact, you could master time. Absolute concentration could stop time in its tracks.

He concentrated. The lighted skylight filled his consciousness. He dominated it, willing himself toward it, slowing down his forward motion. And finally, there it was in front of him, gradually sliding beneath him. His movement came to a complete stop. He was at the absolute extreme point of the arc. He uncurled his hands and released himself.

He fell. He fell slowly, in a slight arc—feet first, a little ahead of his arched back and raised arms—aware of every inch of space beneath him. He fell as his dad used to fall, aiming directly at that small target, with the ghouls below watching breathlessly to see whether he would miss. The hot air began to rush past his cheeks and race up his nostrils. The skylight came toward him. A doubt entered his mind: Would he miss it? Then, as he continued to fall and he realized that the skylight was beginning to disappear out of sight beneath his feet, another doubt seized him: Had he released too late? He could sense the far parapet of the roof coming toward him, without being able to see it. Would he crash into it? Worse, would he overshoot it and sail past the building completely, splattering himself on the broken pavement of Sixty-seventh Street?

The chain of imaginative horror that was generating doubts in his mind finally broke. His feet struck some solid surface; his knees flexed automatically. He rolled to his right—once, twice—taking the main shock of the landing on his shoulder, and came to a stop with his face up against the low parapet that marked the forward edge of the roof.

It took him a moment to realize that he'd made it. It scarcely seemed possible, after the doubts he'd had during the last swing forward. Yet why shouldn't it be possible? God Almighty, who was there in this godforsaken city who could match him, who could come anywhere close to him? Doubts be damned! He'd never imagined for a moment that he couldn't do it! As a stunt artist, he was the greatest!

He turned, got to his knees, and put his hands on the edge of the skylight. He took a couple of deep, slow breaths to steady his pulse; then, brushing the sweat out of his eyes with the back of his sleeve, he lifted the unlocked skylight and painfully eased himself through. He hung for a moment over the stairwell before putting out a foot and resting his weight on the stair rail. A moment later, he was turning toward Fay Coburn's door.

Burton rode down Columbus with Blue at his usual station, a foot to his right and six inches behind his rear wheel. The air was no easier out here in the street than it had been on his deck. But the season, like any other, had its compensations. Sure it brought out the roaches, but it kept down the oil bills.

The traffic was light: a few taxis dropping back into midtown after taking the swingers and the disco freaks back up to Riverdale. The first of the garbage trucks were picking up the black plastic bags from the sidewalks. He was going to turn east on Seventy-ninth, but when he got to the intersection, he still kept south. He thought he might just go down to Sixty-seventh, ride past her place, see that everything was okay.

At Seventy-second Street he changed his mind. What the hell had happened to his self-respect? Was he a free guy or just another West Side crossbred hanging around a bitch in heat? Anyway, riding past her place wasn't going to tell him anything. He'd have to go in, and he'd never get past the security lock on the house door.

He turned into the park. The sky was lightening beyond Fifth Avenue—pale blue at first, then pink. Another day. They'd have sorted everything out again by evening. The sight of the skyline silhouetted black against the rising light lifted his spirits, the way it always did. He knew every tracery: the severe classicism of the Hotel Pierre running into the baroque extravagance of the Metropolitan Club; the Sherry-Netherland, south of Sixtieth Street; the great monolith of the General Motors building competing with the Plaza Hotel for the domination of Grand Army Plaza; beyond, fragmenting the first rays of the rising sun, the towering candle of stainless steel that Citicorp had lit to God. He turned toward the shimmering images and put down his head and kicked his feet into the pedals. The air flowed over him, hot, damp. Christ, it felt good! The park almost empty; the streetlights still burning all the way down Fifth . . . He'd been right to get out. Stuck there in that room with only his own thoughts to think about was never any good.

The sense of freedom didn't last. Every now and

then, some memory would pluck at him. He'd pass some tree; maybe she'd commented on its shape, or they'd hung on a moment while Blue watered the place. At the Conservatory Pond, he could hear her comments again about the bronze statues of Alice and Hans Christian Andersen. She was always trying to teach him something, in bed or out. By the time he'd reached the Metropolitan Museum, where they'd had that workout with the cops, he couldn't stand it anymore. It was no good just running off energy. It still left a jungle in his head. He had to be doing something with his hands, something useful, if he was going to get his mind off her. He turned west, making for the shop.

"C'mon, Blue," he called.

It took Blue a minute to figure out this change in routine—he was into the bushes by the East Drive—but when he caught sight of Burton swinging left toward the north perimeter of the Great Lawn, he threw back his ears and raced after him.

It was full daylight by the time Burton got out of the park. He turned left. Blue checked, then turned with him.

"I know what you're thinking, you old bastard," Burton snapped. "I'm behaving like an eighth-grader. If I lifted one of her handkerchiefs, I'd sleep with it under my pillow. Okay—so what? Keep your snout out of it!"

He made a right at Sixty-seventh and crossed Columbus. It was just as he'd expected: The window of her bedroom was wide open. There must have been another fifty thousand windows on the West Side that looked exactly the same that morning. Everything was just the way it ought to be. He hesitated, left foot resting on the pavement. Behind her building, the black skeletal structure of the crane reared up into the early-morning sky. The red lights still burned along its length. A rope dangled motionless from halfway up the jib. The crane looked ridiculous—incongruous—standing there amid that peaceful, sleeping scene, and as he looked at it, he felt that strange unease that had pulled him out of bed in the first place. He figured he'd just go up and ring her bell, check that everything was all right.

He turned toward the building, but as he did, he could imagine her poking her head out of her window, looking down at him standing like some lovesick kid on the stoop, asking him what the hell he thought he was playing at. He stopped and looked down at Blue. The dog was standing on the sidewalk with his tongue lolling, looking up at him. *Jesus,* he thought suddenly, *what the hell must he be thinking of me?* He turned and headed north.

The morning sun blazed down the whole west side of Columbus, bouncing off the glass storefronts, highlighting the newly painted façade of the Copacabana restaurant. He opened the shop and stood his bike against the wall inside. He knew exactly what he was going to do: He was going to go right to the phone and call her. But when he picked it up, he hesitated. What was he going to say when she answered? "Hi there, honey. Just checking that you're okay. Couldn't sleep. I had this . . . funny feeling."

It wasn't yet six. By seven-fifteen she'd be thinking of taking her morning ride around the park. By then he'd have figured out some casual approach that didn't have the ring of panic behind it—and didn't compromise his position, either.

He picked up the bike that Thomas had been working on. The kid was good, no doubt about it. He had good hands. He'd be quite an engineer when he grew up. It was a shame his old man was taking him west. There was no point in running away. When things got rough, the only thing to do was hang in there, make it even tougher for the bastards putting the squeeze on. If you dug your heels in deep enough, any guy would finally have to lay off you. He put the bike down and turned to his own work.

By seven, the first commuters were coming down from Westchester in their Firebirds and Monte Carlos. The towaway trucks had started to prowl. Burton still didn't pick up the phone. Every argument he'd rehearsed in his head had fallen down in the end. He leaned back against the bench and said to Blue, "Listen, hound, suppose I was to tell you straight out I was in love with you. Suppose I was just to lay it on the line and say, 'Don't let's mess around. Don't let's have this casual junk about meeting now and then, living our own lives, getting into this Plato's-Retreat crap. Let's just get married, find a nice apartment. You go on teaching if that's what you want; I'll stick with the shop. Vacations, we'll go up to Maine, maybe now and then down to Florida. Build up a life together.' Eh? C'mon now, what would you say to that? That sound dumb to you?"

Blue lay on his piece of sacking and looked at Burton.

"You old bastard." Burton, squatting, took the dog's head between his hands and rubbed his ears. "You know damn well what I'm saying. You don't fool me none. But you're not gonna commit yourself, that right? Well, okay. Just don't come to me for advice when it's your turn. Remember, now: I told you."

There was something about Blue that didn't feel right. He wasn't relaxed, the way he usually was after a run. Normally he'd let the whole weight of his head rest in Burton's hands. Now he was holding back. When Burton let go of him and stood up, Blue got to his feet and walked slowly to the door of the shop and stood for a while looking out. Finally he returned to the piece of sacking, but he didn't lie down; he just stood there looking at Burton. Maybe he was figuring what his own position would be in this new setup Burton was proposing. Sure as hell *something* was bothering him.

"Hey, you like her, don't you?" Burton said. "You don't think it would make any difference to *us,* do you? Why, you crazy old Kraut."

He went over to a new consignment of packing cases and picked up a ripping bar from the wall rack behind. He'd seen a piece in *The Times* that said cycling had peaked out. That wasn't his experience. As far as he was concerned, they couldn't ship them in fast enough. He put the chisel end of the bar between the planks of a case and began levering it apart. Inside, he could see the protective pads of polystyrene and the tape-wrapped chromework. The sight of the new machine didn't excite him the way it usually did, though. His mind was still on Blue. The dog was standing beside him, watching him. Something was wrong; Burton knew it in his soul.

"What is it?" he asked. "What you trying to tell me?"

Blue never took his eyes off him.

Burton put a hand down and patted Blue's head. "Come on," he said, "let's have the truth. You think it's a lousy idea? You think I oughta give her up?"

Blue continued to stand. Finally he walked over to the pile of scrap chains that Callaghan had brought back. He sniffed at them, then turned his attention to the remains of the bike that McGlade had rented. As he sniffed, he gave the softest of little whines.

"So what is it, then?" asked Burton.

The dog knew something; there wasn't any doubt in Burton's mind. He knew something that Burton didn't know. Something had happened. He'd never seen Blue so uneasy. Blue didn't have the usual human limitations; he had insights. He'd had an insight about Fay. He'd accepted her right away the first time he saw her. He'd had an insight about McGlade, had gone for him the minute the bum walked into the shop. On both counts Blue had been right.

Burton began to put the two names together: Fay . . . McGlade . . . Oh, Jesus, no! The dog was wrong this time. McGlade wouldn't be *that* dumb—not after having been warned off.

He dropped the ripping bar and ran to the phone. He couldn't get his fingertips in the holes fast enough. Why did they have to make the fucking things so small? The number rang at last. He could imagine the room at the other end of the line. He could see the phone sitting there, one of those new, red press-button things, just to the left of the big potted fern. She'd have picked it up by now if she'd been in the living room. Maybe she was still in the bedroom. If she was in the tub, it could take her thirty seconds to get a robe around her and walk the half-dozen paces down the little passage and cross the room.

Still it rang. He gave it another few seconds. A glance at his watch told him it was 7:10. It was early for her to be in the park. There was still no answer. Finally he hung up.

Something was wrong. He picked up the ripping bar and grabbed his bike. Blue was already waiting for him in the doorway.

The door to the apartment house was locked. Burton, his thumb on her bell push, kicked at it and yelled, "Fay!"

Nobody came and nobody called from the open window above.

"Fay!" he yelled again, without letting up on the kicking, without removing his thumb from the bell push.

A male voice hollered, "For Christ's sake, cut that out! You want me to call the cops?"

Burton looked up. A couple of houses to his left, he could see a guy's head poked out of a third-floor window. "Yeah, you!" the guy yelled. "You hear me?"

Burton ignored him. His finger was still on the bell push, but nobody opened the door. Jesus, was everybody deaf?

He couldn't wait. His face was a lather of sweat. He had to know. He rammed the chisel end of the ripping bar between door and jamb and leaned on the other end. A long splinter of wood came away, exposing the edge of the lock. He got in again with the chisel.

"Jesus!" he muttered, working the bar. "Let me be wrong!"

Blue crouched behind him on the stoop.

It took him fifteen seconds to bare the mortise. All the time, the guy at the window was screaming, "I've called the cops, you bum, you hear me? They're on their way!"

Finally, the lock ripped out of the woodwork and he was in. Blue leapt past him and up the stairs.

Later, Burton couldn't recall even seeing the stairs, the landings, the doors opening off into the other apartments, any other tenants. The first thing he could remember was putting his hand on the door of Fay's place and finding that it wasn't locked. Even the guard chain wasn't in position. His guts began to turn to water.

Yet nothing was out of place inside. It looked as if she'd simply walked out and forgotten to drop the latch. The living room was just the way it always was —the stereo set up along the left-hand wall, the big fan slapping away in the window.

"Fay?" he called.

There was no answer.

She hadn't cooked breakfast, by the look of the kitchen, but that didn't mean a thing. She usually left it till after her workout in the park. The bathroom was empty. He didn't even bother to turn the light on. It was the bedroom he was making for, a couple of yards ahead of him. The door was half open. Blue was already inside.

It was too late. He knew it, long before he pushed open the door and heard Blue whimpering. He'd known it from that moment in the middle of the night when, unable to sleep, he'd got up and gone out on the deck. Blue had known it, too—all that padding around the deck, all that tension in the poor dumb bastard when they were together in the shop. This was what it had all been about. Blue had been trying to tell him all the time. He just hadn't wanted to listen.

He expected to find her body lying across the bed, face puffed and purple, the bicycle chain still around her throat. The sight of the empty bed with the sheet ripped off was almost more of a shock. He hadn't been prepared for that. He stood in the doorway, trying to take in the scene. There was blood and grease on the mattress, and spatters of blood on the wall behind the bed. The bedside table lay shattered by the window. On the floor beside it, her little alarm-clock radio lay with its plastic case smashed and its works hanging out. The bedside lamp with the Tiffany shade had been knocked over and the glass trodden into the carpet. Jesus Christ! If that psycho had done this to dumb furniture, what had he done to Fay?

Blue gave a soft little whimper, barely audible against the hum of street sounds coming in through the open window. Burton caught sight of his tail, sticking out from around the far side of the bed. For a second he thought his heart was simply going to stall. His imagination went crazy. He wanted to turn around and walk out of the place and slam the door on the scene. He didn't want to see what it was that Blue had found. But he had to know. He finally steeled himself and went around the bed.

He couldn't figure out at first exactly how she was lying. He could make out Blue, standing quite still, his nose down toward the carpet. The two pillows that Fay always slept with had been tossed against the wall. In front of them lay the tangle of sheets and her pajama top. But where was Fay?

Blue looked up at him and whined. He'd been leaning over Mr. Tibbs. The cat lay on her side, in that posture of total relaxation that cats adopt when asleep. Burton looked blankly at Blue. He was in a state of shock, not from what he had discovered but from what was missing. There was no body—no Fay. Finally he bent down and touched Mr. Tibbs. The cat was stiff and chill, the white fur spattered with blood. A bicycle chain had been wrapped around the animal's neck and wrenched so tight that it had burst an artery. A puddle of blood had soaked into the carpet and half dried.

Burton lifted the corner of the sheet and dropped it gently over the cat's body. Where had McGlade hidden Fay? He checked under the bed, then went to the bedroom closet. Her clothes hung on a rail, and when he touched them, they gave off her perfume; but she wasn't in the closet.

"Fay!" he called. "Honey!" What the hell was he doing! If McGlade *had* got to her, she wasn't going to be able to answer Burton.

He checked the bathroom and the kitchen and then walked into the living room. The smell of her was everywhere. She pervaded the place, as if she had just that second left to pick up a carton of milk from Food City and would be coming back up the stairs any moment. All the time, he kept thinking of the bicycle chain. How many did the kook carry with him? Not more than one, surely. One was enough for what that bastard had in mind. And if he'd put it around the cat's neck, what had he done with Fay?

She wasn't in the living room—not under the table, not dumped behind the sofa, not wedged into the big pine chest she used for storing linen. The more he looked, the more the idea grew in his mind that McGlade had taken her with him. It wouldn't be tough for him to terrify her into silence. The name "Bald Eagle" had terrified the whole city. All he'd have to do was breathe it to her and she'd keep quiet, anything he told her to, go with him anywhere he wanted. What woman wouldn't? But where would McGlade want to take her—the park? down to the riverside? The thought that there was nothing he could do to help her drove Burton frantic.

He went back into the little entrance hall, put his hand on the door leading to the stairs, then hesitated. Was there anything he'd missed, anywhere he'd failed to look? He turned to Blue, standing quietly in front of him. Then he noticed the refrigerator, just inside the kitchen. He'd ignored it when he'd taken his cursory look into that room earlier. Now he noticed the fingerprints around the handle on the white enamel door. They were smudges of blood and grease. Oh, sweet Jesus . . . !

Burton stood immobile. Was it big enough to take her? Sure it was big enough! He knew damn well it was, he just didn't want to bring himself to believe it and open the door. In that space she'd be hunched double. He didn't want to remember her like that— deformed, desecrated by the crazy pervert. He wanted to remember her as he still saw her—full of life, riding with him in the park, lying with him in bed with her yellow hair spread around her on the pillow. Finally he stepped forward and pulled open the door.

The motor hummed as soon as the warm air from the kitchen triggered the thermostat. The sound made him start, and he realized that he was on the very brink of going crazy himself. There was an open container of Half and Half on the top shelf, and another of orange juice. On the shelf below lay a slab of cheese wrapped in plastic. There was a half-empty gallon container of Deer Park spring water, plastic tubs of cholesterol-free margarine, an open bottle of wine—the usual detritus of Manhattan living. It was any fridge in any single's apartment in any part of the city. Except for the card. It looked like any ordinary business card. But what ordinary businessman left his card propped against a jar of A&P marmalade inside a fridge?

Burton picked up the card. There was a smear of

blood and grease on it where a thumb had gripped it —a deliberate smear, it seemed to Burton; something to heighten the horror, to make him lose his judgment. But it was more than that. It spoke volumes to Burton in those seconds he stood there with the card between his finger and thumb and the door of the fridge still open. It had been placed there for *him,* Burton, to find. Only *he* would understand its real significance. The precisely drawn picture of a bald eagle and the words beneath—"I Love a Clean New York"—were no more than superficial symbols. They were for the press, the cops. The real message was a personal one from McGlade to Burton. It said: "She's with me. Come and get her."

Burton picked up the ripping bar from the top of the fridge, where he'd laid it down, automatically closed the fridge door, and walked out of the apartment with Blue at his heels.

There was frantic whispering from below. As he reached the stairs, he heard the doors of apartments snap to and guard chains being dropped into position. The place was swarming with people. Why had nobody gone to help her?

"You're shit!" he yelled over the banister rail. "You hear me? Garbage!"

The place was absolutely silent.

He'd reached the entrance hall when a woman's voice screamed down the stairs, "I know you! What d'you mean breaking in here? You won't get away with it!"

"You bitch!" he screamed. "How come you never had your ears open when it mattered?"

Burton rode up Columbus against the traffic. It was heavy now, cars and trucks steaming southward to keep the Apple cooking for another day. He didn't give a fuck if any of it hit him. The whole West Side could come crashing down on his head. He'd welcome anything that put a stop to what was going on in his mind.

That kid McGlade had killed in the rotunda weeks back—she'd been a Fay to someone. There'd been some guy expecting to see her again, wondering how come she was in Riverside Park so early in the morning, trying to make sense of it. He should have let Blue finish McGlade that time in the shop. Blue had known the truth all the time.

He was kidding himself. Manhattan wasn't Indian country anymore. He'd been dumb to live as if it was. He should have gone to the cops straight off, whatever hassle it let him in for. That way, she'd still be alive. Looking after Number One was a great idea, as long as you knew where Number One ended and the rest of the world began. He'd never had any doubts about that boundary till Fay came along and pulled up the markers. She'd become part of him. Looking after Number One had got to mean looking after her as well. Jesus, once you got into that kind of thinking, where did it take you? If he was responsible for Fay, was he responsible for Thomas and Blue and the whole West Side? If so, what was *God* responsible for?

He dragged his mind back to the present situation. Fay was dead now; that was one thing he didn't have any doubts about. No way was McGlade going to let her live. But if Burton was too late to save her, he wasn't too late to avenge her.

Stern opened the door of the liquor store when Burton rapped on the glass. "You looking for Thomas?" he asked.

"Where's McGlade?" asked Burton.

"In his room, I guess."

Burton pushed past him and made for the hallway into the back room.

Stern yelled, "Where d'you think you're going?"

Thomas was having breakfast. When he saw Burton, he started to get up.

Burton asked, "Which way to the stairs?"

Thomas pointed to his left. "Through there," he said, pushing his chair back. When he saw Blue, he said, "Hey, boy, what is it?" Blue ignored him.

Burton began to take the stairs two at a time. He knew where McGlade's place was in relation to his own. Stern was still hollering from below. It didn't concern Burton. He was trying to figure what he'd find when he got to the top floor. He'd still got the ripping bar, so getting through the locked door wasn't going to be any problem. But would McGlade be there? Would he be waiting just inside, ready to swing a baseball bat down on Burton's head, or would he be holed up some other place? No, he'd be there. Why else had he left the bicycle chain and the business card? They were personal invitations to visit.

He steadied himself as he made the final turn. His problem was going to be keeping his cool once he found McGlade. The bastard was strong and rough and a killer. If he got the first blow in, Burton wouldn't have a chance. Coolness wasn't Burton's thing. All he could do was try. The one thing that would throw him would be the sight of Fay's body. He just prayed that McGlade had left it someplace else.

He took the last flight on tiptoe. Halfway up, he paused. Blue ran into him. He waved the dog back. Should he rap on the door and make out he was somebody else—insurance salesman, some guy from Con Ed? Or maybe he ought to announce himself, but act as if he didn't know about the killing yet. He could say he'd come to discuss the rental bike, now that it was damaged.

The waiting was too much for Blue. He couldn't control himself. He slipped past Burton and flung himself at the door, snarling, shoving his nose into the gap between door and floor. If McGlade *was* inside, there was no way of surprising him now.

Burton put his hand on the doorknob and turned it.

The door wasn't locked. He flung it open and took a couple of steps inside, the steel bar gripped in both hands. A second later, the air was ripped apart with noise. He found himself spinning to his left, slamming the door shut with his elbow, sinking down, finishing up with his back wedged against it.

Blue lay on the carpet a few feet ahead of him, blood spouting out of his side.

CHAPTER 14

Stern had got as far as the first landing when the shots exploded above him. He froze. For more than thirty years he'd never heard a shot fired in anger. Now, in the past couple of days, the world had gone mad. He turned and ran right back down the stairs.

Thomas was standing trembling at the bottom, hands to his mouth. "Pa, what is it?" he cried.

"Get out of here right now! Take the train to Queens!" yelled Stern.

"What's happening, Pa?"

"Thomas, get out!"

"Are you okay?"

The boy was in tears. The sight of him standing there broke Stern's heart. If something happened to this one, too . . . Again he yelled, "Get out! Now! Just get out!"

Thomas broke down. "I'm not gonna leave you here! I heard shots! I thought——"

Stern grabbed him by the shoulder, dragged him down the passage, and shoved him through the side entrance into the street. "Get out!" he screamed. "Go stay with your mother! Don't come back till I call!" Then he raced back to the hallway and phoned the police. It seemed a lifetime before somebody answered. Half his attention was still focused upstairs. Any second he expected to hear Burton coming down again, but there wasn't a sound. What the Christ did it mean?

"Officer Callaghan?" he asked, when a voice finally answered.

"He's out."

"This is an emergency!" cried Stern. "There's been a shooting!" He could feel his control beginning to slide.

"Lemme get a pad."

"Are you hearing me?" yelled Stern. "We've got a murder going on——"

"Okay," the voice interrupted, flat and mechanical. "Lemme have your name."

"Stern's liquor store, corner of Columbus and——"

"Just lemme have your name."

There was a hammering at the shop door. Stern saw the police car first, parked at the curb with its lights flashing; then he saw Callaghan trying to peer around the door shade. He stared at the phone. It seemed like magic. He hung up and ran to the door.

Callaghan came in, followed by his partner. "Where is he?" he asked, his hand on the butt of his gun.

"Upstairs."

Callaghan pushed past Stern. "How long?"

"Five, six minutes."

"Jesus Christ, Tony, are you crazy?" asked Callaghan. "I told you to keep that girl of yours in Queens!"

"What're you talking about? She *is* in Queens."

Callaghan turned back to him. "Yeah? Then, what's he want upstairs?"

"I don't know," said Stern. "He asked for McGlade."

"McGlade?" It wasn't the way Callaghan had been figuring it.

"There's been a shooting. I was trying to call you——"

"Shooting? Here? Upstairs?"

"That's what I said."

"Stay here," said Callaghan. He nodded to his partner and they walked through the shop toward the back. It was going to be a whole new ball game if that cocksucker had a gun.

Stern followed them. "Look, I've gotta know what's happening!" he cried. "All these years I've never had any kind of trouble. Now . . ."

Callaghan turned to him. They'd been friends a long time. The guy looked terrible. Callaghan said quietly, "The bastard's been after another woman, down on Sixty-seventh. Only this time he left the bicycle chain, and we got a witness. One of the tenants called. My partner spotted his bike outside your place. It's about time we got lucky."

"Hey—what're you saying? Burton? From the bike shop? You telling me that *he's*——"

"That surprise you?" asked Callaghan, drawing his gun and checking the chambers. "We should've picked him up months ago, but you can't tell these new guys anything. They want it on film before they'll believe you. Experience—that they can do without."

"But my boy was working there!"

Callaghan nodded. He might have said, "I did try to tell you, Tony," but he wasn't that kind of an asshole. He dropped the gun back into its holster and asked, "Which room are we looking for?"

Stern hesitated. Maria was absolutely right. If he'd had any doubts about leaving Manhattan, this had resolved them. "All the way up. Door on the right," he said.

"Anybody else up there?"

Stern shook his head.

Callaghan climbed the stairs, his partner a couple of steps behind him. He took his time. There'd already been shooting. Whatever damage had been done couldn't be undone now.

He paused on the first landing and took off his shoes. He knew kooks like Burton. In the end, it was firepower that was going to matter, not surprise. But he was too close to a pension and that two-bedroom cape in Brighton Beach to take any chances.

He stopped when he reached McGlade's door, then nodded to his partner to take up a position on the far side. He took a final mop at his forehead with a handkerchief; it wouldn't do to have some salt-soaked ooze trickling down into his eyes at the crucial moment. Finally he wiped his right hand on his pants, drew his .38, and thumbed back the hammer.

He listened. There was no sound from inside the room. He wondered what kind of cannon Burton was armed with. What were they going to be facing when they finally got the door open?

He glanced at his partner and nodded. The guy was standing braced, feet apart, covering the door with his gun. Somewhere on the way upstairs, he'd slipped a stick of gum into his mouth and now he was gently jawing on it, the way he always did when he was in action.

Callaghan called, "Okay, Burton—police! Throw the gun out first. Then come out with your hands on top of your head."

There was no answer.

"Save yourself some trouble, Burton," called Callaghan. "You've gotta come through this door. There's no other way out. You could get yourself hurt."

"Keep out of this," said a voice from inside. The guy sounded as if he was right behind the door and speaking from about knee height.

Callaghan gave a couple of quick raps on the door with the gun butt and called, "Come on, you bastard, open up!"

"You deaf, Callaghan?" the voice called. It was coming from right behind the door.

Callaghan's partner mouthed, "That him?"

"I guess," mouthed Callaghan. It had to be Burton's voice, but it didn't ring right. Maybe McGlade had hurt him during the shooting. "McGlade!" he called. "Can you talk?"

There was no answer.

Callaghan turned the doorknob slowly with his left hand, keeping against the wall, out of the line of fire. But the door wouldn't budge. He gave a quick thrust inward, checking to see whether it was locked or not. There was an immediate yell of pain from the other side. The bastard *was* hurt; no question about it. He must be sitting right up against the door so nobody could get in.

"McGlade?" he called again.

There was still no answer. It didn't look good.

Callaghan's partner lowered the muzzle of his .38 and aimed at the lower half of the door. He looked at Callaghan questioningly.

Callaghan remembered all the insults the bum behind the door had handed out to him. He thought of all the beautiful young women who'd been butchered. All he had to do was nod. It would sure clean things up. Why let the bastard go to court and maybe buck the rap on a plea of insanity?

But Callaghan was a cop. Despite the years of hassle, most of the old ideals he'd had were still there under the garbage. In the end, he shook his head. It didn't give him any satisfaction.

He waved his partner across to him. "Get down to the car," he whispered. "Tell 'em we're gonna need some help. I figure we've got a hostage situation. They'd better send in the boys with the baseball hats." He had a pang of nostalgia for the old days, when a cop's individual judgment still amounted to something.

"You figure McGlade's still alive?" his partner whispered.

Callaghan shook his head.

"Why would he kill McGlade?"

Callaghan shrugged. Motives were for the courts. He

was way beyond trying to figure why anybody did anything.

When his partner had gone, he turned back to the
door. "Okay, Burton," he called, "just take your time.
Gimme a call when you're ready."

McGlade was speaking. "I knew I'd get to you in
the end," he was saying, looking right at Burton.

It didn't make sense to Burton. He was trying to get
things together in his head. If he didn't think clearly
now, he wasn't going to live to think again. Everything
distracted him: McGlade, sitting on the sofa opposite,
holding a gun on him; the cop outside, still chasing the
wrong guy; Blue, pouring his guts all over the carpet.

McGlade, "You beginning to understand me?"

"I guess," said Burton. Keep it cool, he thought,
cool. How long had it been since he'd called to Callaghan?

He was still sitting with his back against the door.
He couldn't take anything more than shallow breaths,
and he couldn't lift his left arm or move his shoulder.
That shove of Callaghan's had just about finished him.
But he wasn't dead, and he still had the ripping bar and
one good hand. What would it take to reach McGlade
before the bastard took him out with the gun? He was a
dozen strides away. Burton eased himself up a couple
of inches. The pain seared through his chest, and the
distance between him and McGlade was suddenly vast.

"You're not fireproof, are you?" said McGlade. The
bastard was pleased with himself. "That stuff you're
covered in—that's not asbestos, after all! You're flesh
and blood, like the rest of us."

Outside, the life of the city went on. Through the
open window facing him, Burton could hear the familiar noises, smell the familiar smells. He was drawing
new strength from the city. He'd been street wise from
birth; it gave him that special kind of patience that no
outsider ever mastered. Right now, things didn't look

good. But he was going to make it in the end. No matter how many bullets McGlade pumped into him, the guy was finished. He wasn't a survivor. And in this city, the will to survive was better than a storeful of flak jackets.

"You trying to figure out where she is?" McGlade asked. He was half smiling. The look on his face was one of crazy triumph. "She's in the bathroom." As he spoke, he nodded toward the door on his left without taking his eyes off Burton.

The door was closed. Burton's imagination began to run wild. He could see the scene beyond the closed door: the cramped tub, the leaking shower head dripping onto the stained enamel beneath, the toilet, the cracked washbasin. And somewhere amid that outdated equipment lay Fay—maybe on the floor; more likely in the tub. The fact that in his present state there was nothing he could do about it drove him mad. He sat with his jaw clenched and his eyes half closed, his head resting against the door behind him.

"It was quick," said McGlade. "I'm good at it. I wouldn't want you thinking she felt any pain. She didn't feel a thing." He sniffed. He was watching Burton the way he might have watched an injured animal he'd been hunting. He was looking for the best place to deliver the *coup de grâce*. "You wanna know how I got her here? I told her you'd been hurt. She couldn't get here quick enough. Can you imagine? She damn near ran! Don't you think that was smart? I figured at first I was going to have to get rid of her down there, maybe leave her right in her apartment or drag her out back and dump her near the garbage. But when I told her you'd been hurt, there was no holding her. You know what? If I'd threatened her, she wouldn't have moved. But a little persuasion . . . I guess I'll never figure women."

When Burton didn't reply, McGlade snapped sharply, "You hearing me, you bastard?"

Burton had got his mind into focus at last. He couldn't take McGlade alone. He had to have help. He was going to have to go to the cops. He listened. How far was Callaghan from the door?

"Why . . . did you kill her?" he asked. He spoke as deliberately as he could. He didn't want any misunderstanding from Callaghan this time. He could handle the pain, now that he knew what he was doing.

McGlade didn't answer, but he shifted his position, and the gun muzzle dropped an inch. He was getting high on success; Burton could feel it.

"D'you think . . . she meant something to me?" asked Burton. "I mean, *really* meant something?"

"If she didn't mean something, what're you doing here?" McGlade asked. The gun came straight back on target. "You trying to make a monkey out of me?"

Jesus! Burton was going to have to take it slow and easy. Not that he'd any alternative, the way he was feeling. "I guess you're right," he said.

"You *cared* about her!" cried McGlade. "Say it!"

It wasn't difficult to say; it was true. "Yeah, I cared about her."

"That's all I wanted to know," said McGlade. "There was *something* you cared about!"

"And that's why you killed her?" asked Burton, very slow, very precise.

Could he get the bastard to admit it? He'd have liked to give Callaghan a chance to rig up a tape recorder, something that would stand up in court, but he wasn't dealing the cards.

"What goes on in your head?" snapped McGlade. "*You're* responsible for the killings—all these young women. Don't you see that yet? If you'd gone to the cops, like any decent citizen, none of it would have happened. It's *you* that's poisoned the city. *You're* the murderer, not me! All I'm trying to do is get people to take notice, face the disease we're up against. I'm doing a service, the same as the garbage collectors, same as the cops, except I do it out of conscience, like a priest. I don't cost the taxpayers!"

He was sitting on the edge of the sofa, breathing heavily, the gun clamped tightly in his hands. How long was it going to be before he lost control and pulled the trigger again? Burton could feel his own strength steadily ebbing. Visions of Fay, warm, still full of life, kept coming back to him, but he pushed them to the back of his mind. He still had to get that confession if he was going to get the help from Callaghan he needed. There was no point in pussyfooting.

"Okay," he said. "But you gotta admit it was you who used the bike chain, not me."

A look of sudden exasperation came over McGlade's face. It was puffed and red. Sweat dripped off his mustache. "Why am I wasting my time?" he cried. "I thought I'd made it clear——"

"Sure, sure," said Burton, trying to lower the pressure. "You've made that clear. But I'm not talking about responsibility. I accept that. I guess there's millions of us between the Bronx and the Battery, all got some share in the guilt. It took a guy with a lot of courage—a lot of vision—to show us that. All I'm trying to get clear is who the guy was. It was you, wasn't it? That's all I'm asking. It was . . ."

His focus was slipping again. He fought to bring it back. The pain wasn't a problem now, but he had to keep his concentration. If he could just hang on for another couple of minutes . . .

He said, "It was you put the chain around that woman in Riverside Park. It was you killed the girl that night of the concert, back of the Met. It was you killed my woman on Sixty-seventh. Right?"

All he wanted from McGlade was that single word: yes.

McGlade didn't give it to him. Instead, he said, "You're not talking your way out of this. I'm gonna kill you. Right here in this room."

"I know that," said Burton, struggling to keep the momentum going.

The gun never moved. McGlade had both fore-fingers on the trigger. Burton's head swam. He wasn't going to make it. McGlade had admitted nothing.

Time oozed away. Burton glanced at Blue. He wasn't going to get any help from that poor bastard, either. "Okay," he said. "I guess you're right. I've asked for it."

McGlade took his elbows off his knees and gradually sat up. "Sure I killed them," he said at last. "Those and the two before. All five of them. I left the cards. I took a lot of trouble with them. I wanted everybody to understand. Nobody did. I watched the whole town go hysterical—City Hall tearing its hair out, the media having a picnic, cops running around like ants. But that's not important." He lowered the gun. "What's important is *why* I killed them. Nobody's asked the right question. It's always been: What's wrong with this guy Bald Eagle? They shoulda been asking: What's wrong with this *town* that makes a citizen have to do these things? We're inside a garbage can, a sewer! Everything's rotting around us! Nobody cares! Some-body's gotta stand up and . . ."

Burton nodded slowly. It was everything he'd hoped for. That loose-gutted mick standing outside had final-ly got what he wanted: Burton had gone to the cops. Okay. Now to see what they would come up with.

Callaghan had heard none of it. The minute he'd sized up the situation, he wanted Stern out of the place. The guy had been through enough. He couldn't see any hostage squad talking Burton down. There was going to be a shoot-out. The bastard was on a Murder One already. What did he have to lose?

"Don't argue, Tony," said Callaghan, walking Stern steadily down the passage toward the side entrance. "There's nothing you can do."

"You don't understand," Stern protested. "Everything we've got——"

"Is there any way he can get down except the stairs?" Callaghan interrupted. He had the door open, easing Stern through it and onto the sidewalk.

"No," said Stern.

"I'll look after the place, Tony. Go to Maria. She needs you. Take Thomas with you."

"Thomas?"

"Yeah, Thomas," said Callaghan. "He's hanging out over there." He pointed across the street.

Thomas was standing on the corner, looking back at the liquor store.

"Hey!" yelled Stern. "You stay there! I'm coming over!"

He stepped straight into the traffic and began to work his way through it. Callaghan watched him till he got to Thomas; then he closed the door and shot the bolts. Poor bastard, he thought. It didn't matter how far he ran—Minnesota or the Philippines; he was shipping all his problems with him.

He took a chair from the table in the back room and sat down facing the open doorway to the stairs. With the side entrance locked, anyone trying to get out would have to get past him. He listened. There was no sound from above.

His partner came in through the store, his walkie-talkie crackling. "They want ten more minutes."

"Let 'em take a week," said Callaghan. "It's better in here than on the street."

"Some kids have ripped his place off."

Callaghan looked up at him. "Burton's?"

His partner nodded, keeping the gum in his mouth moving. "Somebody forgot to close the door. They just walked in."

"What did they take?"

"Everything—bikes, spares, cash."

"Well, ain't that something." Callaghan grinned. "How'd they take care of the dog?"

"No sign of a dog."

No dog, thought Callaghan. That place meant everything to Burton. He'd never go off and leave the door open unless the shepherd was on guard. So what had got into him this time? Come to think of it, where *was* that fucking dog?

Burton began to have doubts about what he'd done. Could Callaghan really handle the situation? One dumb move was all that was needed to spook McGlade.

There wasn't a sound from the landing outside. What the Christ was happening? The waiting was going to kill him. A radio blared through the open window. The city hummed. A siren wowed in the distance. He looked at McGlade. The kook was actually smiling.

The first footsteps on the stairs reached Burton without his realizing it. His attention came off McGlade and turned back to the door. Way below, there were noises.

A voice called, "Mr. Burton? You hear me? I'm coming up. I just wanna talk, okay?" It echoed up the stairwell and around his head.

Who was this guy? It wasn't Callaghan. Jesus, if he could just get his head cleared! Half the time, he couldn't tell whether the sounds he heard were coming from inside his head or from outside. Maybe what he'd heard had been his own heart pounding. He listened. Silence. Then he heard them. Footsteps—steady, very solid. He hadn't imagined it.

Again the voice called, "I'm coming up, Mr. Burton. All I wanna do is talk, okay?"

It was a cop, somebody special. Callaghan must have called for him on his personal radio. But why hadn't Burton heard him? And why was the guy asking for Burton? Hadn't Callaghan told him it was McGlade they wanted?

McGlade yelled suddenly, "You stay where you are!"

It threw Burton, the sudden change of focus. He looked at McGlade. The creep was still smiling.

"All I wanna do is talk," the voice called.

"You hear me?" yelled McGlade. "Keep outa this!"

Again the voice called—very calm, very matter-of-fact. "I'm coming alone. I don't have a gun. I just wanna talk."

More footsteps—slow now, very deliberate. The guy was getting close.

Suddenly Burton's head split. The room exploded. Something slammed through the woodwork above his head. Splinters fell down on him. The footsteps retreated.

"Okay, okay, cool it!" the voice called. "I don't wanna give you any hassle. I'll stay here till you change your mind."

McGlade had put a bullet through the door. He was watching Burton. What was it the kook found so goddamn funny?

"You're on your own," McGlade said softly, lowering the gun. "Callaghan didn't hear you."

Burton nodded. He figured the statement must mean something; what, he didn't know.

"D'you think I'd have talked that way if Callaghan had been outside?" McGlade asked. "He went down ten, fifteen minutes ago. I guess you didn't hear him. You wasted a lot of energy. You're gonna be sorry." He sounded very rational.

It took Burton a while to put it together. When he'd managed it, he felt as if the whole of Manhattan had split apart. He'd lost his footing. He was falling into the night. It couldn't be true! All the sweat, all the blood, all the pain he'd put into it . . . It *couldn't* have been wasted.

"Call him," said McGlade. "If he's out there, ask him if he heard."

The hope that had been sustaining Burton evaporated. He was suddenly weak. No wonder this psycho was smiling.

"What kind of a dumbbell d'you take me for?" McGlade asked. He knew he'd won; it showed all over his face.

"I guess . . . that's it," said Burton.

"You could say that," said McGlade.

Burton felt sick. For the second time in his life he'd gone to the cops, and the bastards had let him down again! He began to get mad at himself, and anger gave him a new kind of strength. Why had he compromised? Never trust a cop. Never trust *anybody*. He'd learned that as a kid—learned it the hard way. It was still true. All along he'd been right; he knew that now. If you want something, trust yourself, nobody else! Why had he ever doubted it?

He was on his own again. He glanced at Blue. The dog's ears were laid back and his eyes were closed, but his chest was still moving. The way things were going, he'd outlive Burton.

It wasn't a complicated situation. If Burton could bring the ripping bar down on McGlade before McGlade took him out with the gun, that'd be it. Except there was fifteen feet between them. No way could he cover that before McGlade pulled the trigger. He had to shorten the odds.

He glanced around the room. It was neat as a showcase. There wasn't a wrinkle in the bed coverings to his right. Magazines lay stacked precisely on the coffee table beside Blue. On the cabinet along the left wall, a formation of bright-colored toy soldiers stood rank on rank, not a man out of place. It showed Burton the kind of mind the guy had, but it didn't give him any fresh ideas. It came back to Blue. If he could get to him, he'd have cut down the distance by half. Could he persuade McGlade?

"Let me go to the dog," he said.

"Stay there," said McGlade.

"Look at the poor bastard," said Burton. "He's finished."

"Let him die."

"Jesus Christ! You say you care? You've got the whole suffering world on your shoulders and you haven't got room for a dog? Look at him. You let him lie there in the middle of your carpet bleeding to death and you expect me to take you seriously. You're a kook, McGlade, a psycho! Admit it. You never amounted to a squirt of cat.piss. You never will. You're a failure!"

"Don't ever say that!" McGlade snarled. "I got into that apartment house on Sixty-seventh. Nobody else could have done that. That was one of the great stunts, you understand me? One of the *great* . . ." He paused, considering other stunts he'd seen or heard of, comparing them with what he'd done to get onto the roof of Fay's building. After a moment, he said, "Dar Robinson couldn't have done that. Davy Sharpe couldn't have done that. Even my dad . . . Yeah, even my dad couldn't have done what I did today! I'm not a failure, you asshole, I'm a success! I'm the greatest stunt artist the world's ever seen!"

He was flushed. His eyes were wild. Burton cut in quickly, "Then, let me take a look at the dog. What've you got to lose? He's not gonna live; you can see that."

McGlade glanced at Blue for a moment, then looked back at Burton. Gradually he came out of the dream he'd slipped into. Burton waited for him to agree, but when McGlade finally spoke, all he said was, "No."

"What harm's he gonna do now?" Burton pleaded.

"You set the bastard on me the first time I came into the shop. He damn near killed me in the Ramble! Let him lie where he is."

Burton snapped, "For Christ's sake, wake up! You set him on yourself. It's his job to protect what's mine!"

"I said no! He's not a dog; he's a wolf. He shouldn't even be around."

"A wolf!" cried Burton. He let his head fall back against the door and gave a long, soft laugh. The whole of his left side throbbed. He was walking on eggs. How far could he taunt the bastard? "Look at him," he said. "A wolf? He couldn't swallow a canary. Lemme help him die."

McGlade eased up. There was the smile back on his face. *"You're* the kook, not me," he said. *"You're* the psycho. By now we're surrounded by cops. You hear the helicopter? They'll be putting a couple of men on the roof in a minute. There isn't a thing that ties me in with these killings. As far as the cops are concerned, *you're* the guy they're looking for. You're the only evidence against me. When I've killed you, there won't be anything left."

Burton nodded toward the bathroom. "What about . . . the body?" he asked. "What're you going to say about that?"

"Nothing. They won't find it," said McGlade. He was very sure of himself.

"What if they search the place?" asked Burton.

"Why should they? *You're* the guy they're after. I'm only an innocent victim. When they've picked you up and stuffed you into a plastic bag, they'll close the case. They've got other things on their minds."

"You're crazy! They've got reports to fill out. They'll want to poke around. They'll find something—some of your visiting cards, tire treads from that bike you rented, gloves . . . How'd you get the scars on your hands?"

"You said you'd figured that out."

"Sure I figured it out. How're *you* gonna explain them?"

"I keep telling you, I don't have to," McGlade said irritably. "I don't have to explain anything. I'm not a suspect!"

Burton nodded toward the bald-eagle print over the

desk. "How about that?" he asked. "They can't miss seeing that."

McGlade shrugged. "They cost a couple of dollars on Chambers. I'm into conservation."

Burton's mind went back to the bathroom. It was true: As long as the cops thought he was Bald Eagle, they weren't going to bother McGlade. The bastard had thought of everything. He asked wearily, "How are you going to get rid of . . . the body?"

McGlade looked at him for a moment as if he was some out-of-town hick. Finally he said, "You've got to be joshing me! Getting rid of a body in New York City? That's like . . . like getting rid of a cigar butt. I'll dump it, along with all the rest of the garbage."

Somewhere outside the window, Burton could hear the faint tick-ticking of a helicopter. He could see from the way McGlade was looking at him—amused, triumphant—that he was listening to it, too.

McGlade said matter-of-factly, "I figure this is it. Time for you to join the lady." He leveled the gun very slowly.

"How're you going to explain the shooting?" It was a pointless question. The way McGlade's head was working, he could explain anything. All Burton was doing was trying to delay the inevitable. They both knew it. McGlade didn't object. He had the whip hand, and his expression showed that he was enjoying it.

"They'll pull me in for carrying a weapon, maybe," he said. "It's Stern's, not mine. I'll say I had it up here cleaning it. I'll be out on bail in an hour. When it comes to trial, who's gonna blame me? It was self-defense. I'll be a hero. I'll be in the papers again, interviewed on TV. With the reward money, I can start life over——"

"Who are they gonna be looking for when the killings start up again?" Burton cut in.

McGlade stared at him. "There won't be any more killings," he said slowly, as if he was explaining to a kid. *"You're* the disease I was after. With you out of the way, why should I need to kill anyone else?"

"If it was me you were after, why d'you kill the women? What did you have against them?" Burton tried to keep the exasperation out of his voice. It was no time to spook McGlade. He had to be humored. But it taxed all Burton's self-control to keep his feelings in check.

McGlade looked puzzled, as if he couldn't see why Burton didn't understand. He said slowly, "They were essential. I couldn't have done it without them."

"You're too smart for me," said Burton. "I don't follow you." It wasn't so much that he didn't follow McGlade as that he couldn't bring himself to listen to his ramblings much longer. What the guy was saying made some dumb kind of logic—as long as you accepted his crazy premise. And who could do that but some other psycho?

"I wanted to make this city *care,*" said McGlade, in the same slow, quiet, explanatory tone. "Nobody *cares* —that's the Manhattan disease. I changed all that. People care about young things, beautiful things. All the women I picked were young and beautiful. I was careful about that. I didn't want to waste people's lives for nothing. And they weren't wasted. I got everybody caring. You could see it in their faces every time there was a killing. You could feel it on the streets. For the first time in history, everyone in New York City cared!"

He was elated at the thought of his own achievement. There was an expression of such intensity in his eyes that he seemed possessed. Then, gradually, the ecstasy faded as he became aware of Burton again, still sitting on the floor in front of him. He added, "Except you." His voice had the ring of lead. "I could never get to you. When Rudi told me that you wouldn't go to the cops after the killing by the river, I wondered why. I couldn't believe that anyone would care so little about the death of a young woman. I realized then that

I had to teach you to care. My God! I paced this room night after night wondering how to go about it. I stood at this window looking down at you sitting with that dog on your deck, trying to see some vulnerable chink in you, some humanity! I never could. Until I saw you with that girl. And then I knew how to make you care. My God, I knew!"

"But why didn't you kill *me?*" gasped Burton, every breath sending a stab of pain into his chest. "For God's sake, why *her?*"

"How could I kill you until I'd taught you to care?" yelled McGlade, suddenly angry again. "Don't you listen? Don't you follow me? The killing's not important; it's the caring that matters. You had to be made to care!"

There was a wall around his crazy mind with no way through it. He'd rationalized everything.

"Sure," said Burton at last. "I follow you now. I called you a failure. Well, I was wrong. I wanna apologize. You're a success. The town cares—if you call terror 'caring.' I care. What you said before, that even your dad couldn't have pulled off the kind of stunt you pulled off to get on that roof . . . I figure that meant a lot to you: to have done something your dad couldn't do. And I wonder . . . I wonder if maybe there wasn't somebody your dad cared about more than he cared about you. Some woman, maybe? Someone who stood between him and you."

It took McGlade a moment to realize what Burton was saying, and then suddenly he was galvanized with energy. He leaned right forward, the gun out in front of him. "You're dead!" he snarled. "Dead, dead, dead——"

"Okay, okay"—Burton put up a hand, palm open toward McGlade—"I give up. I came here to kill you. I guess I've lost. I guess *I'm* the failure." He'd needled McGlade as far as he dare. Now he had to make one final attempt to put his original plan into action. He held out the ripping bar toward McGlade. "Here, take it," he said. He gave it a gentle little toss. It fell on the carpet, a foot to the left of Blue. It was perfect. Once he'd got to Blue, he'd have it right beside him. "So now can I go to the dog?" he asked.

McGlade looked at Burton for a moment, his eyes blazing with hatred. Then, gradually, his expression softened as some new scheme began to generate inside his head. At last he put out his foot very deliberately and kicked the bar way over to the wall. The half-smile of triumph was back on his lips. "Sure. Go to the dog."

Burton sagged back and closed his eyes, his head resting against the door. It was over. He'd never reach the bar now. "For Christ's sake," he said, "get it over with."

"Why should I waste a slug? If I sit long enough, you'll bleed to death. So go help the bastard. Come on, move! It'll speed things up."

Move? What was there to move for now? thought Burton. The thing was over. Blue was dying. He was dying himself. He couldn't help Blue anymore. Blue couldn't help him. Suppose he did move, get right up to Blue. What could he do without a weapon? It was getting tougher to hold his focus. The room was starting to tilt, slipping away from him toward the window. He could see Fay, lying right there in front of him—naked breasts, limp arms growing cold. He couldn't leave her like that! He had to get to her—cover her up, at least. He leaned forward and put out his good hand, and as he did, the image faded. McGlade came back into focus, still holding the gun. Was that the last thing Burton was ever going to see—that smile of triumph? He dredged his soul and found a last pocket of strength.

Turning on his side and hooking his legs under him, he went forward on his knees, left arm cradled in his right. He could forget about the arm—it was useless—but the rest of his body was up to it. He got to Blue and put a hand on his shoulder. "How you feeling, Blue?" he whispered. "Anything you want, pal?"

Blue's wound had stopped bleeding. The hair around it was matted now with congealing blood. He'd been hit between the neck and the shoulder. There was no way of telling how much damage had been done, but he was still breathing and his heart felt strong. Burton knew they were in touch.

He lifted the dog's muzzle. There was no blood around the mouth. Maybe, after all, the slug had missed the vital organs. But the poor bastard was in shock. He was shivering now and his eyes were only half open. It didn't look as if he recognized much. He knew Burton only because of the sound of his voice and the feel of his hands. But there was life in him, all right.

Burton was six or seven feet from McGlade. One great drive with his right leg and he'd have the bastard pinned against the wall. But how would he get under the gun?

Blue broke into his train of thought. Something was happening to the dog, Burton could feel it as he knelt there, nuzzling Blue's head between his right hand and his thigh. Blue was conscious again. Burton began to wonder.

He leaned down to Blue, hand now patting him gently. "I gotta ask one last favor," he whispered. "Think you can make it?"

Blue didn't register. Had he heard? The clatter of the helicopter filled the room.

"Okay," McGlade snapped, "I know what you got in mind. Kiss the bastard good-by!" He had the gun straight out in front of him, a couple of feet from Burton's face.

The muzzle was a great black tunnel. Burton couldn't see through it or past it. It filled the whole of his field of vision. Time had run out. Another second and this asshole would have won. What had any of it amounted to—Fay, the times they'd had together, the long, hot

summer? McGlade was going to blow it all away.
There'd be nobody left as a witness, nobody to avenge
her or carry the memory of her in his head. She'd be
just a name on a police file—another kid snuffed out
by the city. . . .

Oh, no! Not if he could help it! He gave a soft, low
whistle through his teeth.

The dog didn't stir. It didn't affect Burton's deci-
sion. If Blue couldn't help, he'd do it alone. He shifted
his weight over his right knee and put his left arm back
into his right. He was going to drop his head and drive
himself right under the gun. With luck, he had a chance
of beating that first shot.

Just as he got ready to move, he saw the smile of
triumph drop from McGlade's face and the gun begin
to swing. The next moment, Blue had the bastard by
the wrist and they were rolling together on the floor.

Burton got to his feet. He couldn't see how to help
Blue, they were moving so fast. The coffee table
smashed, scattering magazines over the carpet. A chair
spun over, and now they were up against the desk. Mc-
Glade let off a shot. It smashed into the ceiling. Blue
hung on, but his strength was fading.

Burton turned. The ripping bar was still by the wall.
He bent and grabbed it.

One blow with it was enough. McGlade took it
square on the head, and the gun fell out of his hand.
But one blow couldn't satisfy Burton, couldn't make up
for everything he'd been through. He came in again
and again, going for the head, the neck, the back—
whatever was exposed. What drove him on was Fay.
Not the dead girl lying in the bathroom, but the woman he'd loved. The one with golden hair and satin skin
and eyes as blue as summer. The one who went her
own way, fought him, loved him. The one who fucked
like Venus.

He lost count of the times he hit McGlade. When he
came to his senses, there was blood on his hands and

jeans and splattered all over the bald-eagle print above the desk. He dropped the bar and stood against the wall, nursing his side. There was no pain, simply a numbness. Blue was lying beside him, fresh blood welling from his wound.

It took him some time to get to the bathroom. The effort of killing McGlade had sapped the last dregs of his strength. In any case, it didn't seem important to hurry. There was nothing he was going to be able to do. Yet, as he got to the bathroom door and began to open it, he knew that McGlade had beaten him again. It was more than a premonition; it was certain knowledge. There'd been something in McGlade's whole manner that had been telling him. Burton opened the door wide and pushed back the shower curtain over the tub.

There was nothing in the tub and nothing on the floor. All the time he'd been facing McGlade, McGlade let him go on thinking it. But she wasn't in the apartment; she wasn't anywhere in the building; she'd never been near the place. She was lying somewhere in the rubble in back of Sixty-seventh Street. Maybe by now some dog had sniffed her out, or one of the construction guys had stumbled across her.

He turned and walked slowly back to the apartment door and opened it. His head was beginning to swim, so that he found it difficult to focus his eyes. He figured he'd lost more blood than he'd realized. He was in shock, and the only thing that had delayed it had been the need to concentrate all his energies on getting to McGlade. Now that that was over, he had no resources left, and consciousness began to slip away from him. It was over. He'd survived. McGlade was dead. Nothing mattered anymore.

He crossed the narrow landing outside the room, steadying himself with his left hand on the doorjamb, and leaned against the stair rail. "Hey, you!" he called to the guy waiting below him. "You can . . . come up now."

He heard the footsteps hit the stairs beneath him, then voices, low-pitched, intense. But the sounds were a long way away and didn't concern him. He was slipping out of that world and into some other reality. He figured that if he got lucky, he might catch up with Fay again. The idea made him smile. Jesus, wouldn't that be great! To see her again, to touch her, to hear the sound of her voice . . .

He felt sick at the thought that he might have saved her. If only he'd gone to the cops when he'd had his first suspicions about McGlade, instead of trying to handle it himself! What bugged him, too, was the knowledge that McGlade had been right: Burton *did* care. He cared about Fay and he cared about poor old Blue and he cared about that kid of Stern's. He cared about a whole lot of things and he'd never realized it. McGlade had known him better than he'd known himself! It had taken that crazy psycho to show him the truth.

There were hands under his shoulders trying to support him. He made no effort to help. There didn't seem any point. He let himself slip through them and onto the bare wooden floor.

"Jesus Christ Almighty!" somebody muttered. "You ever seen anything like it? We need a body bag. Make that two. There's a dog in here as well."

Burton wanted to say, "That's not a dog; that's Blue! Check him out! Don't go stuffing him into a plastic bag and burying him. Check him out first! He saved my life. If it hadn't been for Blue, you'd never have got to Bald Eagle."

But nothing came out of Burton's mouth, and after a moment of trying to force himself to speak, he gave up. There was nothing more he could force his body to do. It had been knocked about too much already. The world dissolved in front of him, his last faint struggles against unconsciousness faded, and he slipped into darkness.

▼▼▼▼▼▼▼▼▼▼▼▼▼▼▼▼▼▼▼

CHAPTER 15

▲▲▲▲▲▲▲▲▲▲▲▲▲▲▲▲▲▲▲

The sky above Burton's head was white. There was an unbroken cloud ceiling a couple of thousand feet above the earth. The sun had somehow got below it and was shining full in his face. It was an odd sun, not the way he remembered it. When he turned his head to look directly at it, it went out of focus. When he looked away, there it was again, bright and sharp, with a halo of gold around it.

He was lying on his back. He figured he must be in the park or down by the river, and he'd laid his bike down and dropped onto the grass beside it to take a little snooze. He put out his hand and called, "Blue!"

When Blue didn't come, he tried to prop himself up on his left elbow to take a look around. The pain stabbed deep into his chest and down his side. He dropped back at once and let out a groan.

It began to dawn on him that he wasn't lying under the open sky at all but in bed in some room. The white sky was the ceiling, and the sun was a big central light. The smell of antiseptic hung heavy in the air.

It came back to him slowly—the shoot-out with McGlade, the cops coming up the stairs, Blue lying on the carpet bleeding his guts out. But they weren't the most important things. There was something else. "What is this place?" he asked.

Nobody answered him.

Then he remembered—the empty bedroom on Sixty-seventh Street, Mr. Tibbs lying strangled beside the bed . . . He called, "Fay!"

There was no reply.

Time neither moved nor didn't move for Burton; he was outside it. Fay had turned his life around, and it wasn't going to amount to a bag of beans without her. God Almighty, how easily he'd let her slip through his fingers! She'd made all the compromises; he'd made none. This dumb insistence on his own independence had killed her!

Two figures loomed by the side of the bed. This was a scene from a film: Burton was the victim of some terrible accident, groping his way back to consciousness after hours under anesthetic. Dr. Kildare came into focus, dressed in pristine white, the way he should be, hands deep in the pockets of his coat, head bent forward gravely, personal bleeper stuck in his left breast pocket. He was nodding. His face wasn't clear, but it was clear enough for Burton to figure out that this wasn't Richard Chamberlain. Chamberlain was Anglo and this guy was black.

"It's not that it will hurt him," Dr. Kildare was saying. "But I doubt if you'll get much sense out of him. It'll be another hour before he finally shakes off the effects."

"I realize that, Doctor," the other guy said. His voice was soft, easy. It sounded a lot more reassuring to Burton than Dr. Kildare's voice. The guy was of average height and thickset, and his open-necked white shirt had heavy sweat stains under the arms, as if he'd just been jogging in the park. He turned to Burton and asked quietly, "You able to hear me, Mr. Burton?"

Burton turned his head a couple of degrees to his left. The big light hanging from the ceiling behind the guy's head made it hard for Burton to make out the details of his face or his expression. "Sure I hear you," he said.

"I'm a cop," said the guy. "I thought you might be able to tell me some things."

"Like what?" asked Burton. He knew the guy was a cop. Who else would you expect to find in a scene like this? Then, after the cop had gone, the patient fell in love with the nurse and everything came out dandy.

"You went down to Sixty-seventh Street. You broke in. Right?"

"Sure," said Burton. He was trying to figure out where the cameras were placed. From what he'd heard of moviemaking, you had someone telling you where to look and what to say. Nobody was telling him anything. This sure was a funny film.

"Did you look in the fridge down there?"

The guy had a look of intense concentration on his face, as if this was a question the answer to which might change the shape of the story line.

"Yeah," said Burton. He'd had no idea how much it took out of you, playing in a film. He was having real trouble getting his head to work.

"What did you find?"

He remembered the fridge. That was after he'd seen Mr. Tibbs in the bedroom. Blue was standing just behind him, waiting to leave the place. A sudden worry struck him: Had Blue come down the stairs with him, or was he still waiting in Fay's apartment? He tried to recap on Blue. No, Blue had left with him, he was sure. He remembered him running past him on the stairs, then trotting beside him all the way up Columbus. It was in McGlade's place that he'd lost touch with Blue. Sure. Blue had got himself shot! He was lying on Mc-Glade's carpet with blood running out of him. He asked, "You see Blue?"

Dr. Kildare looked at the cop, and the cop looked at Dr. Kildare. The patient must be pretty sick, thought Burton. Dr. Kildare shook his head. The cop turned back to Burton, leaned forward with his hands on his knees, and asked, "Blue?"

"My dog," said Burton. "German shepherd. He was shot, up in McGlade's place."

The cop was nodding. "Sure," he said sympathetically. "He's being taken care of. Don't worry. I figure he's going to be okay. Now—what did you find in the fridge? Can you remember?"

It didn't surprise Burton to know that Blue was okay. Whoever had written this script certainly knew Blue. Blue could survive anything. Blue was a real New Yorker. Burton turned his mind to the cop's question: What had he found in the fridge? He remembered opening the door and seeing all the half-consumed food lying on the shelves. He remembered the cold striking him full in the face. He remembered . . . Oh, Christ! Fay! Fay was dead and nobody knew where. That dumb, crippled psycho had got to her despite Burton's warning to him! He turned his head aside and tried to get away from the light glaring down from beyond the cop.

"What did you find in the fridge?" the cop asked again, very calm, very patient.

"There was a card," said Burton, "with the Bald Eagle's——"

"Did you touch it?"

"Sure," said Burton. He had his eyes closed now; the light hurt them. He could see the card again, propped up against the jar of marmalade. He put out his hand and took it. There was a greasy, bloodstained fingerprint on it. He read it.

"What did you do with it?" the cop asked. The voice was a long way away from Burton. He wasn't sure the cop had really asked the question or whether it had been generated inside his own head. "I . . . don't remember," said Burton at last.

"Try," said the voice, still patient but now very insistent.

Burton remembered the one driving emotion of that moment in the kitchen—revenge. He wanted to get the hell out of the place and kill McGlade. He remembered picking up the ripping bar from the top of the fridge. He remembered . . . Yes! "I tossed it on the floor," he said.

The cop's manner changed. "Your fingerprints were all over it," he said, voice now cool and impersonal.

"What d'you expect?" Burton snapped, suddenly nettled. "I handled it—didn't I just tell you?"

When the cop didn't respond, Burton opened his eyes. The cop's face was still without recognizable features. "Hey, come on!" growled Burton. "*I* didn't kill her."

"Kill who?" the cop asked quickly. "We didn't find a body yet."

"You dumb bastard," Burton groaned. "D'you *still* think I'm this Bald Eagle?"

There was a long pause. The cop stood with his thumbs in the waistband of his pants, looking down at Burton. His whole manner had eased. Finally he shook his head. "No," he said, "not me. I've seen too many hostage situations. If you'd been Bald Eagle, you'd never have let me into that room. Anyway, you didn't do any shooting; it was the other guy. You didn't have any powder traces on your hands. It was his hands that gave him away in the end. You could count the links of the bicycle chain he'd used. I guess he didn't think we'd check. It's their own damn arrogance that trips these kooks up. They think they're above detection. They're not. Nobody is."

He was about the first cop who'd ever got through to Burton, and Burton didn't know what to make of him. He saw the guy turn to the doctor and whisper something, then walk toward the door.

Burton called, "When you find Ms. Coburn, I'd appreciate being told."

The cop checked his step and turned back to Burton. "Sure," he said.

*   *   *

Consciousness came in short sequences for Burton. It was like walking along one of those claustrophobic streets around Wall Street after dark when some of the offices were still working. Every few steps, you'd come alongside a window. Inside, the lights blazed, people moved around between the desks, guys were on the telephone, and suddenly you were in the middle of life again. Then, just as suddenly, you'd come to the end of the window, and a couple of feet in front of your face was a blank, dark wall. Then another window . . .

He was between windows at this moment. He knew what had been going on; he knew he was in a hospital and why he was there. He didn't feel disoriented anymore, but he was having trouble with reality. This image of Thomas working at the bench in the bike shop with Blue lying beside him—was that "real" or was it some hallucination? The jogger running easily down Columbus with the traffic honking furiously behind him —was that "real" or was it a dream?

He was aware of a door opening to his right and someone calling, "We've found Ms. Coburn. The captain said to tell you."

He figured that that was too important to be a dream. The whole of his life was wrapped up with that information. He struggled to get up on his right elbow. The door was already closing behind some cop in his shirt sleeves, and Burton called quickly, "When? Where? Hey, for Christ's sake, don't leave me——"

The door closed. He didn't know whether the cop had ignored him or simply hadn't heard him. Anyway, the guy had gone. Until someone else came in, all he could do was wait.

He got the impression that he was gradually slipping back into the real world. There was a single fly that had got into the room, and if he half closed his eyes to cut out the glare from the overhead light, he could see it crawling on the cream-colored ceiling above him. He got to wondering how it stayed up there, defying gravity. Maybe it had some kind of glue on its feet; more likely it stayed up by suction. He watched it walk until it was almost out of his field of vision. Then, suddenly, his attention was distracted.

He realized right away that he must be asleep, because Fay was standing at the foot of the bed. She looked just the way she had when he'd last seen her— fresh, vital, beautiful, radiating life. Her hair was the color of ripe corn, and with the light behind her, it looked like a golden halo. Christ, he thought, if she'd been here now and known what he was thinking about her, wouldn't she josh him! Him—Burton—having sentimental feelings about her, just as if he was still a kid!

She'd moved around the bed without his noticing, and now she was standing beside him to his left. If only she'd come around to his right side, he could put out his hand and touch her. But he was all trussed up on his left side and couldn't get near her.

He heard himself say, "I hear they found you. I wish I'd been there when the bastard got to you. I oughta have known. I'm sorry."

She wasn't fooling him. He knew he was dreaming. This was all part of the process of coming out of anesthetic—that and what these butchers in the white coats called "postoperative shock." But it was nice to play along with the idea that it wasn't a dream, though it cut him up like hell for the illusion to be so real. He could smell her perfume as she moved; it drifted over him, cutting through the smell of medication and disinfectant that seemed to ooze out of the plaster on the walls.

She spoke at last, sitting on the bed beside him and bending sideways to look into his face. "How is it?" she asked. Her face was very tender. He'd never seen such concern on it before—or maybe he'd never looked.

"It's okay," he said.

He couldn't understand why there were no marks on

her. Even a hallucination like this ought to have some links with the facts. But the way she was dressed—low-cut cotton blouse and white cotton pants—he could see the whole of her neck where the bicycle chain must have been, and there wasn't a blemish on her skin. Even if McGlade had killed her some other way, he'd have left some visible mark. There was nothing. She looked as if she'd just got out of the shower and come right to see him.

"I . . . honestly didn't know you cared that much," she said. She was struggling with some strong emotion, and the words didn't come easily. "I feel . . . terrible about it. Okay, I wasn't to know what was going to happen, but . . ." She shrugged, then put out a hand and touched him gently on the cheek. The gesture was more eloquent than any words she might have found.

He put his right hand out and covered her hand. "I loved you," he said. "D'you know that? And that's what's killing me now—that I hadn't the goddamn sense to tell you! All I can hope is that maybe you guessed."

She smiled. She was actually crying. A tear ran off the end of her nose and fell onto the back of his hand. He could feel it trickling warm and damp across his flesh. It was so real! He turned his hand without removing it from contact with hers. He could actually see the little line of damp that the tear had made on his skin; it was glistening in the light from the overhead lamp. The sight of it disturbed him. It began to raise doubts in his mind as to how much of a dream this was. The quality of reality was intense. He couldn't ignore it any longer.

"Fay?" he said at last, looking right into her eyes.

"Burton?" she replied, looking right back at him.

"Is it really you?" he asked, still expecting her to fade from view as he watched her.

She didn't fade. She nodded and said, "It's me, Burton. Sure—it's really me."

The truth began to overwhelm him. He fought it at

first, not wanting to face the dreadful disappointment that would inevitably follow if the experience turned out to be no more than an illusion. But the truth was too strong for him to resist. If this girl sitting beside him was nothing more than an illusion, then he'd rather live with illusions than return to reality without her. He struggled to sit up, but she put a hand on his chest to prevent him. As she did, he took hold of her by the left shoulder and pulled her toward him. She hesitated for a moment, then allowed herself to be drawn downward.

She was lying on his chest now, keeping her weight off his injured left side. He could feel the warmth of her skin on his cheek, the weight of her body on his. He could smell her flesh and feel the brush of her hair over his cheeks and forehead. She was alive—here, safe in his arms! Somehow McGlade had missed her, or she'd escaped from him, or else . . . He brushed such considerations aside in the magic of the moment. For now, nothing else on God's earth mattered!

▼▼▼▼▼▼▼▼▼▼▼▼▼▼▼▼

CHAPTER 16

▲▲▲▲▲▲▲▲▲▲▲▲▲▲▲▲

September had come at last. The drumming heat that had crucified the city had finally lifted. In the past three weeks, the air quality had changed from "unacceptable" to "good."

Burton breathed easily, letting the air in and out of his lungs, cleansing the dregs of August out of his system. It was the first time the doctor had given him permission to test himself again on his bicycle. Christ, it felt good! There was a slight ache where the smashed rib was still healing, but it was nothing.

A breeze, gentle and refreshing came up the Hudson from the sea. It was sweet. Across the wide stretch of water that lay in front of him beyond Riverside Park, the new condominiums on the Jersey shore rose high over the Palisades and caught the early sunlight. The first leaves were starting to redden. The joggers were out, grim-faced, plodding determinedly. A few guys were working on the boats moored in the boat basin. A whistle shrilled. A kid with a ginger Afro tore past Burton on roller skates. God Almighty, it was good to be alive and in Manhattan!

Ten yards ahead of Burton, Fay Coburn set the pace. She had her hair tied back with a little silver clip that gave her head a neat, workmanlike appearance. Now and again she'd turn her head around and call, "How's it feel, then?" or "Still okay?"

Watching her trim body move on the machine, he figured he must be about the luckiest guy in the city. He'd been so damn close to losing her. He had Mc-Glade to thank for saving him. If it hadn't been for McGlade, he'd have let her go. He hadn't had the strength then to lose face and apologize, and he'd certainly owed her an apology for the way he'd behaved. Okay, when he'd yelled at her in the park when Mc-Glade was shadowing her, it had been for her own good. But he might have taken time out to explain it to her instead of giving her orders. A girl like Fay, she didn't take orders from anyone. Why should she? She rated an explanation, the same as anyone else. He'd behaved as if he owned her, and nobody owned Fay—that was part of her magic.

And yet, ever since he'd come around in the hospital room and found she was still alive, one question had been gnawing at him. It had to be asked sometime. Maybe this was the time. She wouldn't like it. She'd tell him it was none of his business what she did in her own time. Maybe she was right. But there were some things that had to be said. He'd compromised—God knows he'd compromised; anyone who'd known him earlier wouldn't recognize him anymore—but compromise was a two-way business. A little compromise from her on this vital point wouldn't do any harm.

Blue cut into his train of thought and prevented him putting the question. Blue was managing to keep up okay. Considering what the poor dumb hound had been through, he was lucky to be moving at all. Jesus, when Burton had seen him lying on the carpet bleeding his guts out, he hadn't held out much hope for him. But Blue was tough. Blue was another survivor.

"Hey, c'mon dog," Burton cried, looking down at Blue and snapping his fingers. "What're you limping for? How we ever gonna make the Cloisters at this rate? If you can't do better than that, you'd better get yourself a wheelchair."

"God knows why he stays with you," called Fay, slowing and glancing back toward Burton. "He saved your life; you said so yourself. And now he's a bit slow, you shout at him."

He drew up beside her and they rode together along the riverside path. "He needs me," said Burton. "That's why he stays. Who else would put up with him? He's not the easiest guy to live with."

"My God, you never change!" said Fay. She was laughing as she spoke. He amused her now, whereas earlier his arrogance had made her mad.

"Why should I?" he asked, sitting upright in the saddle and riding with his hands off the handlebars. "When you've got a good thing, you stick with it. Right?" He'd changed, all right; that was a fact. What he was doing now was putting on an act for her amusement. At one time, it would have been for real.

A siren wowed along Riverside Drive. Burton nodded in the direction of the sound. "It's all go for those poor overworked cops," he said.

"Maybe if they got a little help," said Fay. "If people realized they've a job to do—an important job— maybe then we'd see the results we want."

"Well . . . maybe," Burton admitted.

She turned to look at him. "Well, *that's* an improvement," she said. "Do you think that when they had you under anesthetic to remove that bullet, they straightened out your thinking as well?"

Burton stared straight ahead. "D'you think it would have made any difference if I'd gone to them with my suspicions? I still wonder. That cheese-head Callaghan . . . if I'd relied on him, I'd be dead. The guy ought to be mainlining Geritol!"

"When did you first suspect that McGlade was Bald Eagle?" she asked. It seemed to her that he'd finally dropped that impenetrable defensive shell, for the first time, she felt totally in touch with the living human being behind it. It was a fine human being, as she'd always known—a human being she loved.

"When I saw the marks on his hands. There are a lot of things I don't know, but I *do* know bikes. If you've ever put a chain on in a hurry and got a finger trapped between it and the sprockets of the drive wheel, you damn well know about it. It leaves marks on the skin that I'd recognize anywhere. I saw them on McGlade's hands."

"Couldn't he have got them the same way you did —by putting on a chain in a hurry?" she asked.

"On *both* hands?" said Burton. "You should try it. It's impossible. Anyway, I'd already seen him and put the two things together. It doesn't prove anything, not in the way the cops want proof, but it sure as hell looked suspicious when——"

"You'd already seen him?" she cut in. "When? Where? Doing what?"

He'd got his hands back on the handlebars now, as if he needed all his attention to concentrate on what he was saying. "You remember the killing back there in the rotunda? I'd been over in Queens that night to collect a bike. The guy was way behind in his payments. As I was coming out of the park on the Seventy-ninth Street underpass, some bastard tried to crowd me into the wall. He scuffed up the front tire and knocked up the chrome. I figured I'd have a couple of words with him when he stopped for the lights, but the lights were green and he went right through. I stayed with him. I figured that if he was going to pick up the West Side Highway, he'd have to slow. He was crossing Broadway when I reached Amsterdam. Normally I'd have caught up with him, but the front wheel of the bike was buckled. It kept binding on the brake. By the time I got to Broadway, he'd disappeared."

They were coming up to the Soldiers and Sailors Monument at Eighty-ninth Street. Burton slowed and came to a stop, resting his foot on the ground. Kids were playing around the monument wtih skateboards and Frisbees. Beyond them, the apartment blocks of Riverside Drive rose up into the clear morning air. In a few days the whole atmosphere of the city had changed. The West Side had been a damp, scorching stewpot all summer. Now it had the leisured feel of some civilized Old World capital, with its glazed entrance lobbies, its uniformed doormen, its window boxes of red geraniums.

"Hey, let's take a breather," Burton said at last. He turned to the bench on his right, propped up his bike, and sat down.

"How do you feel?" asked Fay. The wrinkles around his eyes were deeper than she remembered them, and some of the muscle tone had gone from his body.

"Fine," he said. "Give me a couple more days and I'll be right back where I was." He grinned suddenly, a wide-open grin that showed his teeth and made his eyes light up. "Hey," he said, "do I still get to you the way you get to me?"

She nodded. Finally she asked, "Did you find the man—the one you were chasing in the car?"

"Sure I found him," he said. He hadn't forgot what he'd been talking about, but the memories it brought back tired him. He was wishing he hadn't brought it up, except that she deserved an explanation. "I cut right over to the West Side Highway—that seemed the most likely place to find him—but he wasn't there. I cruised the blocks for a while, figuring that's where he lived or that's where the chick he was with lived. I couldn't see the car. He'd just vanished. I was about ready to give up, but he'd made me so mad, what with the buckled wheel and all, that I gave it one final try. I thought that if he wasn't on the streets and he wasn't on the highway, maybe he'd pulled into Riverside Park. I went down there. It was dark as hell, but I figured I'd be able to pick out a car. And finally I saw it, just pulling back into the road off the grass. I started after it, but the bastard was really moving and I knew I'd never catch him. I gave up. That's when I saw McGlade. He was ahead of me and on the left, jogging along the drive in a dark-colored sweat suit."

She found it extraordinary, even now that she knew him so much better, that knowing what he'd known, he hadn't gone to the police. She asked, "Didn't you suspect him then—the next day when you heard about the murder?"

He shrugged. "I didn't give it any thought," he said. "He was a neighbor. I used to see him from my deck, walking up and down in that room of his. We shared the same air space. I'd never even spoken to him till he came in to rent a bike. He did that to give himself more mobility; I see that now. The killing after the concert in the park—I don't imagine he'd have done that without a bike. No, the guy I was suspicious about was the guy in the car. I might even have got around to calling the police about him, except that McGlade was smart enough to do that; he told me so himself. It was after that that Callaghan started harassing me."

"Well, you've got to admit you didn't go out of your way to put Callaghan's mind at rest," said Fay. Just below the surface of this reformed Burton there was the old, intransigent anarchist she'd fallen in love with in the first place. She was glad that nothing could shake his basic independence. It gave him the air of a modern Don Quixote, battling his way against the current of contemporary attitudes. He was as necessary now as his type had always been. Self-reliance, independence of spirit, rabid individualism had torn up the wilderness and built the roads and the cities. America was great because of men like Burton, however you viewed them as people. . . .

He broke in on her thoughts. "You think it would have made any difference if I'd told them?" he asked. It was clear from his tone that he didn't believe it would have. He added, "Jesus—what did it take to stop that bastard in the end? Not the cops, not the National Guard, not the army. Me! One guy! Okay, I had an incentive: I thought he'd got you. Even so, as far as the cops are concerned, I'm a crook. They don't believe a guy has any right to live his own life—run his own business the way he sees best—without explaining every move he makes to them. They're trying to block the reward money, and they haven't recovered a single bike that was ripped off from my shop. A guy like me can't afford to carry insurance. Blue was my insurance. It's gonna take some sweat putting that business back on its feet."

"I imagine you'll manage it," she said.

"Damn right I'll manage it!"

Blue had come back from inspecting the trees and marking the territory, and sat down at Fay's feet. The place where the bullet had entered his shoulder was still obvious. According to the veterinarian, it always would be. Hair would never grow out of the scar tissue. She put down a hand and patted him. He turned and looked up at her. It gave her a deep feeling of satisfaction to realize how completely he now accepted her.

Burton watched her bending over Blue. He figured that now might be the best time to put it to her—the question that would finally decide the way their relationship was going to go. Instead he asked, "You getting another Mr. Tibbs?"

"How would a cat get on with Blue?" she asked, still stroking Blue.

He didn't see the implications of the question right away. "I figure he could live with it," he said. "He copes with me."

"How would he cope with me?" she asked—lightly, almost as if it was simply an academic question. She knew that he wouldn't commit himself until he was quite certain she was seriously asking to come and live with him.

He didn't altogether fulfill her expectations. "What're you trying to tell me?" he asked. "The bulldozers are into your bedroom? You've been given notice to quit?"

"I've given myself notice to quit," she said, turning to look at him and leaving Blue to snooze at her feet. "I don't want to live by myself anymore. I want to move in with you."

He leaned back and crossed his legs and let his arms hang down behind the bench. He felt suddenly that it had all been worth it—the bullet in the side, the rip-off of his shop, the hassle with the cops. She was actually asking to come and live with him, to give the relationship some basis of permanence. It was everything he'd wanted. A couple of smart remarks occurred to him, but he dismissed them. It wasn't the time for smart remarks anymore. At last he said, "Why not?"

He looked at her for a moment. She was absolutely beautiful, sitting there with the late summer sun on her hair and her blue eyes full of tender feelings. He took her hand and put it to his lips and kissed it. "I figure that if we're gonna move you in, there are some things need doing."

He got up and lifted her to her feet. This was the moment he'd been waiting for: Either he put the question to her now and face the answer she gave him, or he put it out of his mind forever. For a moment he hesitated. Finally he realized he had to ask; if he didn't, there would always be this barrier between them. "How come," he asked quietly, "when McGlade went to get you, you weren't home?"

She felt enormous relief. She'd expected him to ask long before this and had decided that when he did, she'd tell him the simple truth. "I had a date," she said. "I told you that when you called."

"What kind—just a casual date?" He was looking at her and she was looking directly back at him. It was a final confrontation, and both of them knew it.

"Sure," she said. "A casual date."

He could see that she was being absolutely honest with him. Her answer wasn't arrogant or defiant; it was a simple statement of fact. "What time did you get home?" he asked.

He began to wonder how he was going to react when she finally told him the truth, because she would, he knew. Lying there in the hospital bed, turning the possibilities over in his mind, he had thought she might make it easy for him, maybe even lie. Yet even as the idea of her lying occurred to him, he knew she wouldn't.

"Around midmorning," she said.

"You'd spent the night with this . . . casual pickup?" he asked.

"If that's how you want to put it," she said. "Why not? You and I were through, as far as I could see. There was no future for us. We'd had some good times, but, by God, we'd had some lousy ones, too. I wanted to forget as quickly as possible."

"And that was your way?" he asked. He'd been a whole summer without looking at another woman because of her. Yet the minute she'd split with him, she was right into bed with some other guy.

"That's right," she said. "That was my way."

"And how do you figure it would work out if I let you come to my place?" he asked. He was cut pretty deep, but he had to admit she had a case. He'd been a shit to her, both in the park and over the phone.

"Who knows?" she said. "All we can do is try."

Try, he thought. *Sure, we can try. But is it worth the effort with a woman like this?* He looked at her steadily. There was no guilt in her expression, no shame in her eyes. She stood straddling her bicycle, facing him foursquare. "Take me as I am or not at all" is what her manner was saying. She was some woman—proud, independent, self-sufficient. He thought of the alternative to what had happened. Without that date, she'd have been home when McGlade broke into her apartment, and it wouldn't have been Mr. Tibbs Burton found in the bedroom; it would have been Fay. *She'd* have been lying there with the bike chain around her throat, face choked with blood and eyes popping. Is that what he would have preferred? Instead she was here with him —alive, beautiful, ready to come and live with him. God Almighty, what was a casual affair compared with that? No, he thought, thank Christ she was still alive! Nothing else in the world mattered.

"If it hurts you, I'm sorry," she said. "But it's the truth; I can't change that."

"Let's start again," he said at last. "Somehow we got off on the wrong foot last time. I'm sorry I hurt *you*. I guess it was the only way I could deal with how I felt about you. This town's not the place for strong emotions; they complicate life."

He had climbed onto his bike and was riding along the path that led toward Riverside Drive. Fay rode right beside him. She said, "Hey, listen—don't go thinking it was all your fault. I guess as long as we're baring our breasts, I ought to apologize, too. I hurt you, I know that. I meant to; I was so damned hurt myself. But it's over. Sure—as you say, let's start again."

Two kids in Yankee shirts were pitching a softball over on Burton's left. He remembered those two kids of Stern's racing after him that morning, telling him they'd found a body. Christ, they were shook up. He could see them now—white-faced, wide-eyed, standing together trembling. A lot had happened since then. A whole summer had gone by. He figured that if he had to live through it again, he'd go to the police when he'd seen the marks on McGlade's hands. And he'd do something else: He'd change that day in the Ramble. This time he'd kill McGlade instead of warning him off!

Poor Thomas, he thought, his mind coming back to the kid he'd got close to during the summer. Stern was crazy, selling everything, going west, dragging the kid with him. What a waste of effort! Where would it get him? In a couple of years he'd be swamped by the same old problems. That's the way he was built. Trouble with guys like that, they were always yapping about roots, but they never thought to put any down. They treated the city like a house of correction. They were all just working out their sentences, filling in time till they could get back home. If Europe meant so much to them, why didn't they go back there? They talked about the "American dream," but all they really had was the "European dream." They spent their time trying to plaster it over America.

It was the same with the blacks, the same with the Hispanics. They had the "African dream," the "Puerto Rican dream." All of them had their own ideas of what America *ought* to be. They never came to terms with what it *was*—a place in its own right, not just an extension of where they'd come from. They were all on the run. The least little hassle and they just turned their backs on the city and drifted west.

Not me, he thought. *Here's where I belong. Here are my roots, right down in this slab of granite. Here's where I stick till I get taken out one way or another. Manhattan, my Manhattan—Sodom, Babylon, Paradise, City of Gold!*

"That's what killed McGlade," he said. "Manhattan."

She realized that he was talking more to himself than to her; yet the statement wasn't entirely incomprehensible. She sensed that McGlade still dominated his thoughts. He must be wondering still what everyone in the city was wondering: What turned an average, caring citizen into a madman who hunted young women?

"They say he was an unwanted child, that his dad beat him, that he was a loner without any friends, that he had some chemical defect of the brain. Oh, my God, everyone's climbing his own bandwagon, pushing his own fool theories. It's all garbage. Manhattan—that's what killed McGlade. It drove him crazy, then killed him. It takes a special kind of talent to survive in Manhattan. He didn't have it. Maybe he was a decent guy. Thomas's brother thought he was great. So did Stern. The cops said so. But Manhattan took him and squeezed him and turned him into a killer."

They were coming up to Ninety-sixth Street. On their right, a guy lay unconscious on a bench, an empty gallon wine bottle beside him. Above the dark façade of Riverside Drive, the sun hit the water towers on the roofs of the apartment blocks. In the distance, a tug was hauling a string of barges downstream. Behind it, the slender sunlit span of the George Washington Bridge was more a part of the sky than of the earth. The city was warm and tender again. Life hummed everywhere.

"How about that?" Burton cried. "That poor dumb psycho was so wrong! He really thought that nobody cared, that something was wrong with Manhattan. Man, nothing's wrong with Manhattan. Wherever you look, people care. I've never known a city more full of caring!"